I'LL MISS YOU THIS CHRISTMAS

LUCY MITCHELL

For my family

CHAPTER 1

EMILY

'Christmas is cancelled,' I shout before sliding down the outside of Felix's bedroom door, tucking my knees under my chin, and bursting into tears. Everything goes blurry except for a small black dog shape moving quickly towards me, carrying something pink. For a fleeting second, I wonder whether Baxter, the miniature dachshund, has finally decided to work with me and not against me, and is now rushing to my aid with the box of pink tissues from my bedroom. The sound of a heavy object being dragged across the floor in Felix's bedroom distracts me. 'I don't care about Christmas,' Felix yells, making me flinch. A sinking feeling takes hold of me – he's using his desk chair to strengthen his bedroom barricade. This child protest is going to go on for hours. I try to muster the energy to go downstairs but I just want to sit here and weep.

A thud is followed by him screaming, 'I HATE YOU, AUNTY EMILY.'

Wiping my damp cheeks and heavy eyelids with the sleeve of my cardigan I bite my tongue and refrain from yelling, 'YOU'RE SO HARD TO LOVE RIGHT NOW.'

Looking down I see Baxter sitting by my foot. A pair of my

cerise knickers are hanging from his little jaws. He's pinched them from the basket of clean laundry on the floor in the bedroom. Why did I even entertain the thought Baxter would help me in my time of need?

I try to grab him, but he hurries back into the bedroom, trots up the makeshift ramp of books, which Felix made for him, and dives in amongst all my clean washing. Why did I leave that basket on the floor when I know Baxter enjoys burrowing deep inside it to hunt for my underwear and Felix likes to encourage him?

After more noises from inside his room, Felix's heavy sobs drift onto the landing. Shame, sadness, and frustration knot themselves together inside my tummy. For the last week every night has ended like this; a huge argument which results in us crying, saying hurtful things, him going to make a lot of noise in his bedroom and Baxter chewing up whatever he can get his tiny black paws on.

The *week* bit is a lie. Felix and I have been at each other throats for months. Sometimes morning and night. Sometimes all bloody day!

Physical and mental exhaustion has turned my body into lead. I've had enough. Assuming the foetal position on the carpet outside my nephew's door I try to close my eyes... but I can't ignore the array of dirt marks in my sister, Vivi's, oatmeal-coloured carpet. Why have I never noticed these before? This carpet is the one she boasted about buying last year. According to her it was heavenly for bare feet and the saleswoman swore it contained some new carpet technology which meant it wouldn't show up the dirt so easily. 'That carpet saleswoman lied, Vivi,' I say, with a heavy sigh. 'Also, not a great colour choice. I think you should have opted for the darker brown. I remember talking to you about it last year. We both laughed at how we were getting our adult kicks from talking about carpets. Once we'd composed ourselves, you said you knew best and ignored my suggestion.'

Pressing my cheek against the carpet I sit up holding my itchy cheek. 'It's NOT soft, Vivi. More like sandpaper.'

I can hear a chuckle from behind the door. It makes me jolt with shock. My heart breaks into a wild gallop. Felix is talking to me. My goodness, this is a miracle.

'Aunty Emily, you shouldn't carpet-shame Mum.'

'Why not?' I say, with a wry smile. 'Felix – have you seen the state of the landing carpet?'

He giggles. 'It's not as bad as the carpet she chose for me.'

I let out a mock gasp. 'What?'

The sound of him laughing against the door makes me forget about why we were cross with each other.

'It's an awful purple colour,' says Felix, before pulling away whatever was resting against the door. He stands before me, puffy eyed and pink faced. I cast my eyes over his ghastly violet carpet which looks more like something Great Granny knitted. What possessed my sister to buy her nine-year-old child such a horrid carpet?

'Yuck. Felix, I want to apologise for your mum's carpet crime. As your aunty I feel like I have let you down by not noticing it.'

He chuckles. I watch him slide down his door, sit cross-legged opposite me in the doorway to his room and whistle for Baxter. My eyes take in Felix's river of freckles which flow over the bridge of his nose and pools around his cheeks, and his chaotic coppery hair (which can't decide whether to stand upright, lean to one side of his head, or just collapse over his forehead, and has decided to do all three and hope for the best).

Baxter returns carrying a blue pair of my knickers which makes me mutter bad words under my breath. To a stranger, Baxter would be viewed as an adorable dog. He looks like someone has dipped him into black treacle but has not managed to coat all of his tin-can-sized body as there are patches of milk chocolate brown on the sides of his paws and belly. His eyes are like two precious black gems which glint in the light. With

Baxter, looks are deceiving. A stranger wouldn't be able to comprehend the amount of carnage and chaos this tiny dog creates.

Felix smiles. Ignoring Baxter's 'come and play' face, he flicks his eyes to his battered old blue trainers and furry, orange socks.

'Arguing is becoming a daily occurrence for us,' I say, wrapping my old bottle green cardigan around myself.

Felix shrugs and tugs at one of his dirty grey laces, which a few weeks ago were white. The sounds of carol singers outside drifts through the open window on the landing. Shame hasn't finished with me yet. This should be a magical time for Felix. Vivi loved Christmas. You'd hear her singing Christmas pop songs from down the street, she'd have spent far too much money on glittery decorations in the Christmas aisles of The Range, her tree would take over the living room, Felix, her only child, would be spoilt rotten, and she'd cook an extravagant dinner which would fill everyone up until New Year's Eve.

Tomorrow is the day before Christmas Eve. As this is Felix's first Christmas without his mum, I should have put up a brightly coloured tree downstairs. There should be a turkey crown sat in the fridge, presents gift-wrapped in stockings, Christmas cards hung on pieces of red ribbon and a festive dog collar on Baxter. I should be busy making happy memories for us, not creating more pain. Nausea creeps up my throat.

'Why did we start arguing tonight, Felix?' I can't even recall how tonight's screaming match began.

He leans inside his bedroom and grabs my silver iPad. 'You got mad at me for using this,' he says, in a tiny voice, sliding it over to me.

I catch sight of Facebook still open. Felix follows my gaze and quickly shuts it down.

If Felix thinks tonight was all my fault he can think again. 'If you'd handed it to me and not flung it across the room, we could have still been downstairs.'

'You were already cross, Aunty Emily,' he mumbles, returning to fiddle with his lace. 'You were doing your angry sewing again.'

Felix knows how to force a smile onto my face. 'Angry sewing – is that a thing I do?'

He nods. 'I can hear you saying bad words as you stab the needle and cotton into the dress you're working on. I always thought sewing made people calm. Not you, Aunty Emily.'

'Really?'

An ear-to-ear smile spreads across his little face. 'You do. I've videoed you doing it.'

'Show me.'

Coming to sit next to me he takes my iPad and brings up a short video clip from tonight. 'This was you after we'd had tea.'

I sit and stare at myself in the video, sat alone, lips clamped shut, eyes flashing with anger and attacking an innocent, dusty pink evening gown with a needle and cotton. Felix turns up the volume and I can hear myself huffing, puffing… and muttering a few swear words.

Oh, God, I shouldn't be allowed near a needle and cotton. I look possessed.

He scratches his head. 'I'd refused to eat my tea again which made you cross but I think it was Facebook which made your face go that weird purple colour.'

I gasp in fright. He's right. I am so annoyed my face has turned a nice shade of … plum.

'Felix – I'm so sorry,' I mutter before pulling him into my arms. 'This is an eye-opener for me.'

I can hear him sigh. 'I wasn't a good boy either, Aunty Emily.' He looks up at me. 'Don't shout but I looked at Facebook too and it made me want to throw things and say stuff which is not very nice.'

Throwing my arms around him I nuzzle my face into his hair and detect my posh coconut shampoo which I have told him a million times not to use. For goodness' sake – is anything sacred with a nine-year old?

Baxter returns from the bedroom, this time with one of my fluffy slippers, which is almost as big as him. 'Did you and your mum ever train Baxter?'

Felix shakes his head. 'Mum took him to one puppy class and the man shouted at Baxter for being naughty, so she left.'

'Why does that not surprise me?' I take some deep breaths and tell myself to stay calm. Felix is gazing at the Facebook icon. 'Social media is bad for both of us, Felix. You're not old enough to be on there and I should delete it.'

A giggle escapes from his mouth. 'You've deleted Facebook and downloaded it again twenty-eight times this month, Aunty Emily.'

'Sorry, Felix,' I say, cursing my lack of self-control with Facebook.

He turns his gaze back to the iPad. 'Christmas is not the same this year, Aunty Emily.' We both go silent, and I find myself wishing I could hear Vivi singing downstairs while she lights all her expensive spiced clementine candles. Felix's finger hovers over the blue Facebook icon sign. 'You're also sad because you want to see what Rory is up to.'

'Rubbish,' I snap, trying to lie my way out of the situation. I don't like to admit this, but a lot of the time Felix knows me better than I know myself.

Felix nods, opens Facebook, goes to my ex-boyfriend, Rory's, Facebook profile and points at the post he's been tagged in. The post, from Beth Harrison, stares back at me. From her profile picture I can see she's blonde, likes to wear bubblegum pink lipstick and enjoys laughing at the camera. I don't want to read the words she's added but my eyes are already focused on them. *Looking forward to my third date with Rory Wilkinson tomorrow afternoon. Feeling festive and romantic xxx*

The urge to take my iPad from Felix and browse the ten

comments which have appeared on the post since I saw it earlier this afternoon is strong. I wonder what people have been saying about her post. No, I can't do that. Shoving my hands under my legs I bite down on my tongue.

To my horror I watch Felix open the post. 'I've read the comments, Aunty Emily.'

'Felix, let's put the iPad away,' I say, with gritted teeth. 'There's a good boy.'

He carries on. 'Rory has invited her over to his flat.'

My mind is now busy creating images of my ex-boyfriend happily lighting candles, throwing rose petals over the carpet, and slaving over a hot oven to rustle up some mouth-watering food. 'Felix, I don't want to listen to this.' Hang on – how does Felix know this. 'How do you know she's going over to his flat?'

Felix points to the one of the comments. 'One of her friends has asked her what they're doing on date three.'

'I don't think it's healthy for either of us to be checking up on Rory's Facebook posts.'

Felix nods while staring at Rory's Facebook page and I try to extinguish the ball of anger, frustration and sadness which is travelling up my spine.

CHAPTER 2

EMILY

'Mum would know what to do about you and Rory,' Felix says, pointing to Rory's Facebook profile. We're still sat on the landing. Felix has not put my iPad away. Like homing missiles my eyes lock onto Rory's handsome face, his curly black hair, his summer-blue eyes and his boyish smile. Inside my chest my heart performs a series of complicated flips and somersaults. Before my mind is flooded with painful memories, I snatch the iPad from Felix and stash it behind me. 'Let's not talk about Rory. He's living his new life in Leeds.'

Felix turns away with what looks like a scowl. I watch him fold his arms across his chest. Before I have time to remind Felix that we're amicable again and scowling is not permitted, I catch sight of the piece of black chiffon material I was looking for earlier. It's hanging off the back of his chair. Irritation makes every muscle in my body clench. 'Felix,' I say, pointing to the material, 'what have I told you about hiding my dressmaking stuff?'

He hangs his head. 'Sorry, Aunty Emily.'

I try to keep my voice sounding calm but it's a struggle. 'Not being able to find that piece of chiffon made me shout a lot tonight. You also lied to me when I asked you where it was.'

Sometimes I wonder whether I should return to my marketing job with the insurance firm. It might be easier as Felix and I would be separated in the day, and he could go to after-school club and holiday club in the holidays. This would mean we would have less time to argue. Starting my own online vintage-style dressmaking business at the same time as becoming Felix's legal guardian wasn't one of my best decisions. Back in May when Vivi died and our lives were flipped upside down, it seemed like the right thing to do. Being at home for when Felix came back from school was my priority, and working till late every night in a marketing office was not going to work. So, I did what any other normal person, someone who had just been through something horrific and was struggling to think straight, would do – I decided to start an online fashion business, Forever Vintage.

On paper it made a lot of sense. Using Vivi's life insurance money I was able to pay off her mortgage and her bills, and there was even some money left over which I set aside for Felix. There'll be things he will need it for as he grows up.

As I've been saving and daydreaming all my life about having my own vintage clothing business, I had my own financial resources to set that up. Making and mending clothes has always been a passion of mine so I thought it might help take my mind off Vivi's death

During the day when Felix was at school I planned to adopt, rescue and repair vintage dresses, in addition to making my own. All of which would sell on my Forever Vintage business website. I would be at home for when he came back from school. I could help him do his homework on an evening, cook us both a meal instead of ordering takeaway, watch TV with him... while at the same time *casually* sorting out dress orders, enquiries, posting dresses on social media and making alterations.

Yes, it was a great idea on paper. It ticked my childcare box, helped me fulfil a life dream and soothed my pain over losing the world's best sister.

In reality my great plan hasn't worked. In fact, it has been an utter nightmare.

I'm Vivi's older sister by three years. When she was born, I became obsessed with caring for her, my baby sister. She became my real-life little doll. This worked for our mother, who was struggling with a drinking problem which we later worked out was connected to Dad's sudden decision to leave us after Vivi was born. Mum unofficially handed me full responsibility of Vivi when I was five because she was drunk a lot of the time and had recently started an affair with a man who lived across the street. According to Mum, Dad went to India to find himself. We never heard from him again. When I was seven, I started making clothes for Vivi's dollies and by the age of twelve I was making amazing party dresses for her, from the forgotten and dust-ridden fancy dresses in the back of Mum's wardrobe. All the mums at Vivi's primary school would beg Vivi for the name of the shop her mother was buying these dresses from, but Vivi never let on and enjoyed being the centre of attention at parties. Mum never found out what I was doing to her dresses. She barely knew we existed half the time.

At school I excelled in textiles and design. After art college and many failed attempts at breaking into the fashion industry, I lost my confidence and pursued a career in marketing. The creative juices never left me and neither did my love for vintage dresses. I have spent the last ten years designing and making extravagant evening and party dresses for my friends in my spare time, and praying for an opportunity to start my own business.

I have learnt the hard way that setting up my online vintage clothing business in the days following the sudden death of Vivi was a huge mistake. All my business decisions were made in the middle of what felt like a hurricane of emotions and I disregarded my carefully crafted business plan, which didn't bode well for my business finances. I have also learnt that when you become the legal guardian overnight of your grieving nine-year-old nephew and his naughty dog, you need patience, energy, and a clear head – all of which I didn't have.

When I was a child and raising Vivi myself, I cooked her meals, tidied up after her, made her clothes, kept her entertained when Mum left us home alone for days, remained patient when Vivi couldn't master riding her bike without stabilisers and made sure she was safe. We rarely argued. Vivi was an angel up until the age of fourteen, when her periods started, and the hormones took over.

'Sorry, Aunty Emily.'

Baxter is back. This time he's got one of my bras and his tail is wagging like crazy. Felix tries to catch him, but he trots away.

I give up with both Felix and Baxter.

Closing my eyes, I massage my temples. Felix and I have argued enough tonight. Everything has once again gotten out of hand. Felix deserves better than this.

Vivi, you must be looking down from heaven and thinking why did I put Emily down as Felix's legal guardian? Opening my eyes, I scan the wall opposite us and spot a photo of Vivi and her two friends, Oliver and Claudia. Why didn't you let them become his legal guardians?

They would make amazing parents. I mean – you only have to look at the photo to see they have their act together. Both are blonde, tanned, and athletic, and Vivi used to tell me at long length about how funny they are at social events. Oliver's got a huge forehead which encases his ginormous Cambridge First Maths brain and Claudia's got a smooth, wide forehead which holds her Cambridge First Physics brain. They take at least three holidays a year to his wealthy parents' family home in the South of France and only wear the best designer clothes. Felix's little life would undergo a serious transformation. Within a year he would be excelling at maths, science, fluent in French, sporting a golden tan from all the school holidays in France and be dressed in Marc Jacobs. Weekly homework struggles, wearing supermarket-branded clothes and spending his school holidays watching me wrestle with clothing mannquins would be a distant memory.

Felix follows my gaze. 'Mum told someone on the phone that Oliver and Claudia were... weird. I heard her.'

Raising my eyebrows at him I make him giggle. 'Do you listen to me on the phone?'

He nods. 'Yes, but you only talk about boring dresses.'

'True.'

Felix continues. 'Mum said Oliver only eats one meal a day and spends all his time on his exercise bike. Claudia lives in the sea shouting at tourists. Mum called her "the angry mermaid". It's true, Aunty Emily. I used to go to their house with Mum. Oliver never came to see us as he was always cycling in his study. Claudia would be walking around in her wet swimming costume. Mum would always go back on her crazy diet after we left.'

I cast him a bewildered look. 'You're quite observant, aren't you?'

Leaning back against the wall I think aloud about whether I could be in the 'weird' camp. 'Felix, I don't eat much, because I sometimes forget to feed us. I also do a lot of angry sewing and I shout a lot. That puts me in the weird camp too.'

Felix nods and rests his head against me.

'After watching that angry sewing video, I definitely think I'm weird.'

He sits up. 'Do you think I'm weird, Aunty Emily?'

I smile at him. 'Out of all of us, Felix, you're probably the normal one.'

Something flickers across his hazel eyes. He lowers them to

the floor. 'Mum told someone on the phone I was weird. I heard that too.'

Ruffling his hair, I give him a hug, tell him not to be silly... and try to bury the memory of Vivi telling me the same thing when I came over to babysit on that dreadful night when life... well... imploded. In my head I can hear my sister saying how she was worried about Felix acting weird. She nagged me about getting Rory to take him to the football at the weekend. Back then I was more concerned with finding out where Rory was and not being able to contact him than what my nephew was up to. I think I was half-listening to Vivi and jokingly said something like, 'Leave him alone. Anyway, Vivi, you were really odd growing up and we just left you to get on with it.'

How I wish I'd listened to my sister about Felix being weird. It might have helped me with him now.

'Come on, let's go downstairs.'

Picking up my iPad and grabbing the black chiffon material from his chair I lead the way. Felix, holding Baxter (still carrying my bra) follows. 'Aunty Emily, I know you said Christmas was cancelled but can we go to London tomorrow?'

On the stairs I turn back to him. 'London?'

He nods. 'I want to see the London Christmas decorations. Everyone at school says London is cool to visit at Christmas.'

Once we get down the stairs, I head for the living room. We're greeted by my four dressmaking mannequins who preside over the corner. All are wearing the vintage dresses I recently bought from the grandson of a lady in Worthing who had passed away. He'd found them in his grandmother's attic and by chance had seen my business Facebook post about buying vintage dresses. I couldn't believe my luck when I saw the dresses: a 1970s original BIBA Maxi dress with their iconic embroidered gold-on-black square label, woven with a black and gold thread, an original Louis Feraud vintage dress in hot pink; a 1950s brocade evening dress in silver; and a stunning 1960s kingfisher-blue silk ruffle evening dress which made both Felix and me gasp in amazement. All were in decent condition and my only issues were a few missing buttons, a ripped hem, and a tear on one of the waists. To my surprise he didn't want any money for them. Instead, he asked me to donate to the Stroke charity which he was supporting after his grandmother had passed away.

Hanging up on hangers hooked over the picture rail are my handmade, off-the-shoulder, red polka-dot swing dresses which have sold like hot cakes online for Christmas parties, and now I have a long list for the new year celebrations. This latest batch still needs some work. Going to London tomorrow will put me behind schedule. My 'to do' list for the business gets longer by the hour and my online site needs updating, which will take me forever.

'I should start working on this lot...' I say, catching sight of Felix's drooping smile.

He clasps his hands together. 'Please, Aunty Emily, it's Christmas.'

I think back to our chat on the landing. He came out of his room to talk to me tonight. Normally I creep downstairs to sew more dresses while he bangs and thuds inside his bedroom. Tonight, I made progress. If I'd known that carpet shaming Vivi would have got Felix out of his bedroom I would have done it sooner.

Scanning the room, I can only see dresses, an old sewing machine, embroidery cases, scissors of all sizes, bits of fabric, paper patterns, books, magazines, tins of buttons and bags of sequins. Vivi's old living room is hiding underneath all this dressmaking chaos. Between the dresses I can see a few violet flowers from Vivi's wallpaper poking out, Baxter's leopard-print dog bed and her extensive ballet DVD collection gathering dust on pine shelves.

When I moved into her house it didn't feel right to change the furniture and I felt Felix needed some stability. However, my dressmaking business has taken over the living room. Being surrounded by patterns, pieces of material and dresses has kept me sane.

I can't see anything remotely festive in this room. Turning my attention back to him I notice Felix is squeezing the life out of his little hands and they're almost white. He deserves a nice day out even though he pinches my fabric, fiddles with my bags of sequins, throws my iPad across the room, backchats me at every opportunity, refuses to eat his dinner and regularly shouts he hates me. Felix isn't a bad kid. I know that.

A memory of Rory and I taking Felix out for the day last year pushes itself to the front of my mind. We had taken him ice skating while Vivi went on a date. I don't think Rory, Felix and I stopped laughing all afternoon on the ice. Felix kept making hilarious comments about me and Rory's dreadful ice-skating skills while impressing us with his fancy moves. At one point Rory turned to me and we both gushed in unison about how great fun Felix was. It was one of those weird experiences where you say the same thing and just stare at each other for ages.

Felix is a great kid. He lost his mummy all those months ago. At nine years of age that's unthinkable. I need to keep reminding myself of this.

Fuck it!

'Yes, we can go to London tomorrow.'

Watching my nephew jump for joy makes me feel light-headed. He rushes over and wraps his skinny arms around my waist. 'Thank you, Aunty Emily.'

'It will be good fun. We need it.'

After making myself a cup of tea, I return to the living room. Felix is sat on the sofa between two large dress carriers, one of my many sewing boxes, two bags of material from the stall at the craft market I visited last week and a pile of paper patterns. Baxter and my bra are on his lap.

I place one of my sewing boxes on the floor before sitting

down. Felix is next to me and I can see that he's fiddling with my iPad again. Seeing me he swiftly places it on the coffee table and shoves his hands under his legs. 'Sorry, Aunty Emily. I should have asked.'

I'm too weary to fight. 'Use it. Let's not get upset with each other any more tonight.'

He nods as I take a mouthful of tea. 'I don't like Beth, Rory's new girlfriend.'

The tea somehow lodges itself in my throat. I'm now choking and spewing tea all over one of my dress patterns. Felix springs up from the sofa and races to get some kitchen roll so I can clean up the mess I have made.

Once my paper dress pattern is drying out on the radiator I sit back. Felix cuddles up to me and Baxter runs off as he's bored with my grey bra. 'Rory's new girlfriend makes you sad, doesn't she, Aunty Emily?'

'Don't be silly, Felix,' I say, blinking away tears. 'Rory has moved on with his life. I don't know why he keeps appearing in my newsfeed. I don't know why we are still friends on Facebook. Maybe we should unfriend each other and then I won't have to see his dating exploits.'

'Mum was always secretly unfriending people on Facebook,' mumbles Felix. 'Please don't unfriend him?'

I let out a heavy sigh. 'He's not my boyfriend anymore. Felix. It looks like he's about to become Beth's.'

Felix hangs his head. 'Beth makes me sad. How far is Leeds, Aunty Emily?'

'A long way away,' I murmur, recalling the day Rory turned up on our doorstep to announce he had accepted the new job in Leeds. Pain engulfed my chest as I forced out a smile and reminded myself that this was the best decision for both of us.

'My maths teacher at school, Mrs Atkinson, says that if two people love each other, love will find a way to reunite them.'

I cast a look of bewilderment at Felix. 'Mrs Atkinson needs to get back to teaching primary school maths.'

Felix shrugs.

'Life has taken Rory and me in different directions,' I say, ruffling Felix's hair. 'The best we can do is hope Rory finds happiness with... Beth.'

CHAPTER 3

FELIX

*C*rawling underneath his desk, Felix makes himself comfortable by leaning against the warm radiator. He holds up the phone and presses *record*. 'Mummy, it's me. Every day I worry Aunty Emily will find all my videos for you on your phone. There's not much to see as I record under my desk. Just my weird-looking face.' He pulls a silly expression and peers into the camera. 'I would get told off for using your phone for videos.'

He admires his mum's old silver mobile phone. 'I like talking into your phone. It feels like you're still here with me. Do you think God might let you watch these videos? I hope he does because that would be naughty of him if he didn't. I wish you were in your bedroom watching TV in bed. Do you remember how I would climb into your bed, and we would snuggle up and watch a cartoon? If I was a good boy, you would bring me a cup of warm milk and a biscuit. I had to promise not to get crumbs everywhere. There's no one to cuddle in my bedroom. Baxter is downstairs chewing up Aunty Emily's bra and doesn't want to be cuddled. Aunty Emily doesn't like big cuddles anymore. I wish you were here, Mummy.' Tears stream down his cheeks. At first, he wipes them away with the back of his hand but soon grabs an old sock lying on the floor near him to stem the flow.

'I miss you, Mummy.' Pressing the sock over his mouth he tries to muffle the sound of his sob. 'Sometimes... missing... you... hurts...' His sobs force him to pause. 'It hurts me so much I have to ask Aunty Emily for some medicine.' Rubbing his chest, he tries to get his breath.

'When I can't get to sleep, I think about what you're doing up in heaven. Aunty Emily says you're working on God's newspaper. I do ask Google and Siri a lot whether God has a newspaper, but they don't seem to know.' He wipes his face again with the now-damp sock.

'Today, Amelie, Ronnie, Sai and I walked to the sweet shop. Amelie carried Baxter as it was cold, and she was worried his paws would freeze. We talked about you working on God's newspaper in heaven. Amelie thinks her grandpa will be working on God's newspaper too. According to Amelie, he loved writing poems. Although she did say her grandpa was rubbish at Scrabble. She beat him every time they played. I can believe that as she always comes top in spelling tests. Amelie asked me to tell you to check his spelling. She's the only friend who knows about these videos for you. Ronnie said his dad is in heaven too, but he thinks you and Amelie's grandpa will be writing about him in God's newspaper. He was a lifeguard and was always saving people who couldn't swim. Ronnie said before he got sick and couldn't be a lifeguard anymore, he once saved five people in one day. Amelie reckoned Ronnie's dad is now one of God's lifeguards. Ronnie googled to see whether there is sea in heaven. Sai said his parents have told him that when you die you come back as someone or something else. Amelie said her grandpa loved eating smelly fish so she thinks he might come back as a kipper. Ronnie said his dad loved fast cars so he will come back as a Formula One driver. The thought of you, Mummy, coming back as another person made me sad so I talked about watching

Santa travel the world on Christmas Eve.' More tears make their way down his cheeks so he wipes them away with his sleeve.

'In our street there is a huge Christmas tree in every window. Aunty Emily is too busy sewing dresses and doesn't have time to put up our tree. Amelie says her mum has gone Christmas-tree mad this year. Her mum has bought a giant one for the lounge plus littles ones for every bedroom – even the spare room. I told Amelie about last Christmas and how we had to have a trolley at IKEA for all our decorations and a man had to help us to the car because we'd bought so much stuff. Tomorrow Amelie is going to do something sneaky. She's going to put the little tree in their spare room in a carrier bag and drop it off on my doorstep.'

He takes a deep breath. 'I have not been a good boy again today. I threw Aunty Emily's iPad across the living room, and she got very angry. It was a bad thing to do. I also didn't eat her casserole. Mummy – it was horrible. I loved your casseroles. One bit of meat took me twenty minutes to chew and it made my teeth hurt. I also stole a piece of her dress material, so I got into trouble for that too. Mummy, I know you are busy with God's newspaper, but I get so sad living here without you.' He buries his face in the sock and cries. 'Aunty Emily has changed. She used to be a fun person. We used to have hugs and play fights. All she does now is sew dresses with a scary look on her face.'

He reaches across his carpet for a new sock to wipe his face. 'Rory still has his new girlfriend called Beth. There's no change from when I spoke to you at the start of the week. Aunty Emily lets me use her iPad, so I log on to her Facebook and see what Rory is up to. The other afternoon when Amelie, Ronnie and Sai came to call for me I showed Amelie, Ronnie, and Sai Beth's photo on Aunty Emily's iPad. Aunty Emily was on the phone shouting at someone who was complaining about one of her dresses and she didn't see me sneak out of the door with her iPad. Amelie thinks Beth is a top model, Sai says Beth looks like the woman from the football TV show he watches, and Ronnie says she looks like his brother's new girlfriend.' Felix blows his runny nose into his new sock.

'Rory and Beth are having their third date at his flat tomorrow. Ronnie is going to ask his older brother what happens on a third date. Amelie says the third date is where you cook a meal at home, light candles on the table, post a couple of selfies on Instagram and then the other person gives you their feedback on your cooking and your room design. Sai thinks it's where you watch a sad film together. His dad said his mum loved to watch sad films when they met. Amelie reminded us about how she loves horror films, especially the ones which are rated fifteen and banned by her mum. They would give me bad dreams. Sai says the third date is also where you let the other person choose the first chocolate in a selection box. We all agreed Sai will struggle with this when he has a girlfriend. Sai also agreed.' Felix giggles at the thought of his friend's love of chocolate.

'Ronnie is sure his brother will know as he's had lots of girlfriends at university, and he overheard his mum telling his stepdad that she's worried his brother is spending too much time with his girlfriends and not studying.' Felix fiddles with a loose strand of purple carpet.

'Every time I think about Beth, I feel angry. Aunty Emily shouts a lot after she has looked at Beth's photo. Her mouth goes all twisty when I show her Beth's Facebook page. I think Aunty Emily is sad too. She loves Rory but won't admit it. I know I'm right. I've just sent Aunty Lizzie an iMessage on Aunty Emily's iPad about Rory and Beth. Aunty Lizzie will talk to Aunty Emily for me.' He tugs hard at the loose strand, but it refuses to part from the carpet.

'Amelie asked us today what we want for Christmas. Before they all could answer I said I wanted the old Aunty Emily and Rory to get back together and adopt me. Don't be cross, Mummy. I know you won't be coming back. God needs you for his newspaper. I will miss you forever, but Amelie keeps telling me I must think about who is going to look after me now that I am an orphan. I told her I have a dad, but no one knows his name. I said he looks like a pop singer from long ago. Amelie says being an orphan is cool. In all the books she's read orphans are always the characters who everyone loves and who get to do crazy things. I have asked her to name some, and she said, Oliver Twist, Peter Pan, Mowgli, and Harry Potter. Pretty cool, huh?'

He takes a deep breath. 'Amelie asked me who I would want as parents if I could pick anyone in the world. She says that if she was an orphan, she would want Spiderman and Ariana Grande to adopt her. I said I would pick the old Aunty Emily as my new mummy, the one who laughed a lot, chased me around the park, took me to the arcades on the Pier and made me cool waistcoats for parties. For my dad I would pick Rory, as he watches ballet DVDs with me, he loves Marvel films, we have wave jumping contests down at the beach and he loves Aunty Emily. He also knows my secret. I can't tell you my secret yet, Mummy. They would be great parents for me.' He sniffs and goes to wipe his nose on the sock but feeling that its damp he wipes his nose on his sleeve.

'Mummy, you always told me I have good ideas. Well, I have a plan about how to get Emily and Rory back together. I must do it. Today I told Amelie, Ronnie, and Sai about my idea. Amelie hugged me which was nice. She always smells of cola bottles. Ronnie high fived me and Sai said thinking about my plan made him feel sick. He had to sit down outside the sweetshop and tell us about how his parents would ground him for the rest of his life if he did anything like that. We all think it's funny how Sai always worries about things. I also spoke to Miss Hemingway next door about my plan who said she was pleased I had told her but was now going to have a sleepless night and worry a lot about me.

'Earlier I persuaded Aunty Emily to take me to London tomorrow. This is part of my plan. I told her I wanted to see the

Christmas lights. Please don't worry, Mummy. It's a good idea. Trust me.'

Leaning his head against the inside of his desk he sighs. 'Before I started this video, I did something very naughty. You must believe me when I say it's part of my plan. Aunty Emily thinks I am up here buying her a Christmas present. I am buying something but it's not a present I can wrap up.'

Sitting up he bangs his head on the bottom of his desk. 'Oh, I must go, someone is knocking at our door. Speak soon, I love you, Mummy.' He presses his lips against the screen, leaving a saliva imprint, and saves the video.

CHAPTER 4

EMILY

*F*elix has gone upstairs with my iPad. Apparently, he wants to check on my Christmas present. Hearing him talk about sorting me out a gift for Christmas shocked me. After everything we have been through, all the arguments and the countless times he's screamed about how much he hates me, I didn't think he would buy me anything.

He's also checking out the train times for tomorrow's trip. I did offer to look for them on my phone, but Felix wants tomorrow to be his day.

A knock at my front door makes Baxter and me jump. It's Lizzie, my best friend, and lifelong partner in fashion and chaos. She's an exceptional human being who's put up with me since we were thirteen. Tonight, Lizzie is wearing her hideously expensive, full-length Marlborough trench coat in red tartan, which she bought a few weeks ago during a moment of cocktail-fuelled online shopping madness, and has been threatening to return it as there is now a crater-sized hole in her savings. The sight of her coat with its double-breasted front, fitted shape and belted waist lights me up inside. Together with her striking shiny black hair, which is cut into a sharp French bob, Lizzie looks amazing. Underneath she's wearing the cute evening dress in black crepe with puff sleeves and gathered waist I made her last year for her birthday. One of the many benefits of having Lizzie as a best mate is that she'll always make you look cool when you go out with her.

'Felix messaged me on Facebook to say you still love Rory and he's got an *awful* new girlfriend,' she says, before pulling me into a warm hug and air kissing me with plump lips coated in the boldest of red shades. She stands back and places her hands on my shoulders. 'In my horoscope for today the astrologer did say I would get a mysterious message and have to act on it straight away.' I watch her check to see if her bob is still in place. 'Obviously I would have preferred a mysterious message from the cute Irish barman I have been lusting after for months and that could still happen later tonight, if he stops gazing longingly at that Cara woman from my office. Anyway, here I am answering Felix's distress call.'

I stare at her in bewilderment. 'What?'

My heart is thumping in my chest. Why did I let Felix borrow my iPad?

Lizzie coos at Baxter and scoops him into her arms. He rests his head on her arm giving her the impression he's angelic. She sighs and heads for the living room. 'Blimey, Ems, this room gets more overcrowded every day.' I hear her screech. 'Why is there a pile of chewed up knickers by this chair?'

Rushing in I curse at Baxter and pick up the remnants of my silky underwear. 'That dog has been sent to test me.'

Lizzie hugs Baxter. 'Sounds like you're getting blamed for everything, my sweet boy.'

I also move a pile of patterns and glossy fashion magazines from the armchair. She plonks herself down and surveys my new swing dresses. 'Wow – they look great. Do you want me to model one now for you?'

Lizzie is Forever Vintage's model. As she has a perfect

hourglass figure and is adored by any sort of camera, she models all my clothes on a regular basis. Without Lizzie's modelling support I don't think I could have got Forever Vintage off the ground.

'I thought you were on your way out?'

Lizzie places Baxter on the floor before pouting and striking a model-like pose with her hand touching her face. 'I'm in the mood for some modelling and later when the Irish barman asks me what I do for a living I can show him the pics of me wearing one of those fabulous dresses.'

She undresses and I help her into the swing dress which is nearly finished. 'I can't believe Felix messaged you,' I say, making sure no pins holding the back panels together stab her.

Lizzie shrugs and once I have finished making sure the dress is ready, she lets her eyes wander over the messy room. 'Do you think tidying up in here might be a good idea? Some models would refuse to work in such terrible conditions.'

Folding my arms across my chest I shake my head. 'No, it's organised chaos.'

Lizzie frowns at me. I clear her a space near the far wall. 'Right, Kate Moss, strike your best pose.'

Taking out my phone I snap away as she strikes an array of elegant poses. 'Lizzie – I don't know how you do it, but you always bring my dresses to life.'

She pouts and makes me laugh. 'It's all the Milan fashion shows I do, darling, when I'm not sorting out payroll queries and undertaking staff disciplinaries at the factory.'

By day Lizzie is Head of HR for a factory which makes cheap electrical goods and by night she's Forever Vintage's top model.

Once I have got the perfect shot, she makes her way back to the chair she left her clothes on and I head for the sofa. 'Good news,' Lizzie says, 'Bill is going to move into the flat with me and take your old room.'

Before Vivi died, Lizzie and I shared a flat together,

overlooking Brighton seafront. I got very emotional on the day I moved into Vivi's house. Our little flat was a true palace. It was the place where we happily failed at being responsible adults. We spent a lot of our time wrapped in duvets on the sofa comparing hangover symptoms, sat in the bathroom dyeing each other's hair, crying over subsequent hair distasters and partying far too much. We had our own makeshift seventies cocktail bar in the living room, a square of wooden floor for dancing away our troubles and a silver disco ball hanging from the ceiling. The parties we threw in our flat were not the coolest ones in Brighton. Lizzie and I changed into comfy slippers the second everyone started dancing in our living room and by midnight we would both be in our PJs.

We also had a chalk board in the toilet with a long list of the men who had broken our hearts, and a selection of Lizzie's paintings from her artist life phase. Lizzie goes through many phases. Her artist phase is mine and Bill's favourite. Her still life artwork of vases, bowls of fruit and plants was ghastly. She was hopeless at painting faces, arms, backs, shoulders, and legs but she discovered a unique flair for painting naked male bottoms. Her teacher gushed at the use of her shading. Proud of her creative talent, Lizzie adorned our hallway with her finest artwork focusing on male buttocks in different settings, and to this day she will still give visitors to the flat a guided tour of her journey of self-discovery into male bums.

I gulp back a wave of emotion. Bill is one of our friends. Both Lizzie and I used to work for Bill many moons ago when we worked in a customer services call centre and he was our team leader. Fresh out of university, Lizzie and I found ourselves temping in a customer services department answering the phones, and we had to report in to Bill. Being a new team leader of eight young people wasn't the best career choice for Bill, who had recently relocated to Brighton from Wales. He admits his brief spell in a semi-managerial role was a mistake. At his daily morning team meetings, Bill spent more time talking through all our boyfriend, girlfriend, and marriage issues than he did setting team goals for the week. His own romance issues were always interesting, especially when he started dating a local Brighton DJ and could get us all on the guest list. When we were supposed to have our 1-2-1 appointments Bill would take us for a coffee in the café and for an hour we'd sit and talk about the meaning of life. In terms of productivity, our team was the worst, and one day Bill was demoted. After that Lizzie and I decided to make him part of our friendship group. He's been a close friend ever since.

My sadness has nothing to do with Bill. He's a great friend and it's good that he'll be getting out of his pokey bedsit, with brown running water and his neighbours who seem to have noisy sex day and night. Moving in with Lizzie will be amazing for him. They will have a lot of fun together. I miss living with my best mate, we had such fun. I think I'm in mourning as that part of my life died too when Vivi passed away.

Lizzie has picked up on my quivering bottom lip. She shoots up, jumps over a pile of dresses, nearly loses her footing on an empty plastic dress carrier lying on the floor, dodges a pile of books about the history of dresses, hops over a confused Baxter and lands before me. 'Talk to me,' she whispers, shifting a half-finished stitched dress which was stretched across a part of the sofa and plonking herself down.

'I'm not enjoying living here, Lizzie,' I sniff as tears shoot for freedom down my cheeks. 'I feel so guilty for saying that, but all Felix and I do is fight.'

Lizzie pulls me against her. 'It was always going to be frigging hard to move into Vivi's house and look after Felix 24/7, Ems, but you're doing a great job with him.'

Shaking my head, I pull away. 'Lizzie, I'm the worst person to be his legal guardian,' I say, grabbing a tissue from my cardigan to stem the train of snot which has shot out of my nostrils.

Lizzie squeezes my arm. 'Come on, don't say that. I'm sure most kids who have just lost their mum would act the same as Felix.'

'He tells me he hates me every evening.'

Lizzie casts me a warm smile. 'That's a normal kid thing. I was always telling my parents I hated them. I think it's a part of growing up. You and Vivi must have told your mum that?'

A memory of Vivi shouting at our drunken mum who was lying in an empty bath, fully clothed and downing a bottle of vodka surfaces in my mind. 'Yes, we did, but she never listened to anything we said.'

Lizzie strokes my cheek. 'You are doing a good job, Ems.'

'I sometimes forget to cook tea, Lizzie. When I do cook something, he spits it out in disgust, I yell and scream at him, and then I go ballistic when he hides my dress material.'

I hear my best mate let out a sigh. 'Again, all standard stuff. My mother couldn't make toast, I would feed her attempts at a casserole to the dog, she would scream from morning until night, and she would go apeshit when I nicked her cigarettes.'

We both smile. Lizzie picks Baxter up, who lovingly licks her face. 'This dog is bloody adorable, Ems, I don't believe all the bad stuff you claim he does.'

Shaking my head, I grimace at Baxter. 'When he's not burrowing into my clean washing basket, chewing up my knickers, he's having a tantrum about his dog food. Vivi spoilt him rotten. I also think he doesn't like me so that's why he's so naughty.'

Lizzie strokes Baxter's velvety black ears. 'With dogs you need time to bond with them.'

I roll my eyes. 'I don't have any time for dog bonding. Baxter doesn't like me because I replaced his dream dog owner.'

Lizzie sighs. 'Right, what's the deal with you and Rory?'

I can feel myself deflate. 'Rory is going on a third date tomorrow with someone called Beth.'

Lizzie studies my face. 'Felix is right – isn't he? You do still love him.'

Hanging my head and letting my unwashed for several days, auburn hair drop over my face. 'No. Well, I'm working on *trying not to love* him.'

Lizzie chuckles. 'That plan of yours has never worked for me. You know I've been trying not to love Robbie Tulloch from school for years.'

I plunge my face into my hands. 'I can't end up like you and Robbie Tulloch.'

At school Robbie and Lizzie were like David and Victoria Beckham. Robbie was the handsome, blond-haired football striker and Lizzie was stunning with her silky black hair and model looks. Everyone said they'd marry and have beautiful children. They broke up in sixth form after he cheated on her. It was a dark day for romance and there were rumours of year seven and eight girls crying in the school toilets over their breakup.

Lizzie sighs. 'If Robbie thinks I am going to go out of the back of the pub with him on New Year's Eve this year and do unspeakable things in an alleyway while his second wife chats to her gym friends in the bar he can think again. I have to put a stop to our annual meet up.'

'I'm buying you a padlock for your knickers for Christmas.'

She nudges me. 'It's okay to still love someone after you break up with them.'

We go silent. The day before Rory and I split up rushes back to me. We were out having a lunchtime drink with his work colleagues. It was a week after Vivi had died and it was the day Felix returned to school. I don't know why I let Rory persuade me into going. The world felt like it was made of cotton wool, and everything was sort of weird and echoey. I was still in shock. After a few sips of wine, I remember telling Rory I needed the loo. It was a lie. I wanted to go into a toilet cubicle and cry my heart out about losing my wonderful sister.

There had been a woman in the bar carrying a handbag like Vivi's Radley bag. The sight of it slung over her shoulder made the bar go blurry. After I'd cried hard against the toilet door I emerged with red, puffy eyes and mascara tramlines plotting a course down to my chin. Anna was there waiting for me. Anna, with her endless, slim legs, her happy, smiley face and glossy raven mane of hair which was so long it almost touched her bum. Rory's work friend. She'd joined Rory's company a few months before and knew someone from Rory's university days, so they had a lot to talk about. He had been spending a lot of time with her during the weeks leading up to Vivi's death, going out for drinks and lengthy meals where they talked nonstop about old memories. I knew they were just old friends and I trusted Rory but a little piece of me didn't like the fact that Anna had Rory's full attention.

She placed a hand on my shoulder as I washed my hands. 'Emily, I'm so sorry about your sister,' she said in a sweet, sincere voice. 'I can't imagine what you're going through.'

The toilet mirrors went blurry as I desperately tried to hold everything together.

'How's Felix? Rory says he's gone back to school?'

I didn't know where to start with putting an answer together. How was Felix doing after losing his wonderful mother in such a tragic way and having to come to terms with his Aunty Emily looking after him? He'd locked himself in his bedroom after I told him his mummy had gone to heaven. A neighbour had looked after him while I was at the hospital with Vivi, then Felix had watched me come up the path to the house. I placed my hands on his shoulders, but he'd batted them away. 'Where's Mummy?' he demanded. In the days that followed he spent a lot of time thudding and banging in his bedroom. Every half hour I'd knocked on his door to ask him if he was okay. He'd yell at me to go away. When he did venture out, he shouted at me, threw things, and had tantrum after tantrum.

'He's being brave,' I replied, shaking my wet hands and heading for the dryer.

Anna nodded. 'Poor lad.' She watched me wringing my hands under the hot air. 'How do you feel? Rory said you're Felix's legal guardian now.'

I shrugged. 'I'm Felix's family now.'

His father was someone Vivi had had a drunken fling with while on a Butlins holiday weekend. She didn't know his name, or where he lived, but she did know he'd been there for a stag do. When she discovered she was pregnant with Felix I pleaded with her to try to remember some useful detail about her fling to help us identify him. All Vivi had said was that he looked like Rick Astley, complete with an elaborate Pompadour hairstyle and square black glasses. I spent hours trawling through Rick Astley lookalikes on Facebook for her, in a bid to track him down. It was only after I had given up with mental exhaustion that Vivi remembered him saying he wasn't on Facebook. Vivi could be very frustrating at times. Our father hasn't been in touch in thirty years and my mother is dead so there is only me.

Anna walked over to where I leant against the dryer. 'It's a big thing what you're doing, taking on young Felix. I really admire you.' She sent me a warm smile, before shifting her gaze to her reflection in the mirror. 'What will you and Rory do now? I mean he's not the settling down type – is he?'

Once the questions had left her lips they'd headed straight for my mind, burying themselves deep inside.

I'd not given much thought to my relationship with Rory up until this point. Grieving for Vivi, looking after a devastated Felix, and trying to figure out what the hell I was going to do with my upside-down life had taken up all my head space. At that moment, I decided to bat away her questions, make up an excuse about needing time to clear my head and return to Rory.

Those questions echoed in my head until I started to see my boyfriend in a new light. It was like someone had placed a filter over my eyes. Thinking of a future together with Felix felt like I was being cruel to Rory. He loved his commitment-free life, his socialising, his drinks after work, his bike, and his football. I also couldn't see Rory as the stand-in father either. He did take Felix to watch the football every Saturday, but I think Rory enjoyed it more than Felix. It was clear he wasn't ready for children.

Lizzie rubs my arm.

'Rory is not at the settling down stage and that's fine.'

Lizzie nods. 'There was his friendship with that Anna woman.'

Anna appears in my mind. Who wouldn't find Anna gorgeous? She had no emotional baggage and also had some connection with him from the past. 'She was more suited to him.'

Lizzie gives me a poke in the ribs. 'You can cut the negative self-talk out. Anna had nothing on you, Emily, she had the personality of a snake, could not be trusted and I don't know why Rory spent so much time with her.'

'Well, it hardly matters anymore. She's in Brighton and he's in Leeds. And I have to get on with my new life too, I guess.'

'When did you last hear from Rory?'

Despite the living room looking like a hurricane had brought the dress fitting department from *Strictly Come Dancing* and dumped everything on the floor, my eyes swiftly locate Rory's Christmas card. It's poking out of my handbag which is under the coffee table. 'Three weeks ago. He sent me that card.'

Lizzie nods. 'That was the card where he…'

I finish her sentence. 'He wanted to know whether I still loved him.'

'And you replied with…'

It hurts to force the words out. 'I texted him to say I didn't love him. It would have been cruel to say anything else.'

Lizzie frowns. I hold my hands up. 'Rory and I are over. I just need to get him out of my system.'

Lizzie pats my arm. 'Maybe you should date someone else?'

'What?'

My best mate smiles. 'You could date a handsome single father, someone who isn't having a thirty-something crisis like Rory and wants to be a great dad.'

CHAPTER 5

RORY

'*E*mily, kiss me, again,' I say, stroking her leg. 'I've missed you.' I can't believe that after weeks of trawling the Leeds city centre bars, I have found my ex-girlfriend.

Why didn't she tell me she was in Leeds? I've had a lot to drink. Fuck – I am very drunk. That last cocktail has not done me any favours. Still, I'm back at her hotel and when I wake up, she'll be in my arms. I wonder where Felix is tonight. He's probably back in Brighton at a friend's house getting excited for Christmas.

Emily's blurry face comes close to mine. To my dismay she stops undoing my jeans belt, places two hands on my chest and forcibly pushes me away. 'I'm NOT Emily, I'm Cassie. You are blind drunk – aren't you?'

I extend my hand. Emily's playing a joke on me. 'Come on, let's go to bed.'

My hand is whacked away. 'I am not sleeping with you if you can't get my name right.'

'Emily, please… we're back at your hotel.'

I can hear a frustrated yelp. 'I'M NOT EMILY and we are not at a hotel.'

Staggering to my feet my cocktail-saturated mind picks up on the Northern accent. Emily is not from the North. This is not Emily. She lets out a heavy sigh. 'For goodness' sake, why have I brought an idiot home?'

A new voice enters the room. It's female too. 'Who is this?'

'An idiot from a bar in town.'

I lose my balance and topple over to what feels like the sofa again or it could be the hotel bed.

The voices carry on and are oblivious to me lying helpless over here.

'He's a good-looking idiot.'

'Yes, he is. He keeps calling me Emily but he's a good kisser. We got a taxi home and it's been nonstop Emily this and that.'

'What do you want to do? Shall we kick him out?'

I can hear someone yank a curtain across a window. 'Have you seen the snow?'

'Yes, it's coming down fast. The taxi driver, when he wasn't moaning about the idiot over there looking like he was going to throw up all over the inside of his car, was telling me how the forecasters are saying it is definitely going to be a white Christmas.'

'Maybe we should let the idiot sleep on the sofa? He wouldn't survive outside,' says the new voice.

I hear Emily screech. 'Kate, he's a stranger and we're going to let him sleep down here? He could attack us in our beds tonight.'

'Hang on a minute, Cassie, when I came downstairs about ten minutes ago you were busy kissing his face off on the sofa and we both know what would have happened next if he hadn't have called you Emily.'

Emily or Cassie is sighing again.

'Rob's coming over in a bit,' says the new voice. 'By the time the idiot comes round my rugby-playing boyfriend will be here to protect us.'

Cassie giggles. 'Won't you and Rob be busy doing something else?'

'What's that on the floor by the idiot?'

I can hear footsteps get nearer. Someone is close. It's either Emily or Cassie, I can't see properly, they're just a blur of colour.

'It's a gold chain with a locket on it,' says Cassie. 'The idiot has good taste in jewellery. Emily is a lucky lady if this was meant for her.'

'Right, stick it back in his pocket. I'm off to bed.'

'Shall we leave the idiot down here?'

A blanket is thrown over me and a pillow hits me in the face. 'Right, idiot from bar, as my flatmate and I are feeling festive you can sleep on the sofa. If you try anything on you will be escorted out into the snow by Kate's six-foot-five, weightlifting, rugby-mad boyfriend. Do you understand?'

My world goes dark.

The vomit flies out of my mouth and spatters against the sofa cushion before I have a chance to properly open my eyes. Fuck! My head feels like someone has been hitting it with a shovel for hours. The stench of my own sick is making me heave again. Rubbing my sore eyes, I see it's still dark, but a thin slice of silvery moon has lit up where I am sleeping. In front of me is a dark fabric sofa cushion adorned with my yellow puke. Where the hell am I?

Hauling myself to my feet I stand and stare at the sick. Why did I drink so much last night? Whoever owns that sofa is not going to be impressed with me. I need to clear it up and I need to drink some water. Staggering towards a door I almost fall into a tiny galley kitchen. After drinking a pint of ice-cold water, I grab the kitchen roll and by the light of the moon clear up my mess. After putting the kitchen roll in the bin, I return for a cloth and some washing-up liquid. Desperately trying to not be sick again I dab at the cushion and fight waves of tiredness.

Come on, Rory, you need to get out of here.

Opening the front door, I gasp. The world outside is covered in thick, white snow. An icy wind whips at my face and nearly knocks me off balance. I've no idea where I am or which part of Leeds this is. Instead of venturing outside I close the front door and rest my head against it. Fuck. Reaching into my pocket I find my phone. My heart sinks as I realise it's out of battery. My wallet is still safe in my jeans. What about Vivi's locket? Oh God, I hope it's still there. As I slip the phone back into my pocket my fingertips touch the locket.

'Ugh – have you been sick?' A voice behind me makes me jump and so does the blast of the yellow living room light. 'It stinks!'

Turning around I see a young woman, wrapped in a fluffy pink dressing gown and snowmen pyjamas. She looks familiar with her shoulder length auburn hair, her almond shaped brown eyes, and her wide smile. She also has a look of Emily about her.

'Erm, yes, I've cleaned it up,' I say, sheepishly. 'I'm really sorry.'

She nods and points outside. 'Is the snow bad?'

Rubbing my forehead and wishing the pain radiating out of it would ease I nod.

'Fancy a cup of tea or coffee before I call you a taxi?'

I'm led away from the sick-stained sofa and into the blue galley kitchen. At the far end there's a tiny breakfast bar with two red leather stools.

'I'm Cassie by the way,' she says with a grin.

Why does that name sound familiar? A memory of kissing her in a bar last night comes rushing back to me, bringing with it a tidal wave of nausea. Oh, God, did I have sex with her?

'No, we didn't sleep together,' she chortles, reading the look of panic on my face. 'You kept calling me Emily even though I'd made it very clear I was Cassie.'

Shame casts its heavy cloak over me. 'I'm so sorry.'

I watch as she places two mugs of steaming tea on the wooden breakfast bar. The clock on the wall above our heads tells me it's six in the morning. 'Have a seat.' She also slides across a little packet of paracetamol. 'You might want some of these too.'

We both sip our tea and I wait for the paracetamol to deal with my throbbing head.

'So, who are you and who's Emily?'

I clear my throat. 'I'm Rory. Emily is my ex-girlfriend.'

Cassie nods and takes a mouthful of tea. 'You still miss her?'

I cast her a look of shock. Does she talk like this with all her dates?

A smile forms at the corners of her mouth. 'I like helping people, especially drunken idiots. Do you miss Emily?'

I hang my aching head as it grows heavy with all the memories of Emily racing out and clambering to get my attention. 'I shouldn't miss her, but I do.'

'You shouldn't miss her? What does that mean?' Cassie asks.

My eyes focus on the swirling tea below me. 'It's a crap situation. I just need to get on with my life.' I take in a lungful of Cassie's kitchen air.

'Oh,' says Cassie, 'do you still love her?'

I trace the rim of the mug with my fingertip. 'I'll always love her, but I have to move on with my life. It's for the best.'

'I'm so glad we didn't sleep with each other,' sighs Cassie with a wry smile, making my stomach knot with guilt.

With a heavy sigh I take a sip of my tea. 'I'm sorry. Going out and getting blind drunk is my way of getting Emily out of my system.'

Cassie shakes her head. 'Rory, let me tell you something – she's *not* out of your system. That plan of yours is a shit one.' I watch her wrap her fingers around her mug. 'When we kissed on the sofa you thought I was her and we were in a hotel together.'

Rubbing my stubble-clad chin, I pray for Cassie to stop reliving last night. This is torturous.

'By the way, last night, a gold chain with a locket on it dropped out of your coat pocket. Is that Emily's?'

I take the chain and locket from my pocket and lay it in the palm of my hand. 'Sort of.'

'What do you mean?'

In my hand I hold the chain and let the golden locket dangle in front of me. The kitchen light bounces off it and it begins to twirl. 'Her sister, Vivi, asked me to buy it for Emily. It was meant to be a surprise birthday present from Vivi. I never got the chance to give it to Emily.'

'It's so beautiful,' gushes Cassie. 'Where's the box for it?'

Hanging my head, I mumble, 'I've lost the box.'

Cassie is glancing between me and the locket. 'You've lost the box that the locket goes in?'

I nod. 'The thing is, I like having the locket on me. It stays in my pocket a lot of the time.'

'But the locket is not yours – is it?'

CHAPTER 6

EMILY

*F*elix is asleep on the sofa making cute murmuring sounds. The sight reminds me of when he was little, and I'd come over to babysit. Vivi would have dressed him in pyjamas adorned with teddy bears and his freshly washed hair would smell of strawberries. We'd watch one of Vivi's ballet DVDs as she reckoned it was the fastest way to get young Felix to sleep. She was right. After an hour of *The Nutcracker*, he'd curl up beside me and fall asleep.

Felix came down while Lizzie was still here. She had a cuddle with he and Baxter both on the sofa. I watched Felix giggling as Lizzie kept telling me to tidy up the living room. I made us all a huge bowl of oven chips. We sat and ate them saturated in tomato sauce, surrounded by dressmaking chaos. Lizzie showed us photos on her phone of the Irish barman she fancies, and Felix told her at length about our trip to London tomorrow. Lizzie asked him what he was excited about seeing in London and to our surprise he said the giant Christmas tree in St Pancras station. Lizzie cast me an odd look and asked him why that station and not see the Christmas lights in Oxford Street, Regent

Street or Covent Garden. He shrugged and said that was what he wanted to see.

I've been trying to attach this button to a dress for the past half hour, but I keep getting distracted by things: Felix's school books which are jutting out from underneath the sofa and an old notebook lying open on the coffee table with Felix's list for Santa. Peering over I smile at his neat, curly handwriting. There are only two things written on it. My heartbeat quickens. Maybe we can enter a shop tomorrow in London and while he's not looking, I could sneak up to the counter and buy them. Craning my neck, I read his list: *1. Mummy to come back. 2. Aunty Emily and Rory.*

I can hear my tears plopping onto the notebook. 'Oh, Felix,' I whisper, wiping my eyes. 'You're such a sweet boy. I wish your mummy was back too and I'm sorry for doing such a rubbish job.'

My attention turns to a photo of Vivi and Felix which is hung on the wall and hasn't been covered up by a dress. I smile at my beautiful sister, her gorgeous silky red hair, her porcelain-like skin and her piercing jade-green eyes. 'I love you, Vivi,' I whisper. 'I'm doing my best here but it's bloody hard.'

In my head I'm whisked back to that dreadful day in May. I recall standing on tippy toes, looking up and down the bustling seafront for Rory. On that evening it was full of bobbing sunburnt heads, inflatable beach accessories being carried aloft, and excitable children sat on the reddened shoulders of weary parents. Behind me was a shimmering, marine-blue sea, dotted with paddleboarders and evening swimmers. Groups of holidaymakers were sprawled across the golden beach; children chased each other across the sand and a group of giggling young women carried heels and bottles of wine over towards a deserted spot.

A longing to call Vivi and make up a lame excuse about not being able to babysit for her tonight gathered momentum inside me. In my head I visualised Rory spending the evening sat on the beach, sipping bottles of beer and eating takeaway. After what happened later, I am so glad I didn't tell a lie.

The reason why I didn't bail on Vivi was because she would have detected my lie. Frustratingly, my dream started to evaporate. Vivi always claimed my voice changed when I was being dishonest. When we were little, she always knew when I was lying to her about not knowing where I'd hidden some chocolate. When we were teenagers, she always knew when I'd been secretly drinking Mum's vodka behind the sofa or kissing the older boy down the street, the one whose lips tasted of cola bottles.

It was gone seven and the oven-like sun was busy roasting my neck and creating yet more damp patches on the back of my blouse.

Where the hell was my boyfriend?

He was coming straight from his office where there had been an absence of both electric fans and air conditioning. I expected to see him walking towards me, his curly black hair clinging to his sweaty forehead and his blue shirt trying to unstick itself from his back.

I still couldn't see any sign of him.

After a flurry of texts at lunchtime about plans for that night we'd agreed to meet on the seafront after work, grab something to eat and head over to Vivi's house to babysit Felix.

I rang his phone. It went straight to voicemail. 'Hey – are you coming over Vivi's tonight with me?'

After twenty minutes I decided to make my way to Vivi's. Maybe Rory was held up and would turn up at Vivi's later?

One of the many things I loved about Vivi's house when she was alive was her kitchen. When I went over I never used the front door and would always head around the back. The door opened onto Vivi's kitchen. It's not posh or anything, her kitchen cupboards were put in about fifteen years ago by her then boyfriend, and were made out of reclaimed floorboards, but they have been painted a variety of different colours since then. Every time Vivi got her heart broken she would always paint her kitchen cupboards. It was her way of mending her heart. By the time she had finished painting them she'd feel better about dating again. I'd always call in after work and she'd be sobbing over a tin of cerise-pink wood paint, surrounded by the contents of her kitchen cupboards. She would refuse my offer of help and reassured me that once she started painting the sixth cupboard near the back door she would be singing and smiling again. One year, however, she did make me laugh as I found her coating her cupboards in a rich purple colour. I asked her whether her boyfriend at the time had been horrible to her. She shook her head and said their relationship had got dull and she'd fancied a change in her kitchen. After telling him it was over she'd rushed to buy some new paint.

Vivi's kitchen was always full of colour, warmth, and laughter. All her white electrical goods were adorned with her extensive fridge magnet collection from the many places she'd travelled to before Felix came along. One of the walls in the kitchen by the door had no appliances against it so Vivi had covered it with postcards, letters from friends, Felix's school letters, the newspaper articles she'd written for the local paper and silly photos of her and Felix. Her radio would always be blasting out something from the eighties and if she was going out, she would be doing her make-up on the old wooden kitchen table. To this day I don't know why my sister chose to apply her make-up in the kitchen. Whenever I burst through the back door she would be singing along to some tune while holding up a little mirror to apply her mascara. The coffee machine would be gurgling away in the corner, there would be something amazing bubbling away on the stove and Baxter would be sat obediently on the floor by her legs. As you can imagine, the kitchen is a place where Felix and I now try to spend as little time as possible.

On that night I noticed something was different. There was

no radio blaring, nothing cooking on the stove and no make-up chaos strewn across the table. She was leaning against her work surface rubbing her neck. I did notice she was wearing the dress I'd made her at the start of the summer. (It was based on an outfit I'd seen Princess Anne wear in the seventies, a gorgeous blue-and-yellow floral print, with a ruched bodice, balloon sleeves and gently grazed her open-toe silver sandals.) 'Alright, Ems,' she said, softly, as I stepped inside her cold kitchen. 'That nagging headache I texted you about at the start of the week. It's still here.'

'Oh... have you taken stuff for it?' I asked, flinging down my handbag and walking over to her.

She nodded and smiled. 'Yes, but nothing has worked. I think I need to go out and get very drunk.'

'Are you due on? I get terrible headaches near my period.'

Vivi scratched her head. 'No, I don't think it's that. I've been really stressed at work lately, so I think it's that.'

I rubbed her shoulders. 'Vivi, you need to look after yourself. Your health is more important than work.'

She chuckled. 'Try telling my editor that.'

A loud thudding noise above our heads made us both look up.

'What the hell is that?' I asked, staring at the kitchen ceiling.

Vivi rolled her eyes. 'Felix is always banging around in his room. I have no idea what he does in there.'

I smiled at the thought of my nephew. 'I thought he'd be down here to greet me.'

More bangs followed. I remember waiting for Vivi to go shout at him for making such a din and nearly coming through the ceiling. Instead, she sat down at the table, rubbing the back of her head. 'Felix is going through a weird stage.'

'What?'

She nodded. 'Secretive, quiet and banging about in his room.'

The words *secretive* and *quiet* made me think about Rory. Instinctively I reached for my phone and saw that he'd not returned my call or sent me a text.

Vivi sighed. 'I've given up with Felix. Maybe he'll start acting normal again soon.'

Preoccupied with my boyfriend's whereabouts I nodded, still looking at my phone, and made a joke about Vivi being weird when she was younger.

'Where's Rory?' Vivi asked as Baxter came into the kitchen. He trotted over to her, and she made a fuss of him.

I shrugged. 'No idea. He's probably had to work late.'

Vivi touched my hand. 'Will you ask him if he can take Felix to the football at the weekend?'

I remember groaning. 'That will take all Saturday afternoon, Vivi. Rory and I have been invited to his mate's barbecue. I really fancied going as all his work mates will be there and Anna's NOT going for once. Also, I'm not allowed to go with him and Felix when they go to football.'

Vivi cast me her best begging face. I have spent a lifetime unsuccessfully trying to ignore this face and stick to my guns on something. My sister knew I struggled when she tilted her head to one side, widened her green eyes and stuck out her bottom lip. On that night it brought back the memory of seventeen-year-old Vivi pleading for me to drive her to the party where she was planning to show her ex-boyfriend that she'd moved on and didn't care that he wasn't in her life anymore. Being driven to the party was essential as she'd spent hours putting her hair in curlers and didn't want the evening air to dampen her huge curls. I was supposed to be driving in the opposite direction to see Lizzie. Vivi spent a good hour repeatedly casting me that very face... until I cracked and agreed to drop her off.

'Please, Ems, Felix always comes back transformed after one of Rory's trips to see the football.'

I let out a heavy sigh. 'I'll ask him.'

Vivi smiled in victory and rose from the table. 'You are the best sister.'

Putting away my phone I watched her grab her silver clutch bag. 'So, who is this date with?'

A grin broke out across her face and a sparkle appeared in her left eye. 'Paul from the printing firm next to the café where I buy my morning coffee.'

'Oh,' I sang, making her laugh. 'Tell me about Paul.'

She squealed. 'Mid-thirties and separated, and if I squint, he looks a bit like David Beckham, and he owns the most divine pair of desert boots.'

We both laughed before she left the house moaning about her headache and promising me to expect a drunken sister coming home. I watched her walk up the street and admired my dressmaking skills.

I made Felix his favourite buttery toast treat, and we watched TV together. We also sat and talked about his school friend Amelie who had cut her own hair while her mum was downstairs watching Corrie. Felix made me smile when he asked me whether I would ever have a mullet hairstyle. Amelie had been asking her mum for a mullet hairstyle for weeks and when her mum said no for the hundredth time Amelie took the kitchen scissors and gave herself what she thought was a mullet. We googled mullet hairstyles from the eighties and Felix said he would have a mullet when he was old enough to have a moustache. He thought mullets and moustaches looked cool. Afterwards he went upstairs to bang around in his bedroom, and I binge watched a grisly crime drama on Prime while Baxter slept in his dog basket.

Rory never turned up. He got a few angry messages from me but then I put my phone away and distracted myself with a handsome, smooth-talking detective. Felix did make a right racket upstairs until about ten thirty when everything went quiet.

Vivi returned at midnight. She was desperate for the loo when she came in. I watched her sprint up the stairs to the toilet. She shouted, 'Stick the kettle on, I need a cuppa.'

I called after her, 'Are you pissed?'

She laughed and I heard the toilet door bang.

The kettle whistled so I poured hot water into both cups and fished us two herbal tea bags from a jar on the work surface. By the time I realised Vivi had not come out of the loo I was sat at her kitchen table texting Lizzie, who was crying in the toilets of a club after spotting the guy she was seeing with his arms around another woman.

I remember wondering whether Vivi had passed out on the loo. She has been known to do that.

Leaving my phone downstairs, I bolted up the stairs. 'Vivi – your tea's ready.'

There was no reply. I knocked a few times on the toilet door. Nothing. My heart began to thump against my rib cage. Turning the handle, I tried to open the door, but Vivi was somehow lying against it. Blood drained from my face and my breathing quickened as I saw my sister's head on the floor.

She'd not passed out. She hadn't drunk that much. She'd suffered a fatal brain aneurism. The doctor at the hospital, the one with tears in her eyes and warm hands, said Vivi wouldn't have felt anything.

For a few days after, Felix and I struggled with using the upstairs bathroom. That was until we came home from buying Felix a suit for his mum's funeral to find Rory painting the walls marine blue and preparing to put new flooring down. It was a welcome surprise.

Felix is stirring. I'm back to the present. Vivi has gone. It's just me and Felix now. I must stop crying. It's late and Felix should be in his own bed, not asleep on the sofa.

Even though I feel like I am doing the worst job at caring for Felix I have to somehow carry on. Tomorrow is his special day, and he deserves a bit of spoiling and magic.

Putting down his Santa list I scoop Felix into my arms and head upstairs for bed.

CHAPTER 7

EMILY

'*R*ory?'

A familiar voice calls out through the wintry darkness. 'Aunty Emily?' The warm, fuzzy feeling inside my chest is replaced with a sweeping wave of disappointment.

Flicking on the bedside light I can see Felix standing in the doorway of Vivi's bedroom. At his feet is Baxter wearing his red lead.

I now sleep in Vivi's bed. This is a three bedroomed house with two decent sized rooms and one small room, which contains all my belongings in storage containers, so really there was no option for me but to sleep in Vivi's bed. I hated sleeping in her room at first and spent the first few weeks on the sofa. It smelt of her Elizabeth Arden perfume, her vanilla-scented shampoo, and her Jo Malone grapefruit body cream. No matter how much air freshener I doused the room in I could still smell Vivi. I even bought myself a new olive-green duvet set from the supermarket. Something completely different to her deep purple duvet. Every time I got into bed it still felt like Vivi was going to appear at the door, with a towel wrapped around her head, telling me to move over as I was on her side.

Eventually, a combination of physical exhaustion and Felix sleepwalking in the night made me reluctantly move from the sofa to Vivi's room. I couldn't bear the thought of Felix injuring himself by falling down the stairs half asleep.

Rubbing my sleepy eyes, I see that he's already dressed in jeans and trainers, and even has his red coat on. 'What time is it?' I croak. 'Why are you up and ready?'

'It's our special day remember?' he says, stepping into the bedroom. As he gets closer, I can see his grey rucksack is on his shoulders. 'I'm ready for an adventure,' he says, with a grin. 'Baxter is also excited about our trip. Why were you saying Rory's name?'

Stifling a yawn, while trying to bury the dream about Rory telling me he still loved me at the back of my mind, I sit up and frown at Baxter. 'We're not taking Baxter to London.'

Felix shakes his head defiantly. 'Baxter loves adventures. He came everywhere with us when Mummy was...'

I interrupt him. 'Baxter is only eight inches tall; he will get trodden on. He'll be flat as a pancake by the time we get back.'

Baxter tilts his head and barks at me to raise his complaint too. This little dog sees himself as the third human in the house so will always add his viewpoint to any argument.

Felix lets out a heavy sigh. 'He hates walking so he will sit in my lap or allow me to carry him or he will sit in my rucksack.'

I have enough worries about today. Baxter will cause trouble, that's guaranteed. 'He stays here,' I say, turning to check my clock. 'It's just gone six, Felix.'

He nods. 'Mum always said the early bird catches the worm.'

When do children start sleeping in? I remember Vivi waking me up as I headed towards the teenage years. It would be mid-morning and she'd be clutching a bowl of cornflakes.

'I'm taking Baxter whether you like it or not,' Felix announces.

I can feel my blood simmering. Why does Felix disobey everything I say?

'It's snowing, Aunty Emily,' Felix explains, before marching over to the window and yanking back the curtains. It's a good distraction as we both gasp at the gigantic snowflakes colliding with the windowpane and the white pile of snow on the ledge.

'We might need to rethink our plans. Trains to London might be cancelled,' I mutter without thinking. Felix's face drops. He lets go of the curtains, scowls, and runs into his bedroom, slamming the door. A few seconds later the usual bangs and thuds on the floor begin.

'Shit,' I say, rubbing my forehead. 'Why did I say that?'

Baxter comes to my side of the bed and starts barking at me.

Guilt wraps its fingers around my chest and squeezes. This was supposed to be Felix's special day and I might have already ruined it.

'Stop barking, Baxter,' I snap, grabbing my phone, I log on to my train app. A wave of relief spreads through me. They all seem to be running. The Met Office tells me that more snow is expected later this afternoon. Felix and I should be back early afternoon.

'FELIX,' I shout. 'The trains are still running.'

His bedroom door opens with such force it bangs against his wall. Within a few seconds he's by my bed, watery eyed and with an ear to ear smile. I can't help thinking his face reminds me of a rainbow which appears after the rain.

As Felix and I smile at each other Baxter runs off with my slipper.

'That dog is NOT coming to London,' I shout as Felix runs after Baxter.

Once the slipper has been returned to me Felix comes into the bedroom with Baxter in his arms and licking his face. 'Aunty

Emily, please rethink about Baxter coming with us. I promise you he won't be naughty.'

'I'll think about it,' I say, scowling at Baxter's cheeky little dog face.

Felix and Baxter hang about upstairs while I shower and get dressed. While I am drying my hair at Vivi's dressing table Felix comes in carrying Vivi's old mobile phone. I've added a new pay-as-you-go SIM card to it and I let him use it when he goes to football matches with Rory, on sleepovers with school friends (he's only been on one since Vivi passed away) and when he goes on school trips. It's my idea of safety. He knows how to use it as apparently Vivi was always asking him how to do stuff on it. Felix knows how to use any piece of technology. He's a whizz with my latest iPhone, my iPad, and my laptop. We've agreed that Vivi's phone is only to be used in an emergency. It has a pay as you go Sim card inside it so he can't run up a bill. 'Can I use this today?'

'Yes, good idea in case we get separated in the London crowds. Is it charged?'

He grins. 'Been charging all night in my bedroom.'

Why do I get the feeling Felix is always one step ahead of me?

My eyes notice his bag. 'What on earth are you taking to London?'

Before I get a reply, he scoots off and thunders downstairs.

Turning back to the mirror, I carry on drying my hair. It looks clean, thick, and glossy today which is a rarity these days. Normally it's unwashed, greasy, and held in an untidy ponytail. Back when Vivi was still alive and I was busy dating Rory and working, I obsessed over my hair. Every morning I would wash it and spend a good half hour straightening the life out of it. My hair straighteners are still in an unopened box which I brought with me when I moved out of Lizzie's flat.

My mind flicks back to the last time I'd used them. It was a few days before the night my life imploded. Rory had stayed over at my flat. He was lying in bed trying to persuade me to climb back underneath the covers with him. We'd spent half the night arguing about how he'd turned up drunk to mine after yet another office night out and, on my couch, had started telling me how wonderful it was to have Anna as a friend. I'd gone to bed in a huff. He'd followed and we got into a heated debate about what my problem was with him going on his third office night out in a week. We'd both turned to opposite sides of the bed and fallen asleep. I had awoken to him wrapping his long arms around me and whispering a lengthy apology in my ear. He looked so handsome in the morning light with his messy curly black hair, his boyish smile, and his athletic, muscular chest. We'd had amazing make-up sex and afterwards we both lay grinning like idiots and gasping for air.

So, there I was doing my hair, showered, and fully dressed for work, watching him in the mirror inviting me back to bed. 'Let's do that all over again,' he said with a grin.

'Rory, I will be late for work,' I replied, turning on my straighteners.

He crawled over to me and began kissing my neck. 'Please come back to bed with me,' he whispered.

Turning on my stool I let him kiss me. Before I knew what was happening, he'd lifted me off the stool and placed me on my dressing table. With a sexy smile he removed my skirt and pants. The sex was great until I burnt my bottom on my poker-hot hair straighteners.

Letting out a heavy sigh I run my brush through my hair and groan as it gets stuck in a huge knot.

'Beth has posted a comment on her post to say she's excited about this afternoon's date,' says Felix, making me jump in fright and yank my hair brush which in turn makes me cry out. I whirl around still with the hairbrush caught up in my tangled hair mess. 'OUCH! What?'

Felix is holding Baxter and my iPad. 'She's had four likes already.'

Carefully I begin to unpick my hair and think about Beth. Forgetting Felix is telling me this I start to think aloud. 'Beth is sounding a bit desperate.'

'I've been on your Facebook page, Aunty Emily, and you rarely posted anything about you and Rory when you were together,' explains Felix.

'That's because I like to keep things private.' The brush is released but decides to bring a clump of my hair with it too. What with this, the snow, our day in London, taking Baxter with us and having Felix keep me updated all day long about Rory's third date, I think I'll need an intravenous drip set up of strong coffee.

We all walk down the stairs.

'Mum never kept things private on Facebook,' says Felix, once we get to the bottom of the stairs.

For goodness' sake – are all nine-year-olds like little spies? How did my sister stay sane with this level of monitoring?

He follows me into the kitchen. 'Mum was always telling everyone on Facebook about her dates and her nights out dancing at discos and moaning about our next-door neighbour.'

'Who is that?' Getting to know the neighbours has been way down my priority list since I moved in with Felix. In fact, I couldn't tell you who lived on either side, and I wouldn't be able to recognise them in a police line-up.

'Miss Hemingway,' explains Felix, 'she's nice and has helped me a lot.'

'Oh,' I reply, switching on Vivi's coffee machine. 'Didn't your mum like her?'

Felix shakes his head. 'Mum called her an old busybody. Miss Hemingway complained about Mum's loud music and her singing.'

I try to stifle a smile but fail. 'When we were growing up your

mother had a dreadful singing voice.' At once my mind is awash
with memories of Vivi standing in the middle of our own living
room, clad in a purple leotard and singing along to *X-Factor*,
using a shampoo bottle as a microphone.

Felix is listening intently.

'Vivi thought she was a songbird, but I used to say she
sounded more like a seagull.'

Felix grins and goes off into the living room with Baxter,
leaving me staring at the array of Vivi's tiny travel magnets.
Almost immediately they go blurry, and I have to grip onto the
work surface to steady myself. I make myself a coffee at high
speed and race out of the kitchen to get away from my memories
of Vivi. I go to find Felix, who is watching one of Vivi's ballet
DVDs. He's in one of his ballet trances, eyes fixed on the TV
screen and limbs completely frozen. His red coat is still zipped
up and his rucksack is still over his shoulders. I often catch him
doing this. It's his way of thinking about his mum. The sight of
him makes me think about Rory. When Rory came over to
babysit with me, he would always put one of Vivi's ballet DVDs
on and he would sit and watch it with Felix. My heart would
swell at the sight of them both snuggled up on the sofa watching
The Nutcracker or *Swan Lake*. They would sit for a good hour
watching the dancers. Even though Rory was always out getting
drunk, going on office nights out and was often unreliable when
it came to remembering date nights, he had a definite connection
with Felix. Rory spent more time with Felix than I did in the last
six months before Vivi died. He used to take Felix to watch the
football every Saturday. My mind reminds me of his date with
Beth this afternoon. I can't think about Rory and him rebuilding
a new life for himself; it feels like someone is scraping out my
insides.

Checking my watch, I see that it is still early and an hour
before the time we'd planned to leave for London. My brain leaps
into action. I could finish sewing the buttons on the dress I was

working on last night and after that I could sort out my website. Felix is still stood staring at the ballet dancers on the screen. Rory's face appears in my mind. If he was here now, he'd allow himself to become as engrossed in the ballet as Felix.

There are so many things to do. I have a horrendous 'to-do' list and I know orders for New Year's Eve will come in thick and fast today.

Felix snaps out of his trance. 'Go and do your dressmaking, Aunty Emily. We don't have to leave until later.'

Guilt twists my stomach into knots as I detect a tone of defeat in his voice.

I take a deep breath, try to remain strong and sit down beside him. 'Today is your day, Felix. No dressmaking today.'

He looks up at me. 'If you don't do your dressmaking, you will be grumpy for the rest of the day.'

Irritation prickles away at my cheeks. I let out a nervous laugh. 'I think I can take a day off from my business.'

Felix shakes his head and says quietly, 'You haven't had a day off since you started it the week after Mum died.'

'That's not true,' I snap. My nephew has such an imagination.

Felix turns to me. 'I'm telling the truth, Aunty Emily,' he shouts, making me flinch. 'You're always dressmaking.' Before I can say another word, he races away in tears and thunders up the stairs. I'm left staring down at an angry Baxter who is growling at me.

Plunging my face into my hands I let the tears flow. Nothing I do or say with Felix is right. Life with him is getting harder. Wiping my wet cheeks, I reach for my phone. I am sure I've taken time off since I started Forever Vintage.

My stomach has just performed an elegant swan dive towards the floor. I feel sick. Felix is right. I have not taken any time off since I launched Forever Vintage. Shamefully this includes weekends, school holidays and the day of Vivi's funeral where I sewed in the evening.

Vivi, if you're listening up in heaven, I still don't know why we agreed I should be Felix's legal guardian if anything ever happened to you. I am sensing he doesn't like me anymore. If I am honest I never realised how hard being a parent could be.

We're all on our way to Brighton train station.

Felix emerged from his bedroom after half an hour of him banging about in his room and me sat in the living room, hating myself for spending all my time setting up my business. In the end I crept up to the landing to sit outside his door. He ignored my initial attempts to persuade him to come out and talk to me. So I played a Christmas song on my phone and pressed it against the door.

It's the song Rory and I danced to last Christmas right here in this very house. 'All I Want for Christmas is You,' by Mariah Carey. Vivi had thrown an impromptu Christmas party and invited everyone she knew. Lizzie, Bill and his boyfriend, Keith, came as well as Rory. Lizzie got off with one of Vivi's old school friends and Bill split up with Keith after a huge drunken argument in the hallway. While Vivi tried to calm them both down and keep an eye on the wild disco dancing which was going on in her living room, Rory took me into the kitchen, played Mariah's song and pulled me into a romantic slow dance. It was the best slow dance I have ever had in my life and even beat my first with Samuel Butters at the school disco when I was thirteen. In the end, just as Rory was about kiss to me, a little voice came from under the table. It was Felix. We both laughed as Felix crawled out of his hiding place. Rory asked Felix why he was under the table, and he said that a couple of Vivi's work friends were kissing on the bed in his bedroom and it made him feel sick. Rory was shocked anyone would think of entering a child's bedroom to get off with each other and like a hero he marched upstairs to drag the randy couple out of Felix's room.

Felix had a huge grin on his face when he opened his door. 'I remember that song from last Christmas,' he said. He broke into a chuckle as he recalled Rory telling off the two people who were kissing on his bed. 'It was so funny, Aunty Emily,' he laughed, 'the man was Mummy's boss at work.' For a few minutes Felix and I forgot our quarrel and reminisced about that party; Lizzie being sick all over Vivi's plant pots outside, Rory's drunken dancing and Bill calling Keith a 'two-timing rat bag' in front of Felix.

Baxter chose to raid my laundry pile again and came waddling out onto the landing with one of my black thongs in his mouth. Red faced with embarrassment I chased after him but failed to grab him as he scooted under Felix's bed. He then proceeded to growl at me every time I tried to get hold of my thong. I swear this tiny dog thinks he's a Rottweiler. As I was busy hissing at Baxter, I caught sight of an overflowing cardboard box. It was piled high with ballet DVDs and on the top was a pair of ballet shoes. I don't remember Vivi joining a ballet class but she did often surprise me, so I wouldn't put it past her.

I suggested we make an earlier start for London. Once Felix had wrestled Baxter into his red dog coat and made him ready for winter weather we finally left.

On our way out of the house Felix waved to our neighbour, Miss Hemingway. She was stood in her doorway staring at her snow-covered path. Her hair was adorned with pink curlers, and she was wearing a blue dressing gown. I would say she's in her eighties and has a stern head teacher sort of face. To my surprise Felix, carrying Baxter, walked over to the little fence, which separates our front gardens, and shouted, 'Merry Christmas, Miss Hemingway.'

She glanced at him and smiled. Her eyes drifted to me, and I watched her replace the smile with what looked like a scowl.

Turning back to Felix she said, 'To you too, Felix. How are you getting on?'

He pointed in my direction. 'Aunty Emily is looking after me. We argue a lot. Sorry about the noise.'

Oh, God, why has he said that, I thought. If he's not careful I will have social services on my door. I tried to hurry him along. 'Come along, Felix,' I hissed.

'Yes, I can hear you shouting most evenings,' Miss Hemingway called out, making my cheeks heat up. My embarrassment levels were soaring.

Felix wriggled away from me and ran to the fence. 'Aunty Emily is sad a lot.'

'FELIX,' I roared, hurrying back to him. In my head I recalled Felix telling me Vivi moaned a lot about Miss Hemingway and referred to her as a busybody. 'Felix, I am NOT sad a lot.'

Taking him by the elbow I frogmarch him up the path, muttering under my breath about why my sister made me his legal guardian.

'I can tell,' shouted Miss Hemingway, making me jump out of my skin. Is my sadness that obvious?

Felix waved back. 'My Christmas present, the one we talked about the other day, will make her happy again.'

Before he could say another word, I dragged him away. Out of earshot I turned to him and barked, 'Why did you say that? Your mother called her a *busybody*. I'll be the talk of Brighton.'

Felix grinned mischievously. 'Sorry, Aunty Emily, I'm sure she won't mention it at one of her coffee mornings.'

'WHAT?'

Felix nodded. 'Miss Hemingway is very popular. Don't worry, I am going to make you happy again, Aunty Emily.'

'I'm not sure if that's possible,' I murmured, picturing Vivi and Rory in my mind. Thinking about what Felix had said to Miss Hemingway I turned to him. 'Have you been talking to her?'

He nodded. 'Out of my bedroom window.' As he walked a

little way in front of me, I found myself thinking about how little I know about Felix.

Huge snowflakes are now descending from the sky and the sight of them is fuelling my anxiety. I hope the trains will get us to London and back later this afternoon. At the edge of my mind are all the swing dresses I have yet to finish, the new photo images I need to upload to Instagram, the changes I need to make to my website and the latest orders I need to process which came through last night. My shoulders and neck are so tense with anxiety they are like rods of iron. I can't stop worrying about Miss Hemingway telling the neighbourhood I shout a lot. All the talk and memories of Rory have taken my heart hostage as well. I am also distracted by Rory's third date with Beth this afternoon. I can't help thinking whether he's slept with her yet. Shards of what feels like jealousy keep torturing my poor heart.

The pavements are coated in white snow which is delighting Felix. I am holding Baxter and watching Felix dance and twirl in the snow with an ear-to-ear smile. He moves with such grace, something I have not witnessed before. My eyes are drawn to his pointed toes and the intricate set of steps he takes before leaping into the air. His thin body arches and all I can do is murmur, 'Wow – Felix, you can dance.' He stops and I notice his cheeks are flame red. Turning on his heel he continues to dance.

Baxter and I stand and watch Felix. My mind drifts. I wonder what Rory is doing right now. Nibbling on a fingernail I think about all my dress orders back home. Guilt creeps up my spine. Today is about Felix enjoying himself. It shouldn't start with me struggling to contain a head full of worries. How I wish I could let all of them go, relax, and enjoy my time with Felix.

The Rory and Beth date also won't leave me alone. What happens if Beth is amazing in bed, and they spend all of Christmas having great sex and he gets so carried away he asks her to marry him on New Year's Eve?

Felix has stopped dancing and is staring at me. 'Are you thinking about Rory, Aunty Emily?'

I let out a nervous laugh. 'Don't be silly, I'm thinking about how wonderful it is to have all this snow.'

Felix shakes his head. 'You do know I can tell when you're lying, Aunty Emily.'

CHAPTER 8

FELIX

Taking his mum's phone out of his pocket Felix looks over his shoulder to see whether Aunty Emily is watching. He spots her a little way behind looking in a shop window. 'Mummy, it's me, again. I must talk quietly as Aunty Emily might hear. We're off to London. Say hello to Baxter.' Holding the phone with one hand and Baxter in the other, he gently presses Baxter's face against the screen and makes a woof sound for him.

'I set my alarm clock early so I could pack my rucksack. Amelie suggested I should take a skipping rope as in all the action films she watches rope always comes in useful. As we passed her house yesterday, she grabbed hers and gave it to me. Ronnie got excited and said a life jacket would also be useful to have in my rucksack. I had to explain to him that I wouldn't be crossing any water. Sai always comes up with good ideas. He suggested I take chargers for my phone and Aunty Emily's iPad, plus, he said, a torch, batteries, and clean underwear. Amelie was really impressed with Sai's ideas. Ronnie went in a mood because no one liked his life jacket idea.' Baxter is wriggling about so Felix rearranges him.

'Wish me luck. I am going to get into so much trouble today.'

He points the phone upwards so that his mum can see the millions of fluttering white snowflakes descending from the sky. 'Look, Mummy, it's snowing.'

After wiping Baxter's head, he goes to stand in a doorway. 'Last night I had a dream it was last Christmas, and you were still here with me. We were in the kitchen making Christmas lunch. I was trying to peel the potatoes and you were chopping carrots. We were singing along to Christmas songs on the radio. I was so happy. There were twinkly lights everywhere. Aunty Emily and Rory came to the door with presents and everyone was smiling. When I woke up, I went downstairs to find you. The house was dark and cold. It was a dream and I cried.'

He nuzzles his face into Baxter's fur. 'Amelie is worried I will get grounded forever when Aunty Emily finds out what I have done, and she'll have to hang out with Ronnie and Sai by herself. Amelie keeps asking me to describe the old Aunty Emily and the new Aunty Emily. She doesn't understand what I mean. I said when the old Aunty Emily picked me up from school, she would be happy to see me, and we would walk home talking. Once home she would make the best buttery white toast and we'd sit on the sofa eating and watching one of my ballet DVDs. Aunty Emily would look at the weather and if it was nice, we'd go down to the beach, roll our jeans up and paddle in the sea. I'd get to stay up late too.' He pauses to check on Aunty Emily. She's rummaging through her handbag and hasn't moved any further from when he last checked.

'The new Aunty Emily looks sad when I come out of school. She's always in a hurry to get home because a dress needs sewing, or an order needs to be posted. When we get home, we get upset and don't feel like talking. I know she cries a lot because I can hear her when I am in my bedroom. She's sad about you and Rory. Amelie said I had to do something. She was the one who gave me the idea for the plan. I told Amelie I was only nine and a half and there wasn't much I could do. Amelie said nine-and-a-half-year-olds can change the world. She said everyone thinks we are silly little kids, and we have to show them our secret powers.'

He checks again on Aunty Emily. 'Mummy, I have to go now. She's walking towards me. Talk later and don't worry about me.'

CHAPTER 9

RORY

'*I* better go,' I say, rising from the breakfast bar stool. 'Once again I am sorry for last night and for vomiting on your sofa.'

Cassie places a hand on my arm. 'Wait – why haven't you given Emily the locket her sister bought her?'

The memory of Emily's tear-stained face greeting me at the hospital unearths itself at the back of my mind. I can still remember holding her crumpled body as she wept on my shoulder. 'Vivi's dead,' she sobbed. 'My beautiful sister has died, Rory.' Every muscle in my body has tensed. I try to send the memory back to the shadows in my head but fail. Between sobs I can hear Emily telling me how she found Vivi unconscious in the toilet. My heart has begun to ache. Emily is holding me so tightly. 'Where were you? I have been calling you all night.' Guilt uncoils itself in my stomach. Where was I? If she'd known I'd gone back to Anna's flat for a late-night coffee, which ended disastrously as Anna had assumed I wanted to sleep with her and had taken off her clothes in front of me, Emily would have broken into tiny pieces. While her sister was dying, I was trying to persuade an emotional Anna to put her clothes back on, and apologising for giving her mixed signals.

'Rory?'

I return to the present day with a jolt. 'Huh?'

'The locket. Why haven't you given it to Emily?'

The gold chain and locket is nestled in the palm of my hand. 'Oh, umm, Vivi, her sister, died two days before Emily's birthday. Emily was in a bad place and didn't want anyone to celebrate her birthday. We were going to do something for her birthday later in the year.' I stare down at the lino floor. 'Then she broke up with me. I forgot about the locket in all the chaos of us separating and made a knee-jerk decision to move to Leeds.'

Opening my hand, I stroke the locket before opening it up to reveal two tiny photos of Vivi and Emily, smiling at the camera. My heart wakes up with a splutter.

Peering over my shoulder Cassie gasps. 'Oh – wow.'

'Vivi didn't know but I got someone to cut and insert the photos. I knew how much Vivi meant to Emily.'

Cassie's chestnut-coloured eyes have dramatically widened. 'Shit – Emily's sister died – was she ill or something?'

I let out a heavy sigh. 'Brain aneurism. Happened quickly. No warning.'

Cassie has covered her open mouth with her hands. 'Oh, God, that's awful. Was Emily close to her sister?'

'Yes, very close, Emily practically raised Vivi when they were children.'

Cassie shakes her head in bewilderment. 'That's so sad. Did you get on with Vivi too?'

Stuffing the locket back in my coat pocket I nod. 'She was a good friend to me. We became mates once I got together with Emily. She and Emily were a force to be reckoned with. It was Vivi who got Emily and me together.' I can't believe I'm telling a stranger called Cassie all this. 'I should be going.'

'No, tell me. How did you and Emily meet?'

The memory of the newspaper clipping comes back to me. 'Do you remember a story in the news years and years ago about two little girls who were found living alone in the woods?'

Cassie stares blankly at me.

'Well, I worked for a local newspaper back in Brighton and I got talking to this woman called Vivi who worked in the advertising team. We were chatting about a story of two runaway boys. Anyway, Vivi took out this old article and showed me it. She pointed at the two little girls, stood holding hands in a forest clearing. Vivi was the younger one and her older sister was Emily. Their mother was a drunk and didn't want to care for them so one day she dropped off her two young daughters at a nearby wood.'

I can tell Cassie is now hooked to my story. Her mouth has fallen open, and her eyes are now as wide as saucers. 'She did that to her own kids?'

'Yes, she did. The amazing thing was these two little girls lived in the woods by themselves for two days.'

'Eh? Two days?'

I nod. 'Emily took care of Vivi by building her a shelter inside of an old tree which had been hollowed out, picking blackberries and strawberries for them to eat, washing themselves in a stream and telling her stories when she got scared. Before their mother had taken them to the wood Emily had shoved a load of biscuits up her sleeves so they had those too. They were found fit and well two days later.'

Cassie's mouth is now gaping with amazement.

I smile. 'I asked Vivi if I could meet Emily as she sounded amazing and she was… amazing.' Why is my voice cracking with emotion? How much did I drink last night?

Fighting back tears I stare down at my hands.

'Rory, that's so sad about Vivi dying. How's Emily doing?'

I find myself sitting back down on the stool and running my hands through my hair. Lawrence's face flashes up inside my head. 'I know what it's like to lose someone. Emily's life will never be the same again.' Feeling dizzy I grip onto the table. 'Vivi had a young son, so overnight Emily became his legal guardian. That's really tough.'

Cassie's eyebrows have travelled so far up her forehead they are almost touching her hairline. 'Is the boy the reason why you can't be together?'

'Partly yes, no one seems to think fatherhood is for me right now,' I say, as Felix's face appears in my head. 'Emily didn't think it was fair for us to be together when she was going through so much and she got it into her head I was not serious about our relationship.'

Cassie blows the air out of her cheeks. 'I'm going to say it again, I am thanking all my lucky stars I didn't sleep with you last night.'

'Thanks.' I'm secretly glad too.

Cassie plunges her face into her hands. 'You were a lucky near miss, Rory. I was pissed off when I went to bed that you hadn't turned out to be the date I wanted, but after hearing all this, I think I might actually be glad we didn't go to bed together.'

'Right, I need to go home. I will walk in the dark and the snow. Might be good for my hangover.'

Cassie nods. 'The city centre is about half a mile walk in that direction.' She points behind her. 'Just keep following the main road. You will probably be able to flag down a taxi.'

As we get to the door, she touches my arm. 'Good luck, Rory.'

I smile. 'Thanks for everything, Cassie, the tea and the chat.'

She studies my face. 'Is fatherhood a bad concept for you?'

Pointing to myself I let out a nervous laugh. 'Look at me, Cassie, do I look like someone's father? Two weeks ago, I lost my job due to cutbacks, I have spent the last few weeks blowing holes in my savings, I go out far too much, get blind drunk and end up having short, meaningless relationships with women who I think are Emily. Also, I was a bit of an arsehole to Emily.'

Cassie opens the front door. 'Did you get on well with the boy?'

The subject of Felix will make me feel sadder than I already am. Ignoring her I stride out into the snow which is lit up by the streetlamps. 'I think I better go. Thanks for everything, Cassie.'

She stuffs her hands in her dressing gown pockets. 'Goodbye, Rory and happy Christmas. Good luck with your life and missing Emily.'

I smile and wave. 'Sorry I was a near miss.'

She frowns and folds her arms. 'Have you ever thought of trying to make it work with Emily as opposed to torturing yourself by looking for random flings?'

'I'll get over her, one day,' I say, staring down at my shoes, which are submerged in fluffy white snow.

I turn and begin to trudge away.

'At least give Emily her locket,' shouts Cassie. 'That is a beautiful locket. The fact you got their photos inserted is so sweet. I would be pissed off if someone had not given me my late sister's gift.'

The thought of sending Emily the gift stays with me all the way back to my flat in the snow. Up until now hanging on to the chain and locket hadn't felt wrong. I don't know why I thought keeping hold of Emily's present from her late sister was all right. It's been in my pocket for weeks, something I've secretly held or stroked whenever my new life in Leeds hasn't felt right. I often find myself opening the locket and gazing at Emily. The more I think about the locket the worse I feel about taking it out of its box all those months ago and carrying it around with me like some good luck charm. Perhaps I could send it back to Emily by special delivery?

Wearily I climb the stairs to my flat as the lift is once again out of order. Once back in my flat I head for the sofa and in the darkness think about what to do with the gold locket Vivi asked me to buy on her behalf for Emily's birthday. I take it out of my coat pocket and hold up the chain so the locket twirls in front of me. Vivi had taken me aside and asked what Emily would like for her birthday. The locket was something I should have bought Emily months before. Whenever we walked past the jewellery shop, she always pointed it out. When Vivi asked me for ideas on something nice for her older sister the locket was the first thing I blurted out. I knew Emily would treasure it.

It doesn't take long for my eyelids to grow heavy and my head to hit the cushion.

'Rory?' My flatmate, Tom, is standing over me, clutching a bowl of cereal. His blond hair is dripping wet and he's wearing his black bathrobe, 'You had a good night? How did it go?' He raises his thumbs. 'Were you successful in our *challenge*?'

With a groan I haul myself up to a sitting position and rub my bleary eyes. It's light outside. I'm not sure I want to tell him about how I pulled Cassie, thinking she was Emily, went home with her, tried to sleep with her but kept calling her Emily, threw up all over her sofa and then ended up pouring out my heart to her in the kitchen. 'It was good.'

Tom grins and slaps me on the back. 'That's the fighting spirit. Did you manage to score?'

I can't lie anymore to Tom. 'No, did you?'

'Ah, no, I wasn't so lucky with our challenge.' He shakes his head. 'I pulled some girl, lovely figure and a sexy smile. We were leaving the club and I saw Suzie. Mate – why did I have to see her in the club?' He groans with frustration. 'Suzie looked amazing. She was wearing that glittery gold dress I like. There I was embarking on our challenge. Suzie yelled she wouldn't take me back even if I was the last bloke on earth and then told the girl everything.'

'I'm hoping the girl you pulled ignored Suzie.'

Tom clamps his hand over his forehead. 'This girl linked arms with Suzie, and they went back into the club together.'

Tom is the guy who owns this flat. He's a newly qualified

solicitor, and when I moved in back in May he was weeks away from proposing to Suzie, who he claimed was the woman of his dreams.

Suzie dumped him after they had a drunken night of revealing their secrets to each other. She'd sold him the idea of having an evening where they told each other *everything*. Apparently, she wanted to know *everything* about her future husband before she got married.

Eager to get started, Suzie confessed to snogging a bridesmaid at her brother's wedding when she was nineteen, having sex in an office supplies cupboard with a previous ex-boyfriend and having an affair with a married bloke at work before she met Tom.

Lulled into a false sense of security, Tom confessed to sleeping with a woman at a work conference in Norwich just after he'd started seeing Suzie. He thought his secret was bulletproof as he explained to Suzie that they hadn't had the *exclusive conversation* until the afternoon he'd got home from Norwich.

Suzie took a different view of Tom's antics in Norwich. She left shortly after he had stopped chuckling, and she'd poured his favourite Scotch all over his head and screamed at him.

'Why did I think it was a good idea to tell Suzie about Carol from Norwich?' Tom groaned.

I watch him shove a spoonful of cornflakes into his mouth.

'Sorry, mate,' I say, massaging my aching forehead.

Tom gestures for me to shift up on the sofa. He sits down beside me with his cereal. 'Neither of us are performing well on this challenge. I don't understand why?'

Blowing the air out of my cheeks I sit back and place my hands behind my head. 'It's not easy sleeping with one other woman let alone ten.'

Tom shakes his head. 'Why is it so difficult for us? I mean we are two thirty-something, handsome bachelors. I thought the women of Leeds would be throwing themselves at us.'

'Your brother must have been lying about this secret challenge. Anyway, I'm not sure I want to sleep with ten women just to see whether your brother is right about his claim that after sleeping with ten women you'll forget all about your ex-girlfriend. I have gone off the idea of this challenge.'

'Rory, my brother was devastated when he split up with Marie from Huddersfield. He didn't come out of his flat for weeks. Then he took up this challenge. After ten shags my brother is back on form and hasn't thought about Marie from Huddersfield for weeks.' He licks his spoon. 'There's still hope for you though. What time is Beth coming over?'

Beth. Shit. I had forgot she was coming. 'Good job you reminded me. I think about midday.'

'I'll get out of the flat so you can have your wicked way and get our challenge started,' he says, with a chuckle.

The thought of getting physical in my hungover state makes my stomach roll over. 'Mate, I feel dog rough. I hope she's happy with an afternoon watching Christmas films.'

Tom bursts out laughing. 'Have you seen Facebook?'

I clamp my hand over my face. 'What has she posted?'

Tom brings the bowl to his lips to drink the cereal-saturated milk. Once he's stopped making his disgusting slurping noise he puts down his bowl. 'I get the feeling she's expecting *Fifty Shades of Grey*, my friend.'

'Mate, I'm a broken man,' I groan.

Tom rises from the sofa. 'This is your chance to get rid of the past. We both need to stop thinking about our ex-girlfriends and get this challenge underway. If I, was you, I'd be drinking a couple of cans of Red Bull from the fridge, taking a shower, dousing myself in aftershave and buying condoms.'

He walks out into the kitchen whistling.

Leaning back, I stare up at the ceiling. He's right. It's time to let Emily go. The chain and locket slips to the floor, breaking my train of thought. I bend down to pick it up and remember what Cassie said about giving it back to Emily. 'Tom – when's the last post?'

I can hear Tom laugh from the kitchen. 'Mate, it's Christmas Eve tomorrow. The last post was last week. You behind with your Christmas cards?'

Guilt wraps itself around my chest. This locket needs to be with the person it was intended for, it should not be with me. The thought of Emily opening a parcel and seeing the locket Vivi wanted her to have as a birthday gift makes my chest ache. She'd want to know what Vivi had bought her. The golden locket might even go some way to easing her pain. I think about how I would have felt if Lawrence, my brother, had got me a gift before he passed away. I feel like guilt is squeezing me so tightly I'm struggling to get a full breath. I would have treasured that gift although Lawrence only ever bought me daft gifts. My mind tries to take me back to that dreadful night all those years ago when he turned up to take me for a pint. I quickly block the memory out. Why the hell have I hung on to this chain and locket? I have missed the last post for Christmas, so how the hell do I get it to Emily in time?

Her face appears in my mind. I picture her face light up as she holds up the locket and that gorgeous smile sweeps across her face. My heart has broken into a wild gallop.

For a few fleeting seconds I'm whisked back to when we used to lie in bed together. She would gaze up at me and I would be lost in her beauty.

Her text from a few weeks ago brings me back to earth. The one where she said she didn't love me anymore. That horrible sinking feeling returns, the one which took hold of me after I'd read her text. It had sent me on a fortnight of heavy drinking with Tom, the start of our challenge and had fuelled me to find someone else to fill the crater-sized hole inside my chest.

Her words; 'Rory, I don't love you anymore', flash up inside my head. Surely if there was any chance of her loving me she would be here with me right now. It's over. Rising to my feet I slip the locket into my shirt pocket. For the billionth time in six months, I remind myself that Emily and I are over. It's time to move on.

I'll send it to Emily after Christmas.

CHAPTER 10

EMILY

*B*righton train station is filled with the sound of a group of early morning carol singers who are singing their hearts out, tiny children dancing and laughing with excitement while holding onto the hands of their parents, and excited chatter.

Brushing snow off our coats Felix, Baxter and I head towards the ticket machines. Two couples who are engaged in a tearful embrace catch my attention. They look as though they are about to be separated for Christmas and are clinging onto each for dear life. One couple, two young women, are emotional and kissing each other frantically.

'Felix, I have to get our tickets,' I say, mesmerised by the romantic scenes while holding on to Baxter's lead. The romance is making me remember when Rory lived in Clapham and I lived in Brighton. We'd almost sprint towards each other and I would fling myself against him.

Felix doesn't answer so I turn around to see what he's doing. He's already by the ticket machine and collecting what looks like orange tickets from the plastic mouth of the machine. How can he do that when he doesn't have the printed-out ticket reference which is in my hand and no method of payment. As I get closer, he stuffs the tickets in his backpack.

'What are you up to?' I ask, studying the mischievous look which has hijacked his face.

'I collect old tickets people have left behind in the machines,' he explains. 'Back at home I have hundreds.'

'Oh, I see,' I mumble, opening out the printed sheet. Old tickets sound like a strange thing to collect but I can't judge Felix as at his age I collected paper dress patterns from the sixties and seventies which I found in charity shops.

Once Felix and I have had an argument about whether Baxter needs a ticket (my knowledge of dogs on trains is limited) and whose lap he's going to sit on for the entire journey (there is no way that little so and so is sitting on mine), I collect our pre-paid tickets. We wander out to have a look up at the huge departure screen. 'Okay, it looks like the Thameslink is closed for engineering works, so we'll just get that train to Victoria in five minutes.'

Felix turns to me. 'Sai said we get to St Pancras from Victoria on the blue Victoria line?'

'What? You want to go to St Pancras?' I thought he would have forgotten about going to see St Pancras station. There are so many other things we can do and see in London. As always, he reads my mind. 'Please can we go, Aunty Emily, I really want to see St Pancras station.'

Reminding myself it is his special day I smile and nod. 'It's on our list. Do you want to go there first when we get there or before we head back this afternoon?'

He scratches his head. 'Can we go there for lunch?'

'Lunch at a railway station?' Surely not? 'I was thinking more like Covent Garden. At Christmas time there is so much delicious food to tuck into.'

To my dismay he shakes his head.

'Felix, you are the organiser of today so we will eat at St Pancras station.'

Felix nods and grins. 'That would be great, Aunty Emily.'

As we set off to board our train, I find myself staring at my nephew. I'm struggling to understand why he'd want to go to a station for something to eat. Maybe he's becoming a train spotter? That would explain the collection of railway tickets. Discovering what Felix is passionate about might help me with his mood swings. We could go for days out and see some train stations. It might not be riveting for me but if Felix enjoys them than so be it. 'Do you like trains, Felix?'

He yawns, wipes his runny nose with his coat sleeve and picks up Baxter. 'I prefer cars.'

I give up. When I looked after Vivi she was always so easy to read and manage. If she ever cried all I did was offer to plait her hair or paint her fingernails. If she was sad, I would go on a chocolate or biscuit scavenger hunt. Felix is different. One minute I feel like I am getting to know Felix and the next we are like two strangers. Surely by now I should be able to know what makes him happy.

We're being swept along by a moving mass of excitable commuters who are making their way towards the train's open doors. As we wait for a gang of old ladies to board the train Felix and I both turn to see a grinning father and mother chatting away to their son who is roughly the same age as Felix. The conversation about what they are all going to do on Christmas Day drifts over to Felix and me. It sounds idyllic as the father is planning to get up early and make a cooked breakfast. The boy cheers and claps. 'Can we have hash browns, Dad?' The mother rests her head on the father's shoulder. She thanks him for his wonderful culinary skills and makes him laugh by saying she struggles to boil an egg. He nods and says his Christmas dinner later will be out of this world. They all smile and talk about his roast potatoes which the mother describes with a chef's kiss. Mild irritation at their happiness makes my cheeks burn. Looking down at Felix I can see he's scowling at them too. I bet the mother doesn't spend all of Christmas Day trying to lose herself in dressmaking, their dog doesn't have a knicker chewing obsession and the son doesn't alternate between storming off upstairs in fits of anger and undertaking an hourly check of her Facebook account.

In my mind I have edited out the man's face and replaced it with Rory's. Nope, I can't see Rory as the father making me breakfast in bed or doing any family stuff. Although I have to say Rory is a good laugh at Christmas. He does come alive after his morning glass of Bucks Fizz, a good helping of Bombay Mix and a dance around the kitchen to Slade. Last Christmas he spent it with me, Lizzie and Bill. We got Bill to cook us a Christmas dinner while we all made Christmas cocktails, stuffed our faces with Quality Street and played charades.

'I wish Rory was here,' mumbles Felix, tugging at my coat.

Ruffling his coppery hair, I gesture for him to get on the train. Today cannot turn into one long Rory conversation. If that happens, I will be an emotional mess by the time we get home tonight. 'Let's forget about Rory for today – eh?'

Felix and I both know this is easier said than done. He jumps onto the train with Baxter under his arm and turns around to watch me board. 'You don't mean that – do you, Aunty Emily?'

'Mean what?' I gently guide him into our carriage.

'Forget about Rory for today.'

I sink into my seat by the window. Felix takes the opposite window seat and places Baxter on his lap.

'I meant we don't have to talk about him today.'

Felix ignores me. 'I think about Rory a lot.'

Laughter from a young couple sliding into the seats opposite distracts us. Their playful relationship banter about the amount of time it took the guy to do his hair this morning for a Christmas shopping trip in the snow fills the air inside the carriage. He's striking model-like poses with his shoulder-length curly brown hair and she's giggling away. Turning back to the empty seat beside me I can't help but think about Rory and me. We enjoyed a lot of cheeky sarcasm and piss-taking. He was the first boyfriend of mine who made me laugh and not just giggle or chuckle, I mean that hysterical, stomach hurting, tear inducing, wet your pants type of reaction.

Felix points at me. 'Are you thinking about Rory now too?'

Raising my hands in defence I turn to him. 'Look, let's change the subject. Rory and I are not together anymore. There's no hope of us getting back together.'

Felix's mouth falls open and his eyes darken. Baxter starts to growl at me like I am a crazed axe murderer.

Oh, God, please don't let us argue on a train the day before Christmas Eve.

'You shouldn't say that Aunty Emily,' he snaps. 'You and Rory still love each other; I know you do.'

A wave of emotion is building inside of me. This talk of Rory is pointless. Why does Felix keep mentioning him and why do I keep thinking about him? It's a futile situation. Rory, in my eyes, was not ready to be a father to Felix and he didn't need all my emotional baggage over Vivi dying thrown into our relationship. Rory needs to be single but not date gorgeous Beth. Her profile photo is seared onto the back of my mind. Oh, God, the thought of him dating other women is so painful. Rubbing my aching chest, I wonder whether I should buy some paracetamol when we get to London.

Felix is not giving up. 'Aunty Emily, if you didn't love Rory, you wouldn't always be thinking about him, you wouldn't do your angry sewing after seeing posts about him on Facebook and you wouldn't shout his name when you are asleep.'

My nephew is pushing all my buttons.

'I do know you, Aunty Emily.'

Vivi used to say Felix went on and on about stuff, but I always assumed it would be about new trainers or games consoles.

Without thinking I grip hold of the table and shout… 'I DO STILL LOVE RORY BUT HE'S NOT RIGHT FOR US. I BLOODY LOVE HIM, FELIX, WITH ALL MY HEART but…' I'm gasping, 'he doesn't want to settle down.'

Everyone in the carriage is staring at us both.

An ear-to-ear smile spreads across Felix's face. Baxter starts to bark with excitement. This is not the reaction I was expecting as, normally, when I lose my shit Felix does the same. 'You do still love him. I knew it.'

I let out a heavy sigh and sit back in my seat. All my energy is oozing out of me. I'm emotionally spent, and we left Brighton station only a minute ago.

'Mrs Atkinson, my maths teacher, says once you acknowledge a problem you can start to fix it.'

Turning away I mutter bad words about sensible Mrs Atkinson who clearly has not lost her shit in a long time.

He starts to rummage around in his rucksack. It's bulky and filled to the brim. I watch him struggle to fasten it back up.

'What have you got in there? From here it looks like you've brought the contents of your bedroom with you.'

I watch him flick his eyes to the plastic table. 'Don't shout, Aunty Emily, but I have brought along your iPad.'

He takes it out and slides it over to me. 'I thought you might want something to do on the trains.'

Tilting my head to one side I stare at him. 'Let me get this straight, you've brought along my iPad for me?'

I can see the start of a naughty grin working its way onto his face.

'Yes, Aunty Emily.'

We both start to giggle, and Baxter excitedly leaps onto the train table. For a few fleeting seconds I smile at Felix and think optimistic thoughts about today's adventure. That is until Baxter cocks his little leg and pisses on the train table.

After I've lost my shit a second time in the space of five minutes, cleaned up Baxter's pee and shouted about how I never wanted to bring a dog with us, I sit and take some deep breaths. My head is awash with thoughts about whether Rory has bought satin sheets to go on his bed for this afternoon's hot date with Beth, whether we will get home in time before the snow gets bad and the emotional breakdown Felix will have if someone accidentally flattens his tin-can-sized dog.

Why do I get the feeling this is going to be a long day?

The train has stopped at Burgess Hill. Someone is standing over my empty seat. I look up to see a woman, wearing a wonderful red-and-gold headscarf filled with a mass of impressive afro box braids. Standing next to her is a girl of Felix's age who has rows of complicated, neat braids, complete with pink and yellow beads. She's wearing an electric pink coat and a yellow scarf. 'Are these two seats free?' the woman asks with a huge smile.

The woman sits next to me. My nostrils are going wild at her perfume, a sweet tangerine aroma. Her daughter sits next to Felix and immediately falls in love with Baxter. She strokes Baxter with a tender hand. I watch Felix's eyes light up at the sight of the girl.

The woman turns to me. 'My daughter, Jade, has been asking for a little dog nonstop for months. What's your cute sausage dog's name?'

'Baxter,' I reply as we turn to see Baxter gaze longingly up at his new admirer. Jade strokes his tiny black head and floppy ears.

The woman grins at her daughter before turning back to me. 'I don't know anything about sausage dogs. What's he like?'

'Hard work,' I sigh, grimacing at Baxter. 'He's very naughty and is gradually chewing up all my underwear. He won't walk very far so one of us ends up carrying him everywhere. He has a lot to bark about, he has tantrums daily, he thinks he's a wolf and doesn't like me.'

The woman's smile evaporates. Jade lifts her head and casts a dreamy smile at the woman. 'Mum, please can we get one like this doggy?'

'I'm going to think some more about getting a dog. This nice lady here has just enlightened me. I didn't realise how hard and challenging a little dog could be.'

Jade casts me a filthy look. I can hear Felix whisper to her, 'Ignore my Aunty Emily, she's angry about Rory.'

'Who's Rory?' Jade whispers back as I glare at Felix.

Before I have time to catch what Felix says to Jade, the woman taps me on the arm. 'Are you going anywhere nice today?'

'Taking my nephew to London for the day. What are you doing?'

Chuckling she turns to me. 'I'm going to ask my boyfriend, Sidney, to marry me.'

I can feel my own smile stretching across my face. 'Wow!'

Calming down her excitable golden hoops with her fingers she giggles. 'Sidney has no idea. He is a doctor in accident and emergency. He'll be working for most of Christmas Day so I will have to propose before he goes to work.'

I watch her lean back into the seat and a goofy happy expression takes over her face.

'That's so romantic,' I find myself gushing.

'It will be if Sidney says yes,' she says, with an unforgettable hearty laugh. 'I have decided to take matters into my own hands. We have a fantastic relationship; we love each other, and I fancy a big wedding.'

I can hear Felix whispering to Jade. 'Do you like Sidney?'

She replies, 'He's cool, he comes to see me play football a lot.' With a quick glance in my direction, she turns back to Felix. 'Will she get back with Rory?'

I desperately try to hear what Felix is whispering to Jade but the woman taps me on the arm again. 'Have you got anyone special in your life?'

Shaking my head, I try to ignore Rory's face which has appeared in my mind. 'I did but we split up earlier this year.'

Jade and Felix are giggling to each other. Felix is showing her something on my iPad.

The woman taps me again and points at Jade and Felix. 'Those two have only just met and they look thick as thieves.'

A sense of unease creeps over me. Jade is peering at what Felix is typing into my iPad. She sneaks a look in my direction, and I grip onto the train armrest.

'Aunty Emily, I need the loo,' says Felix, holding the iPad against his chest. 'And so does Jade.'

I watch them both get up and walk down the carriage towards the toilets. Why must they take Baxter and my iPad with them? After opening my mouth and raising my hand in a bid to stop them I catch sight of Felix flashing Jade the iPad screen as they get near the carriage door. They both giggle and I put down my hand. Felix deserves some happiness and if that means playing games on my Ipad then so be it.

CHAPTER 11

FELIX

Felix, Jade, and Baxter enter the train toilet and lock the door behind them. He brings out his mum's old mobile phone and hands Aunty Emily's iPad to Jade. Holding up the phone he starts to record. 'Mummy, I'm in the train toilet. Meet my new friend, Jade.' He thrusts the phone screen at Jade.

'Umm… hello Felix's mum.' Jade goes back to watching Baxter sit up in her arms. Felix notices how her smile grows wider every time Baxter looks up at her. 'Felix – can I keep your dog?'

Jade waves Aunty Emily's ipad at him. 'Send the message now. Go on do it.'

He wipes his runny nose with the back of his hand. 'Aunty Emily is going to shout but I know she loves Rory and once they are back together, they can adopt me.'

Jade lets out a sigh. 'This is so romantic, Felix. You are going to bring them back together and then you will all live a H-E-A.'

Felix puts the phone on the side and lets it record. Jade stands in front of it holding Baxter. He takes the iPad from Jade. 'What does that mean, H-E-A?'

'Happily Ever After. My mum reads a lot of romance books,

and she cries a lot while reading them. She says it's all about the H-E-A.'

Scratching his nose Felix frowns at Jade. 'My friend Sai has a mum who watches sad films a lot. He says she cries too.'

'Have you sent the message yet, Felix?' Jade peers over Felix's shoulder.

He stares at the iPad screen. 'Aunty Emily is going to shout at me.'

With a giggle Jade dances with Baxter. 'Send it now. That is an order.'

Felix taps out the message. His finger hovers over the send symbol. 'Shall I send it?'

'If you don't press send I will.'

He shuts his eyes. 'My friend says nine-and-a-half-year-olds can change the world.'

'Grown-ups should be scared of us,' Jade declares. 'I tell my mum this all the time.'

'I'm scared of pressing send.'

Jade picks up the phone behind her and speaks to the screen. 'Hi, Felix's mum, will you tell your son to send the message. He's being a total chicken and if he doesn't send it, I will be taking Baxter home with me.' She blows a raspberry at the screen and makes a peace sign. Pointing the screen at Felix, she shouts 'DO IT NOW!'

'JADE... it's sent!'

Both Felix and Jade erupt into cheers and shouts. Baxter barks too.

Jade tugs Felix on the arm. 'Tell me the next part of your plan.'

Grinning he takes his phone back from Jade. 'I can't because Mummy won't be happy with me.'

Jade holds Baxter close to her chest. 'Honestly – can I have your dog?'

'No, you can't have Baxter,' Felix says. 'Come on, let's go back to our seats. Got to go, Mummy. Bye.'

CHAPTER 12

EMILY

I'm Gloria,' says the woman with an infectious smile once Felix, Baxter and Jade have returned to their seats.

Before I can open my mouth and reply, Felix points to me. 'Her name is Emily. My mum died back in May, so Aunty Emily, Mum's sister, is looking after me and Baxter.' I wish Felix didn't like oversharing so much.

Jade gasps and stares at Felix. 'Eh? Your mum died? But you just...'

He glares at Jade and she goes quiet.

Gloria places a warm hand on my arm. 'I am in the presence of an angel.'

I let out a heavy sigh. If only this woman knew about all the arguments I have with Felix. If only she knew how bad I feel about getting carried away with making dresses because it soothes my pain over losing Vivi. I alternate between shouting and getting obsessed about my ex-boyfriend on Facebook. 'I'm definitely not an angel.'

Her hazel eyes lock onto mine. 'You're raising your sister's child. In my book that's angel territory.'

Jade and Felix start talking in whispers. Jade has her back to me so I can't see Felix. I'm straining to hear what they're saying but the carriage is too noisy.

Gloria chuckles at the sight of them. 'Let them talk, Emily. I sense this could be the start of a great friendship.'

'That is what worries me.'

She shrugs. 'Jade is nearly ten. I'm more concerned about the teenage years which seem to be approaching fast.'

The realisation that I will have to endure the teenage years with Felix hits me like a slap in the face. If he's anything like his mother Felix will be a nightmare. Hang on – he's a nightmare already!

Gloria casts me a warm smile. 'Cheer up. Rumour has it, boys are easier than girls in the teenage years.'

'Really?' A teeny tiny glimmer of hope has just made itself known.

Gloria nods. 'You'll be fine, and I'll be the one with the issues.'

I sit back into my seat. 'Do you think it depends on what the parents were like as teenagers?'

Her hearty laugh fills the carriage. 'If that is so, Emily, I am in for a shock. My mother had to send me away as I was so bad.'

Jade and Felix turn around to see what we are laughing at. They soon return to their conversation.

Gloria nods. 'I was sent to live with my grandmother when I was fifteen. My poor parents were beside themselves. Luckily my grandmother was a strong, powerful woman who believed wild teenagers could be tamed through daily housework, strict rules on homework, weeding her overgrown garden and long silences when they couldn't say anything nice. I soon learnt grandmother would happily sit in silence all day doing her embroidery while I stomped about her house moaning about all the chores I had to do.'

Looking after Vivi when I was a child was nothing compared to my time with Felix. Maybe I have edited out the bad parts?

'It's not easy looking after kids – is it?'

Gloria shakes her head which makes all her box braid beads rustle and clink. 'It's hard, but at the same time so much joy can come from it.'

'Really, Gloria?' I say in a low voice. 'There's not been much joy between me and Felix.'

'I'm not surprised given what you've both been through. You need to go easy on yourselves. Time will help you both to heal. Until then look for the things that bring you both joy and do them... a lot.'

'Do you think so? I've made so many mistakes...'

Gloria lifts her hand and stops me. 'Stop being hard on yourself. We all make mistakes with parenting when there is no trauma in our lives. *You* are parenting in the middle of huge trauma. Let the need to be perfect go.' She points at Felix who is now laughing his head off at something Jade said. Baxter is asleep in her arms. 'Your nephew looks happy today.'

I nod and force out a smile.

Gloria leans and whispers. 'What does your nephew enjoy doing?'

'Huh?'

'Does he have any hobbies?' Gloria asks, studying her leopard-print patterned nails.

That is a tough question. Casting my gaze out of the window and across snow-coated fields I try to rack my brains for Felix's hobbies. All I can picture is Felix watching ballet with Rory and Felix jumping around with excitement in Vivi's house because Rory was coming to collect him for football. My heart swells and a little voice from deep inside me whispers, *Rory wasn't that bad when it came to Felix.*

Leaning into Gloria I whisper back. 'He enjoyed watching ballet DVDs and going to watch the football with my... ex-boyfriend.'

Gloria frowns. 'Was this the ex-boyfriend who your nephew referred to earlier?'

I nod. 'Rory and I split up because I didn't think he wanted to settle down.'

Gloria is listening to me, so I continue. 'When my sister died, I knew my life had to change and I didn't think it was fair for Rory to alter his life too. He was also going through something.'

'What do you mean?'

I dig my fingers deep into the train seat. 'He was always going out partying with this woman from his office. I trusted him completely, but I did feel left out. He swore there was nothing going on. She knew someone from his university days, so they had a connection. I just thought it was cruel of me to keep our relationship going when I needed to focus on sorting out Felix and grieving for my sister — and Rory clearly had other priorities.'

She nods. 'Well, it certainly sounds sensible but why do I sense your heart doesn't agree with your head's plan?' I watch her left eyebrow arch at me.

A smile finds its way onto my face.

Felix's voice makes me jolt. 'Aunty Emily still loves Rory. She's always checking out his Facebook page, she gets angry when she sees his new girlfriend and she's sad without him.'

Gloria turns to Felix with a startled look. 'Is that so, young man?'

Felix nods. 'Aunty Emily says Rory wouldn't have made a good father, but I disagree.'

Out of the corner of my eye I can see Jade gazing longingly at Felix.

'Why do you disagree?' Gloria asks.

Felix glances at Jade and then back at me. He takes a deep breath. Why do I get the feeling he's about to say something big? He opens his mouth and then closes it again. 'I just do – okay?' he snaps and turns to look at the window. Jade taps him on the shoulder and gestures for him to stroke Baxter.

Gloria nudges me. 'Is the bit about you being sad without Rory in your life true?'

The urge to lie and tell Gloria that Felix has a vivid imagination is strong. Words are queuing up on my tongue, but I can't force them out. This is so frustrating.

She takes my silence as her answer. 'You still love him – don't you?'

'I'm trying not to love him, Gloria. It's a really tough thing to do – trying to stop loving someone – but I will get there.'

'Were you happy when you were together… I mean before this woman came along, and Rory was not acting like he was on some permanent Club 18–30 holiday?'

Hundreds of happy memories which have been locked up at the back of my mind shoot out and race to the front of my mind. 'It was amazing,' I say, softly. 'He was perfect in so many ways. He knew how to make me laugh, he encouraged me to chase my dreams, he was the perfect nurse when I got sick, and he adored Vivi and Felix.'

'Do you think this new girlfriend could be long-term?'

I shrug and rub my chest. 'Probably, Gloria. She looks amazing and will suit his party lifestyle.'

Gloria taps my hand. 'If you and Rory are meant to be, mark my words, fate will play a hand.'

Out of the corner of my eye I can see Jade tapping Felix on the shoulder and whispering, 'Do it, do it, do it.'

Felix, Baxter, and I are sat in a trendy London café just off Oxford Street. It's mid-morning and Felix and I are sipping hot chocolates topped with fluffy white cream. I managed to persuade him to come to Oxford Street with me first before going to St Pancras. Baxter is curled up on Felix's lap. Being carried the whole morning has clearly been exhausting.

Oxford Street was heaving with excited Christmas shoppers. I had to get keep a tight hold of Felix, who was clutching Baxter. Felix kept asking me when we could go to London St Pancras and didn't seem bothered with seeing Oxford Street.

I've decided we need some refreshments. I'm also hoping to quiz him about what happened on the train earlier. As we walked along Oxford Street all I could think about was what Felix had been showing Jade on my iPad and what he was going to say about Rory when he stopped so abruptly.

'What were you talking to Jade about on the train?'

Felix casts me a strange look and shuffles about in his chair. 'Stuff.'

'Stuff – can you elaborate?'

He shakes his head. 'We talked about stuff. It wasn't anything interesting.'

'Well, you both looked engrossed in this... stuff.'

Felix runs a hand through his spiky hair. 'She was nice. I am going to email her.'

My defences rise. He *has* an email account. I didn't know this. Does it have security on it? Who does he email? 'You have an email account? Did your mum know about this?'

Something flickers across Felix's face. 'Yes – why?'

'Well, you are only nine and I'm not sure what age children are supposed to have email accounts. How do you access the email account?'

Felix squirms in his seat. 'You're not seeing my email account.'

I can feel my neck and shoulders stiffening. He could be emailing anyone and more worrying anyone could be emailing him. My heart has started to thump. 'Why not?'

'Aunty Emily,' he whines. 'It's my email account. Please let me keep it.'

Leaning across the table I hiss, 'I want to see it, Felix. It's for your own safety.'

His hazel eyes flash with anger. 'I HATE YOU,' he snaps, slamming his hot chocolate down so hard it slops out of the mug and makes a mess of the table. A wave of emotion is building inside of me.

'Please stop saying you hate me, Felix, it doesn't make me feel nice. I am trying to help you and keep you safe.'

His face reddens and I can see his eyes filling up with tears. 'I was happy with Mummy,' he sobs. 'She died and now you are here. All you do is make stupid dresses, you hate Baxter and you sent Rory away.'

Every word of his punctures my heart like tiny arrows. He goes blurry and I gulp back a sob of my own. Before I can control my tears, they stream down my face. It's all true. He was happy when Vivi was alive, and I've come along and made everything bad for him.

Taking out my tissues I try to stem my tears. I want to go home and lose myself in dressmaking. I want to find a medium, contact Vivi on the other side and tell her I'm not cut out to be Felix's legal guardian. I want to contact Vivi's rich friends and ask whether they want to adopt him.

Felix has taken out my iPad and is scrolling through it.

Staring down at my hot chocolate I decide to go to the toilet. While I am there I will pray for a miracle.

CHAPTER 13

FELIX

'Hello, Mummy. I haven't got long as Aunty Emily has gone to the toilet. We're in a café. Aunty Emily wanted to go see parts of London, but I need her to take me to St Pancras station. It's part of my plan. Amelie has messaged me to say that she thinks I am cool. Ronnie has messaged me to say he told his older brother about my plan. His brother told Ronnie if he did what I am doing he'd be in so much trouble he would have to hand over his Xbox and all his games to him, and he would take them to his university. Sai has emailed me to say when he thinks about my plan, he gets a belly ache. He says his mum is very scary when she's angry and she would phone his grandmother in Sri Lanka, who is more frightening. He has wished me good luck and hopes my plan makes me happy again.' He leans back in his chair and strokes Baxter.

'If my plan works, it will definitely make me happy again. I know it. Jade, my new friend from the train, said that she would do the same if it was Sidney. He's her mum's boyfriend and he sounded cool like Rory. Jade's mum is going to ask him to marry her on Christmas Day. I asked Jade what will happen if Sidney doesn't want to marry her mum. She said her mum will cry all the way home. Jade thinks Sidney will say yes as he writes her mum love poems, he sends her flowers every week and he talks about them growing old together. Oh, Jade didn't take Baxter with her. She refused to hand him over when we got to the station and got told off by her mum.' He giggles and plants a kiss on the top of Baxter's head.

'Before Aunty Emily went to the toilet, I told her I hated her. It's a horrid thing to say. You would have shouted at me. It was because she wanted to look at my emails. I didn't want her to see them as I have sent a few of these videos to Amelie. She says some made her cry and she made her mum watch one. Apparently they both cried over dinner about my video after you'd died and her dad got cross with everyone crying.'

He sighs. 'This new Aunty Emily is never happy. She sits making silly dresses and takes sneaky looks at Rory on Facebook. Aunty Emily also doesn't love Baxter the way I do.' Sniffing he wipes his nose on his coat sleeve. 'I don't hate Aunty Emily, Mummy. I just miss the old Aunty Emily. She and Rory used to play hide and seek with me when you'd ask them to babysit. Aunty Emily always made me laugh as she'd squeeze herself into your wardrobe and leave her elbow poking out. She was so easy to find. Then we'd go find Rory who was always standing in the shower. Once Aunty Emily turned on the shower when he was hiding and he got wet.' He giggles.

Resting his elbow on the table he props his chin up and talks into the phone. 'I love Rory, Mummy. He told me I wasn't… weird.' He pauses and flicks his eyes to the café floor. 'One day I heard you on the phone tell someone I was weird. I heard you. It was after you'd walked into my bedroom and made me jump. I told Rory about it. He said I wasn't weird and that you didn't mean it. Anyway, he helped me with my secret. One day I will tell you my secret, but not yet.' Sitting up he turns around and spots Aunty Emily coming out of the toilet. 'Must go, bye.'

*B*eth has arrived early clutching two bottles of Prosecco, a huge bunch of mistletoe and what looks like a small overnight bag. She looks good with her poker-straight blonde hair, her slender legs, a brown leather miniskirt and black velvet knee-high boots. After ogling her from afar in the living room Tom made an early exit. He gave me the thumbs up sign behind Beth's back.

'It's nice to see you again, Rory,' she says, sipping a glass of Prosecco and heading for the sofa. I'm busy trying to find a phone charger for my dead phone. There was one in my room, but Tom has nicked it.

'What have you been up to?' She relaxes on the sofa and unzips one of her boots.

I am on the verge of giving up looking for a charger. At this rate my phone will have to remain out of battery. 'Normal stuff,' I reply, sticking my head in the coffee table drawer.

'How's the job hunt going?'

I'm reminded of the snotty email from a job recruiter yesterday who clearly couldn't be arsed to look for a new job for me as it's Christmas, and tried to pass me off with, *I'm in back-to-*

*back meetings all day so might not get a chance to check the database.
Don't worry the job market will be buzzing early next year.'*

'Really well,' I lie, scrabbling around for a charger. 'Why can't
a man find a phone charger?' I wail with mock frustration.

She grins and opens her overnight bag. 'You can use mine.'

I take it from her, and she holds on to my gaze for longer than
necessary.

Sitting down beside her I plug the charger into the wall and
connect my phone.

'I've been looking forward to this afternoon,' she says,
smoothing out her leather skirt. 'It was a lovely date we had last
week. I really enjoyed that French restaurant.'

A memory of our second date comes rushing back to me. We
ate delicious French food and drank a lot of wine. I soon realised
Beth likes to talk. I listened to her chat about how she spent last
summer travelling around America with her ex-boyfriend. There
were photos of her American summer too. She proudly took out
her phone and went through an entire Facebook album dedicated
to her travels. There were lots of photos of her and her ex-
boyfriend. They looked happy together standing by various
landmarks with their arms wrapped around each other and
laughing at the camera. I sat, stifled many yawns, and wished I
was opposite Emily. If we had gone to dinner, she would have
played our favourite game of people watching where she
comments on their choice of clothes, and I would make up
fictional lives for the restaurant customers around us. I can't
remember ever going for dinner with Emily and having a dull
evening. After I'd said goodbye to Beth, I went to a club and
drank my sorrows away with Tom.

'On our last date you didn't say much about your past
relationships,' Beth asks, slipping her hand into mine. 'I want to
know *everything*.'

I let out an inner groan and blow the air out of my cheeks. Do
we have to talk about our past relationships? I heard and saw

enough of her ex-boyfriend on the second date. Emily and I didn't talk much on our third date. We went to a nineties roller skating disco, drank a lot and laughed at each other's terrible dancing on skates.

'There's not much to tell.'

She nods. 'So, how long have you been single?'

'Erm… since the end of May.'

'Tell me about why you and Emily ended?'

Staring at her I wonder how she knows the name of my ex-girlfriend. Emily won't leave my head as it is. Once I start talking about her it will ruin this date. I turn to Beth. 'Let's talk about something else.'

She smiles. 'Tell me about your family? Do you have any brothers or sisters?'

I flinch. This is also a conversational path I don't want to venture down. 'I have five sisters,' she gushes, not waiting for me to lie to her. She launches into a detailed account of each one. After a while she senses I'm struggling to remain interested in why her third sister didn't want to study medicine at university and the many reasons why her fourth sister chose to take a gap year. Placing her glass down on the coffee table she takes mine from me too. 'How about we have a kiss, Rory,' she whispers, then leans in for a kiss.

Her mouth is warm and soft. I close my eyes as she kisses me. She's a good kisser but doesn't come close to Emily. What I love about Emily is that her kisses are tender at first and build up to a passionate climax. Beth's kiss remains at a steady chew on my lips. Shit – Rory, concentrate on Beth.

Her manicured hands find their way under my shirt. I yelp as one of her long, pink talons gets stuck in a patch of my chest hair. That irritates me.

Just then, my phone comes to life and starts buzzing with notifications. Are they text messages? Is someone trying to get hold of me? Maybe it's that job recruiter? One of them could be

Emily. I break away from our kiss, reach over and check my phone. Beth pauses and takes a sip of Prosecco. Amongst a lot of notifications from Beth on Facebook which I have been trying to avoid as I don't see why she must broadcast to the world we are having a third date; I spot Emily has sent me a message. My heart goes berserk.

'You okay, Rory?'

I nod. 'Sorry, I was expecting a message from someone.' With a trembling hand I log on to Facebook Messenger. It reads – *I love u Rory.*

What the hell? Emily now loves me. This is a massive turnaround from two weeks ago.

'Shall I continue?' Beth leans over, takes my phone out of my hand, and kisses me again. I need time to sit and think.

I pull away and break for air. 'Let's take it slowly – eh?'

She giggles and goes back to her Prosecco. 'I always get carried away on date three.'

Blimey, Beth is Tom's ideal date. He would love the speed at which this is going. In a few hours I will on my way to forgetting Emily. A sinking feeling has taken hold of me. Why do I not seem sure about the forgetting Emily part? Emily still loves me so that must mean I am still in with a chance. Is that what I want? Getting back with Emily means a complete life change as there will be Felix to think about. I know Emily thinks I'm not father material and she might be right; I mean I don't have a job right now and I am blowing holes in my savings, but I constantly think about Felix. Somehow, I don't think love is enough in this world.

'Something on your mind?' Beth asks.

I shake my head and switch on the TV. 'Fancy a movie?'

We begin to watch the latest James Bond. My mind is frantically trying to plot a course through these troubled waters I now find myself submerged in.

Beth's hand starts to wander over my chest again. She lifts her leg and drapes it over my thigh.

Oh, God, Beth wants more from me and all I want to do is sit and stare at Emily's message.

Stroking my leg, she pulls away for air and starts to unbutton her tiny black cardigan, revealing a lacy black bra. To my amazement she removes her cardigan and throws it across the room. I help her remove my shirt. Once I'm bare chested she laughs and chucks my shirt across the floor. Vivi's golden locket shoots out of my shirt pocket and skitters over the coffee table. Beth is straddling me and hasn't noticed the gold locket.

My eyes have become glued to the bloody locket behind her. It's staring back at me from the coffee table. In my head I can hear Cassie telling me I should give it to Emily and Tom laughing at me for missing the Christmas post. Emily would be made up to see the locket Vivi wanted her to have. Vivi's death has broken poor Emily and I can't imagine how hard it must have been for her to become Felix's guardian.

I need to block out the locket. 'Excuse me,' I say, lifting Beth off me and picking up the locket. In the act I accidentally knock over the bottle of Prosecco and Beth yelps. Fizzy wine goes everywhere, all over Tom's carpet and sofa. Racing into the kitchen, still holding the locket, I grab a kitchen roll. When I return, I try to clean up as much as I can while Beth sits and watches me. This morning I've done more cleaning up than I have done in weeks.

Carefully I place the locket near where my phone is charging.

Beth gasps. 'What a beautiful locket, Rory. Whose is it?'

I look at it next to my phone. Beth is tapping me on the arm. 'Who does the locket belong to?'

'Oh, no one important. Where were we?' I run my hand over her thigh.

Something flickers across her face. She pulls away. 'Are you seeing other women?'

'What?'

She's stood up. 'Why won't you tell me whom the locket belongs to?'

Shit. This is not going to plan.

'If you must know it belongs to my ex-girlfriend.'

Beth takes a step back. 'Emily – your ex-girlfriend has been here? In this flat?'

I haul myself to my feet. 'No, she's in Brighton. How do you know about Emily?'

She rolls her eyes. 'At the restaurant you called me Emily several times.'

'Did I?' Shit – what is wrong with me? 'Look, the locket was something I was meant to give her before we split up and I didn't.'

Beth's shoulders drop. 'My friends have warned me about you, Rory.'

Scratching my hair, I cast her a puzzled look. 'What have I done?'

She studies my face. 'Take me to bed and let's forget about Emily,' she whispers.

Reluctantly I lead her into my bedroom. We begin to kiss on the bed and all I can think about is how Emily used to make me feel alive when we had sex. Beth has a nice body but it's not like Emily's. What the hell am I thinking?

Kissing Beth's bare shoulder I find myself staring at the framed photo of Emily and Felix from Christmas last year. It's been on my bedside table ever since I moved in. The two of them are standing in Vivi's kitchen, against her extensive travel magnet collection, and both are laughing into the camera. I'd taken the photo after I'd escorted Vivi's boss and his female friend out of Felix's bedroom. Emily, Felix and I were so happy that night. It felt good to be Felix's hero. I remember the warm ball of tingles which rushed up my spine when he jumped up and down with joy after hearing me tell off Vivi's boss for kissing in a child's bedroom.

Vivi was stood behind me trying to get an emotional Bill to apologise to Keith and at the same time telling one of her work friends to stop dancing on her sofa.

Beth has realised what I'm looking at. 'Don't tell me – that's Emily, your ex-girlfriend and your kid.'

'He's not my kid,' I say, with a sigh. 'He's her sister's boy.'

She gets off the bed, walks over to my bedside cabinet, takes the photo, and puts it in the drawer. 'Let's get back to where we were,' she gushes.

Irritation at what she's just done makes me sit up. She had no right to do that to Emily and Felix's photo. 'Please can you put the photo back?'

I watch her smile fade. 'Are you serious?'

'Yes, please put it back.'

Beth stares at me. 'Do you know how weird this is?'

'Huh?'

'Having your ex-girlfriend and the kid stare at us while we are in *your* bed and about to have sex?' I watch as she slams the photo down after getting it back out of the drawer.

We've decided to return to the living room fully clothed and sit at separate ends of the living room. Once she said how weird it was to lie in my bed with the photo of Emily and Felix on show everything felt awkward and odd. Sex was the last thing on our minds and she'd raced back into the living room to put on her cardigan. I grabbed a shirt from my wardrobe. An uncomfortable silence has taken hold of us.

The chain and locket have returned to the palm of my hand. Beth has noticed and is tapping something into her phone. 'Look, Rory, I think we can both agree this date hasn't worked,' she says, casting me a cold look. 'Can I have my phone charger back as I'm going to get off?'

'Oh... well... here it is,' I say, unplugging my phone and letting out an inner groan. 'But it's only charged to thirty per cent.'

Beth shoots out of her chair. 'Goodbye, Rory,' she snaps, grabbing her charger and races for the door.

The door slam makes me jolt. Taking my phone and flicking onto Facebook Messenger I read Emily's message. She loves me. The locket falls from my hand and the chain coils onto the carpet. After picking it up and opening it I stare at Emily and Vivi. My heart begins to gallop. Somehow this locket needs to find its way back to its rightful owner before Christmas.

CHAPTER 15

EMILY

To get Felix to smile again all I had to do was suggest we go see London St Pancras station. The powerful urge to forget about today and go home slowly diminished the more I sat and watched him. There are things about my nephew which always bring a smile to my face, his coppery mass of chaotic hair, his skinny, bean-pole-like frame and his ability to master any piece of technology. Today I've learnt sitting in silence and gazing at him helps me remove my *upset filter*. At home I have a million things to do and sitting still for five minutes is a rarity. When I do this Felix returns to being Felix, my nephew who I love dearly and who is still struggling with missing his mum and adapting to our new muddled life together. As we left the café, I made a promise to myself to try and find a tiny pocket in my day back home where I can watch him fiddle with my iPad, dance in the snow, or play ball with Baxter.

As we stood and waited for the tube train on a chilly platform, he leant his head against my arm. I don't know whether he did it consciously, but it flooded me with warmth.

We're finally at the place he's been desperate to visit. His elfin face has lit up and he's staring in awe at the gigantic Christmas tree and station decorations. He hands me a sleeping Baxter to hold as he gazes up at the gigantic tree and I survey the busy station.

Even though there is a steady flow of London Christmas tourists here at the station there is still a good trickle of suited and tired-looking commuters trying to weave through the crowds. Sadly, Christmas has not started for them yet. I can tell by their agitated expressions that they just want to reach their office or attend that meeting so the day will go quicker before Christmas Eve. Watching a group of women who are all wearing silly festive hats and talking loudly about the mammoth shopping trip ahead of them reminds me of the times I used to commute into London from Brighton. The trains from Brighton to London never ran to time, they were always crammed, to the extent where being able to breathe properly became a luxury, and it always stank of sweat. No matter what time I left Brighton I would always, at some point in my journey, find myself launching into a sweaty sprint across a station or platform. Back then I was a young marketing executive, determined to make her mark in the world and wishing she'd covered her feet in plasters before squeezing them into ill-fitting high heels.

Three friends are taking selfies with their arms around each other. The man looks a bit like Bill with his bushy beard and impressive sideburns. One of the women could be me if I squint and lose a good stone, the other woman has a sort of Lizzie look about her. Seeing them laughing and pulling faces at the camera reminds me of Bill's Instagram feed which is full of us as a crazy trio in various pubs, clubs, and bars around Brighton. The best one is where I am drunk, dressed in a glitzy, twenties style Gatsby dress, and covered in Police tape, the stuff from a crime scene, Bill is dressed as Superman, and Lizzie is trying to do a drunken cartwheel behind us. Whenever I see it, the sight of us all and Bill's caption (which read *Warning: Danger Ahead*), I always giggle.

Felix has found somewhere to sit. He seems fascinated by the hustle and bustle of the noisy station. I sit down next to him holding a yawning Baxter. 'Are you glad you've come, Felix?'

He turns to me and grins. 'Yes, thank you, Aunty Emily.'

'What do you want to do now? There's a lovely mall filled with nice shops if you want to go and have a look?'

I watch him stare up at the departures board. 'No, I would just like to sit here.'

Sitting back in the plastic chair I fight the urge to pester him about going to see the shops.

'Where's King's Cross from here?' Felix is tugging on my arm.

I look around for the signs. 'It's practically next door. There's a sign over there. Why do you want to know that?'

He shrugs and watches a man and woman close to us engage in an emotional reunion.

Even though Felix denied being a train spotter earlier, I think he was lying.

We sit for ages watching station life. I put Baxter down on the floor and let him waddle about while holding on to his lead. All my pressing thoughts about dressmaking have gone away. I'm enjoying sitting watching couples struggle with huge bags of last-minute toy shopping, students wrapping their arms around each other before going their separate ways and excited children dancing about to someone's phone which is playing Slade's, 'This is Christmas' song.

I spot a young woman wearing an enviable dress underneath her coat, it has a clown collar, and the pink, orange and green floral print is warm and pretty. The sight of it is making my fingers itch and my creative mind bubble with new ideas.

My phone begins to bleep. Watching Baxter below me and Felix at the side, I take it out of my handbag and see that it's Lizzie.

'Hello, babe,' she says, 'how's London town?'

'Busy. We're at St Pancras,' I say, before the train announcer above me reminds everyone about the train which is due to leave shortly on platform five.

Lizzie laughs. 'Felix got his Christmas wish then?'

I smile and take a quick glance at Felix who is in a world of his own gazing out across the station. 'Yes, and he's loving being here.'

'Ems,' says Lizzie, 'you're winning today, remember this moment. I have been worried about you lately.'

'Aww, thanks Lizzie,' I gush, feeling grateful for having such a wonderful friend as Lizzie.

The phone is grabbed away from her and Bill's thick Welsh accent booms down the receiver. 'Hello, Little Miss Vintage, I hear you've become a train spotter now and will be spending next year loitering on train platforms.' He snorts down the phone. 'The second after Lizzie Lupin asked me... I moved in. My landlord at the last place had a queue of people desperate to move into Room 20, Floor Two, Passion Heights.' (Bill's last place was not really called Passion Heights. He renamed it that given the amount of his neighbours' sex he had to listen to daily). I giggle at hearing Bill's voice. 'Have you moved into my old room yet?'

'He also wasn't fussed about me staying. I am skint now but happy as I'm living in Chateau De Buttock with Lizzie Lupin. How is Felix the Fox?'

Bill has pet names for all of us. It's a rarity for him to call us just by our proper names.

I turn around to check on Felix with the phone pressed to my ear but there is no one there. Felix is gone. 'He's... not there.' My heart grinds to a shuddering halt. Felix has gone. Frantically I swivel in my chair to see if I can see him. To my dismay there are just loads of people.

'What?' Bill is still on the phone.

'Listen – I've got to go and find Felix. Will call back in a bit.'

Stuffing my phone in my handbag I experience a huge wave of nausea. Where the hell is he?

Baxter is barking at me from the floor. I scoop him into my arms and scan everyone who is milling around the departure screens. With dismay I move on to the barriers by the closest platforms. There's no sign of Felix. Panic surges through my body. 'FELIX,' I shout hoping he's wandered off to look at something and will hear me. He doesn't magically appear. All the saliva in my mouth has disappeared and my stomach is on a fast spin.

Fuck. Fuck. Panic.

All I can see are fast moving bodies, luggage being dragged across the station floor and faces of festive glee. 'FELIX,' I shout again. Perhaps he's gone to buy some sweets?

Do I stay here in case he returns?

Okay, I need to calm down. Kids wander off all the time. Vivi was always doing that to me in sweet shops when we were little. I need to give him a few minutes to return and act like nothing was wrong. Where is he?

On legs like jelly I stand and look around once more.

Tears prick my eyes. I just hope he hasn't been taken away by some horrible person. My breathing has quickened. That last thought has not done my rocketing blood pressure any favours. A cold sweat is breaking out all over my body. Oh, God, what have I done? I took my eye off him for two minutes and now he's missing.

I stare down at Baxter who is in my arms, expecting him to be asleep or interested in staring at a wrapper on the floor, but he's gazing up at me with huge, sad eyes. Something inside me shifts. In the matter of a few tense seconds, he's not the irritating little dog who hates me and spends his life chewing up my favourite slippers, he's a tiny, frightened dog who can sense my fear and doesn't know where his owner is. I hold him close to my chest and find myself pressing my chin to his little furry head. 'It's okay, Baxter, we're going to find Felix.'

He licks my chin with so much affection I can't stop the tears from rolling down my cheeks. Looking up and blinking away my tears I scan the vicinity for Felix. 'FELIX.'

Baxter stares up at me. My heart is hammering away in my chest. I must do something. 'Let's find the police.'

We race in the direction of two police officers talking to an emotional couple. I want to interrupt them and scream, 'MY NEPHEW HAS GONE MISSING' but the woman is upset about something. Tears are streaming down her face and she's struggling to get her breath. The man is telling her everything will be all right. One officer is talking into his radio and the other is frantically looking around.

I turn back to where Baxter and I were sitting to see if Felix has returned – the seats are empty. Felix – where are you?

Vivi – I hope you're not looking down from heaven right now. My poor sister will be beside herself. I remember her warning me when Felix was younger that given half a chance Felix would be off to make his own way in the world. There was the time she was sat in the park, and he disappeared. She found him ten minutes later wading into the park lake as he wanted to swim with the fish. A memory from one of our holidays to Tenby pops up in my mind. Felix ran away on the beach, and we spent a panic-inducing half hour searching for him. We found him at an ice cream van buying himself two large cones.

For goodness' sake, I need to talk to these police officers. Felix could be anywhere right now. I can hear the couple talking about someone called Jack who is also lost. The man is describing Jack who is nine and is wearing a bright yellow scarf. The urge to interrupt them is strong. Felix is also missing. Maybe Jack and Felix are hanging out together? The nausea in my tummy is getting worse. I think I might throw up with worry. The female police officer is telling both parents that it is common for young children to get distracted and wander off. In most cases they are found safe and well.

My phone is vibrating away in my handbag. Oh, God, who is that? I nearly ignore it in my anxiety to speak to the police, but then realise it could be Felix calling me to say he's hurt or lost. With a shaking hand I hold Baxter and with the other rummage in my handbag. To my relief it's Felix calling me from Vivi's old mobile. I answer and shout 'OH, GOD, WHERE ARE YOU?'

The station starts to rotate before my eyes as I hear his voice. 'Aunty Emily, I'm on the train to Leeds. It's due to leave King's Cross station in ten minutes.'

An angry roar rockets out of my mouth. 'WHAT?'

'I am on the train to Leeds. I was going to get Rory for you but now I am scared.'

Before he can say another word, I'm running in the direction of King's Cross. Holding Baxter tight I race towards the station exit.

'This was supposed to be your Christmas present from me.'

I can't find the words. Shock, anger, frustration, and exasperation have joined forces in my gut and are now rocketing up towards my throat.

'Can you hear me, Aunty Emily?' Felix asks.

I can see Kings Cross. 'DO NOT BOARD THAT TRAIN' I gasp picking up speed.

'I'm on the train. It's going at quarter past. I am frightened. If I get off the train, I won't find Rory.' Felix hangs up and a red rage filter slides over my eyes. What the hell does he think he's playing at?

At the platform barrier a guard stops me and demands a ticket. With an angry yelp I race to the ticket machine, push a young lad out of the way and without thinking buy an expensive return to Leeds. I'll worry about the expense later. Felix's safety is more important. There's no time to lose. The Leeds train is going in four minutes.

Racing down the steps and onto the platform I can see the Leeds train. Screaming at the female guard who is closing the doors I bound down three steps and charge to the train. She opens the door just in time, so I leap onto the train.

With a heaving chest and a panting Baxter, I bend over and get my breath. The train doors slam shut followed by a whistle sound. As I compose myself, the train crawls out of the station. Now I am praying Felix is on this train and not still at King's Cross. My bowels loosen at the thought. Beads of sweat are rolling down my face and dropping onto Baxter's outstretched tongue. It seems he enjoys licking a salty tear or two.

Carrying Baxter, I start my search for Felix. Please, please, please be on this train.

Barging through the carriages I stop and search each train seat.

I've looked through all eight carriages. There is no sign of Felix. He's not answering his phone either.

All hope inside of me has evaporated. Felix must be on a different train or back at the station. I dare not think what Vivi must be thinking if she's looking down from heaven at me. I wonder if I pulled the emergency button – would they stop the train and get me back to Kings Cross? I strongly doubt it. What the hell am I going to do?

Baxter whimpers and presses himself into my neck. I hold him close. His little dog heart is hammering away. My own heart aches so much I'm struggling to get my breath. 'It's going to be all right, Baxter, I will find Felix,' I gasp.

CHAPTER 16

FELIX

'Mummy,' Felix shouts and runs with the phone pressed against his ear. 'I'm running towards King's Cross station. My rucksack is heavy and is hurting me. Aunty Emily was busy talking to Aunty Lizzie when I ran away.' He stops, breathless from running. 'Baxter looked sad when I left. He will be all right with Aunty Emily. I know she says she doesn't like him, but she will make sure he's safe.' Placing his hand on his side he groans. 'I have a stitch. I must keep going. Here's the station now.' The sound of two feet running into a busy station can be heard.

'Can you see me at the station?' Pulling a silly face, he peers into the phone screen. 'Look, I am at King's Cross station'. Flipping the phone screen camera, he pans across the station. 'There are lots of people here because it's Christmas. Some are wearing Santa hats. That man over there has a hat which looks like a Christmas turkey.' Felix's laughter at the turkey hat can be heard above the train announcer overhead, the noisy commuters and the group of tiny children and parents singing Christmas carols. 'I have things to do now so will speak when my plan is in action. Bye.'

Eight minutes later.

'Hello, it's me again. I'm hiding from Aunty Emily.' Poking his head out of from underneath a table he looks up the train aisle, past several pairs of feet and legs. 'My plan hasn't gone well. I'm on the train to Leeds. Six minutes ago, I got really scared. I was on my own and I missed Aunty Emily. When I was planning this adventure, I didn't think I would feel frightened on the train. Even though she makes me sad I wanted Aunty Emily next to me. So, I rang her, and she shouted at me down the phone. So now I am hiding from her. She's going to scream and quite possibly ground me until I am twelve. Sai said his mother was scary, but I think Aunty Emily could beat her.' He crawls back underneath the table.

Felix yelps as a man bends down and peers at him. The man smiles and walks up the train aisle making the door let out a whoosh sound. 'That was scary, Mummy. I didn't know who he was. I thought he was one of those bad strangers who Aunty Emily tells me never to talk to.'

Climbing out from underneath the table he sits on the seat. 'The train is moving, Mummy. I'm scared.' He wipes a tear trickling down his cheek. 'Aunty Emily and Baxter might have missed the train. I am scared, Mummy. I think my plan was a silly one. All I want is to see Aunty Emily and Baxter. Bye.'

CHAPTER 17

EMILY

J'm stood between carriages, outside the train toilet, clutching Baxter and trying to see if Felix will pick up his mobile. When I find him, I don't think he should listen to my voicemail messages. There is no doubt in my mind – I will come across as a lunatic.

Half of me is trembling with rage at Felix. When I see him, I will scream, shout, and get emotional. However, the other half of me just wants to hold him in my arms, I want to hear his voice and I want to know he's safe.

For the ninth time the phone goes to voicemail, and I let out a frustrated wail. Tears are filling up my eyes. I'm minutes away from an emotional breakdown. It's time to start bargaining with God. If Felix is found safe and well, I will rethink my approach to being his legal guardian, I'll not lose myself in dressmaking.

The carriage door swishes open and a calm, male voice says, 'Are you all right?'

Wiping my eyes, I can see a tall, male stranger with short brown hair stood in front of me. 'Sorry for asking,' he says, 'but you look like you could use a friend.'

Tears stream down my face as I try to breathe through sobs. 'My nephew ran off at King's Cross. He rang me to say he'd boarded the Leeds train. I raced to get on the train and now I can't find him.'

The man glances back in the carriage he came from. 'How old is your nephew?'

'Nine — although he's quite small for his age so looks more like seven or eight. He's got dark copper-coloured hair and freckles.'

A broad smile spreads across the stranger's face. 'You might want to check out the table seat on the left, halfway down. I saw you come rushing through earlier and I also saw a boy hiding underneath a train table. He's now sat on the seat.'

I follow the stranger's gaze and spot a small head full of coppery hair. Before the stranger can say anything else I burst through the door. 'FELIX!'

He turns around in his seat with a panic-stricken face. As I get nearer, I can see his tear-stained cheeks. Before I deposit Baxter on the table in front Felix, the little dog looks up at me. In that fleeting moment I know that this little dog and I have formed a new bond. Baxter knows we've both been through the seven circles of hell with losing Felix and I kept my promise of finding his owner. He turns his attention to Felix and dives onto his lap.

'Felix – don't EVER do that again,' I shriek, trembling with rage and emotion.

Once I sit down Felix throws his arms around my shoulders, pulling me into an unexpected hug. He starts to weep and sob. It sets me off. Soon we are both a tearful mess. 'I'm sorry, Aunty Emily,' he croaks. 'I'm so sorry.'

I hug him so tightly and inhale the scent of coconuts from his hair. 'Is it that bad being with me that you have to run away to Leeds?'

He shakes his head. 'No, it isn't.'

I stare into his pink-rimmed hazel eyes before planting a sloppy kiss on his forehead. 'You scared me, Felix.'

I watch as he stares up at me and into my eyes. 'It seemed like a good idea yesterday. Jade said it was brilliant and so did all my friends, so I had to go through with it.'

'Who knew about this?'

He looks away and mumbles, 'Amelie, Ronnie, Sai and Jade.' A few seconds later he turns back with a brighter expression. 'Amelie and Jade both said I was cool.'

I watch him wipe his damp face with the back of his coat and silently curse Jade. If Felix gets this carried away by girls at nine, God help me when he's older.

The face of Felix's sensible friend, Sai, appears in my mind. 'I bet Sai didn't think it was cool.' Out of all of Felix's friends Sai is the sensible one. Amelie is obsessed with wanting to be a superhero and will do anything to make this happen. Ronnie is daft a lot of the time and Sai is the one who thinks deeply about actions and consequences.

Felix shakes his head. 'Sai said my plan gave him belly ache when he thought about it.'

Leaning close to Felix I smile and whisper, 'A little piece of advice – next time when one of these mad plans pings into your head, ask Sai what he thinks.'

Felix rests his head on my shoulder. 'I missed you, Aunty Emily, when I was on this train alone.'

I wrap my arm around him and pull him close. 'I love you, Felix.'

He casts me a puzzled look. 'Do you love me, Aunty Emily?'

Swallowing back my emotion I nod, and his sweet little face goes blurry. 'I do, very much.'

Looking around I wonder whether there is a screen which shows me what the next station will be. We can get off and catch a train back to London. I can't see one.

'Felix, do you know where this train stops at next?'

He coughs and mutters, 'Leeds.'

'Leeds?' I say with alarm, staring at the snow-covered countryside speeding past the window.

He nods. 'It's a direct train from London to Leeds – nonstop.'

My groan is loud and heard by people several rows back. 'We are actually going to Leeds. Have you bought a ticket?' I ask.

He nods and hangs his head. 'I bought it yesterday. I used your credit card.'

'What?'

Blimey – after six months in my care my nephew has turned into a fraudster. Nice work, Emily.

A loud sob comes out of his mouth. 'I just wanted to get Rory back. He'll make everything better again.'

'Oh, Felix,' I say as my eyes start to bubble with tears. He's gone to all this trouble because he wants Rory. Felix buries his head in my coat and lets out a loud sob.

'I miss him so much, Aunty Emily.'

I can't help thinking that Rory has moved on with his life and all there will be waiting for us in Leeds will be an awkward looking Rory and a half-naked Beth. While standing in his flat doorway I will notice the floor covered in flower petals and her cheeks will be bright pink after so much sex.

Felix and I need to move on with our lives too. Gently rocking back and forth with an emotional Felix I try to put myself in Felix's shoes. Six months ago, he lost his mum. I move in as his new guardian. His Aunty Emily who he's only used to seeing on Saturday nights when I did some babysitting for Vivi or on fun days in the school holidays. As Vivi was my sister I am also grieving. On top of this the way I deal with my grief is to channel everything into my new online fashion business which means I don't have to deal with hurtful and painful stuff like Felix. I also allow it to take over everything, the living room, and my spare time. Felix's home has been turned into a clothing factory and the poor kid sometimes can't find anywhere to sit. I rarely make tea as I am too busy sewing up dresses and I don't bond with his dog. Guilt and shame grab hold of my tummy and begin to turn it into a painful knot. Added to this is the fact that we both miss Rory – but he has moved on. Why does thinking about this make me feel sick?

'Felix, I miss Rory too, but he's got a new life now.' Pulling him close I nuzzle my face into his hair. 'We have to make home life better. Felix, I know things between us have been strained and life at home hasn't been great but I'm going to change that.'

Felix lifts his face. 'Do you still love me after finding out about your card?'

With a heavy sigh I nod. 'Yes, I do, Felix.'

A weak smile appears on his thin pink lips. 'Can we have a normal living room?'

We both giggle like kids and press our foreheads together. 'Yes, we can, Felix. Let's leave Rory to get on with his new life.'

Felix pulls away. 'I am still going to see him. I have his address in Leeds.'

My neck and shoulders stiffen. 'What?'

He nods. 'I got it off one of his emails he sent you when he moved up there. I have looked it up on Google Maps and it is not far from the station.'

I let out a heavy sigh. 'Felix, we can't just call in and see how Rory's doing. Beth will be there.'

Felix screws up his face. 'I don't like her. Rory will get rid of her when he sees us.'

I stroke his shoulder. 'Felix, it's not that simple. Rory and I split up because he was at a different life stage to me. He still wanted to go partying.'

'I don't mind Rory going to parties,' exclaims Felix.

Inside of me I let out a series of inner screams. Felix has an answer for everything. He's outplaying me all the time.

'Look, Felix, becoming your guardian was a big thing for me. I wasn't going to be the old Emily Rory knew before everything happened.'

He casts me a puzzled look. 'Why can't the old Emily come back?'

'I have to look after you now, Felix. There are so many things to think about when you are raising a child.'

He stares at me. 'It makes you sad – doesn't it?'

'What?'

'Raising me? I know it makes you unhappy, Aunty Emily.'

His words make me jolt with shock. Is that what he thinks? 'Felix,' I croak, 'looking after you doesn't make me sad.'

'That's why you sew all the time.'

I feel like I have just been punched in the stomach. Before my brain can stop the words on my tongue from being released, they shoot out of my mouth. 'I don't feel I am as good as your mum was at looking after you so I distract myself with sewing.'

Felix rests his head against my shoulder. 'You also miss Rory – don't you? That makes you sad as well.'

'Rory is not ready for an adventurous nine-year-old and a sewing-obsessed girlfriend.'

Felix is shaking his head in defiance. 'You have got him all wrong, Aunty Emily. Rory was brilliant to me.'

'Rory is with Beth now'. Why does saying that make me feel like I am stabbing myself in the heart?

'You two look like you are friends again,' says a familiar voice, interrupting our strained discussion. It's the stranger who helped me locate Felix. He's now sat opposite us.

Wiping my eyes with my sleeve I ruffle Felix's hair and let out a nervous laugh. 'We were always friends – weren't we, Felix?'

Felix mumbles something under his breath and takes out my iPad from his rucksack. I turn to the stranger. 'Thank you so much for pointing him out to me.'

The stranger smiles. He has piercing blue eyes, floppy short brown hair and a friendly face. 'No problem. My name's Will by the way.'

'I'm Emily and this is Felix.'

Will nods at Felix but doesn't get a reaction. Felix doesn't smile. He just goes back to the iPad. Baxter, to my surprise, gets up from Felix's lap and lies down on mine.

'That's a cute dog,' says Will.

I stroke Baxter. 'This is Baxter and we have formed a new friendship today.'

Will gestures for me to carry on.

'Let's just say Baxter and I didn't get off on good terms but today we each realised the other is not so bad.'

'Ah, you and Baxter have finally bonded,' says Will. 'I had the same issue with my mother's dog. We were enemies until my mother broke her hip and I had to look after him.'

'You can relate to what I've been through then?'

Will laughs. 'Yes, I can. Cookie the dog and I are the best of friends now.' He runs his hand through his hair. 'So, are you, Felix and Baxter going anywhere nice?'

I open my mouth, but Felix beats me to it. 'We are going to Leeds to see Rory.'

Will nods. 'That's nice.'

'Rory is my ex-boyfriend,' I say to Will. 'And you? Are you going anywhere nice?'

Will fiddles with the cuff of his blue shirt. 'To visit my son. He lives up north with his mum. We're not together anymore. I try to see him every other weekend and at Christmas.' He looks inside his shirt pocket. 'I fancy a hot drink from the buffet car. Can I get you both anything? My shout as it is going to be a long journey and it is nice to have company.'

'Well, that's lovely, thank you. I'll have a coffee, a flat white. Felix – do you want anything?'

'A Fruit Shoot please,' Felix mumbles. 'Apple & Blackcurrant.'

Will gives us a thumbs up and walks towards the far end of the carriage.

My phone starts to bleep. It's Lizzie.

119

'Ems, have you found Felix?' Lizzie's voice is tinged with concern.

'Yes, he was on a train to Leeds.'

Lizzie gasps. 'What?'

'Long story,' I say as Felix casts me a sheepish look.

'I'm not liking the sound of this. So, are you on the train to Leeds as well now?'

I let out a nervous laugh. 'Yes, Felix ran off and boarded the nonstop train from Kings Cross to Leeds so we're going on a little festive trip.'

Lizzie gasps again. 'All the way to Leeds? Don't shout at me but do you think it might be a good time to discipline Felix? Like take that bloody iPad away from him?'

I turn away from Felix. 'That doesn't work.'

'Is this Rory related by any chance?'

'Yes, it is.'

I can hear Lizzie relaying what I'm saying to Bill in the background.

'Are you going to pay him a visit?' Lizzie asks.

Felix can hear Lizzie down the phone. I know he can because he's looking up at me.

'I don't know,' I say, quietly. 'He has his new girlfriend with him.'

'Oh, God, Ems, do you want to do this? You could be walking in on ANYTHING. Just tell Felix you don't want to go see him.'

With a sigh I glance at Felix. 'Yes, I might try that.'

'Stay in touch. The snow is going to get bad later and we will be worried about you both.'

'We're okay.'

Will returns carrying our drinks. Felix goes back to the iPad, and I sip my coffee while listening to Will talk about what he plans to do over Christmas with his son. The way he talks about his son, I can tell he adores him. They always get the same haircut at a local barber shop when they're together, short at the sides and spiky at the front. Afterwards, they go to the nearest Mercedes car showroom and look at the latest fancy cars to buy. Both he and his boy are mad about Mercedes cars.

As Will talks I remember what Lizzie said last night about how maybe I should date someone else and see whether that helps me unlove Rory. I could date someone like Will, he seems kind and genuine. He's handsome but he's not on Rory's level of handsome. Rory's face flashes up inside my mind. My heart somersaults in appreciation of Rory's boyish smile and those blue eyes which would give me permanent happy, summer day vibes. I still love everything about Rory. I remember how happy I felt when we'd meet after work and then go have some fun, the butterflies in my stomach when he texted me and the childlike excitement when I knew he was on his way to see me. He was the most caring boyfriend I ever had with his daily texts to tell me he was thinking about me and, if I was going out with Lizzie after work, I had to call him when I was home, no matter what time, so he knew I was safe. Damn you, Rory. There's no one else in the world who will match up to you.

CHAPTER 18

RORY

*T*he TV weather woman is struggling to point to all the Met Office snow weather warnings on the map. This is not a great time to travel down to Brighton. I wish I hadn't turned on the TV while I pack.

My phone bleeps. It's Tom. *'I'm bulk buying us toilet roll, candles and tinned meat. One of the tabloids has renamed this snowstorm Snowmageddon. They are saying there's going to be loo roll and food shortages plus blackouts.'*

At the first sign of any national concern Tom goes into panic buying mode. He's the ultimate panic shopper and I can picture him now in the supermarket with his trolley laden with loo roll and candles.

Sitting down on my bed I can't help wondering whether travelling this afternoon to Brighton is a mistake. Heavy snow is due this evening and tomorrow. There's a chance the trains could be stopped, and I could be trapped somewhere. I could miss Christmas altogether being trapped on a train between Leeds and Brighton. Maybe I should wait until the week between Christmas and New Year?

I check my phone for any other messages. Earlier I replied to

Emily's Facebook message. For ages after Beth left, I sat and stared at the message Emily had sent me. My fingers hovered over the reply button for so long they ached. I wanted to be sure how I felt towards her. Emily's face from this time last year flashed up in my mind. She was sat on the sofa in her old flat, wearing a festive gold paper crown, casting me one of her beautiful smiles with her curvy pink lips. Her amber-coloured eyes were shining and the beautiful sight of her made me gooey inside. Eventually I replied.

Reaching into my pocket I take out the locket and open it up. Vivi's smile finds me first. She'd want me to give her gift to Emily for Christmas. I can picture Emily's face lighting up at the sight of the locket. It might even help to ease some of her suffering. I know Vivi's death will have broken her. It had an impact on me and I was simply Vivi's sister's boyfriend. With the tip of my finger, I trace Emily's photo. God, I miss her so much it hurts. No matter what I do; move miles away, go on disastrous dates with other women who either look like Emily or remind me of her, I always end up thinking about her. My mind goes back to the locket. I wish I hadn't lost the locket's box. Damn!

My phone bleeps. It's a text from Anna's mum, Denise Parker. My heart grinds to a halt. Has something happened to Anna? Her text reads: *I know you and Anna are not on speaking terms, but I wanted to say I haven't stopped thinking about Felix and I wanted you to know we all miss him. He brings back a lot of memories from years ago. It's a shame to see Felix's talent go to waste. There's a festival competition in March. Do you think he would want to be a part of it?*

With a heavy heart I close her text and push an army of thoughts to the back of my mind. Grabbing my rucksack, I stuff in a few T-shirts, a couple of pairs of boxer shorts, my spare toiletries bag, which has been packed for months in case Emily invites me back down to Brighton, my headphones, my laptop, and three pairs of jeans. I also rummage inside my underwear drawer for as many pairs of thick socks I can lay my hands on and my emergency credit card which is tucked right at the back. My fingers find the card, but they also touch a long, soft package. Yanking out the drawer fully I take out the paper package. Carefully I unwrap it and stare down at the gift. I was going to send it to him. I wrestle with the idea of taking it with me. Felix tearfully told me after Vivi's funeral that he never wanted to think about his secret ever again, so I chose not to give him my gift. Wrapping up the package I place it on my bedside cabinet. I don't want to make him upset.

With the locket safely in my shirt pocket I give myself two lucky squirts of deodorant and a splash of Paco Rabanne. Trying to run my hand through my dense mass of curls causes my fingers to get stuck in one of them. Rescuing my hand, I decide that getting a brush through my hair is going to be too painful, so I hide my hair inside a woollen hat. For a second, I pause and wonder whether I should tell Tom where I am going. He'll only panic if I tell him. Best to let him think I am out Christmas shopping.

I have a love/hate relationship with the lift in this block of newly-built flats. When I moved to Brighton I lived in a flat where there was no lift. Walking up and down five flights of stairs day in, day out broke me both physically and mentally. So, when I moved in with Tom, I had a lot of love and appreciation for the lift. All I can say is that this lift has hated me from the first moment I set foot inside it. You would not believe how many times it has cruelly closed its doors seconds before I've raced towards it on a morning, or in the evening when I am knackered from work. I have been living here with Tom since the summer and I swear I have spent most of my time walking up and down hundreds of bloody stairs. Our lift is a metal arsehole and has spent six months inflicting pain on me.

On the rare occasions I have managed to catch it, the damn thing has broken down with me inside it *eight* times. The lift engineer and I are now on first name terms and have an amusing

WhatsApp thread which basically consists of him sending me funny memes about people getting trapped in lifts.

Walking quickly towards the lift area I know exactly what the metal arsehole is going to do to me – make me walk down all those stairs. Right now, I need to be at the train station and not walking down all those steps cursing the hell out of a damn lift.

Its metal doors are wide open. You see this is what it does to me, lulls me into a false sense of security and then when I am a fingernail away from touching the button it shuts its doors and excitedly races back down the lift shaft like a mischievous kid.

'It's Christmas,' I say, breaking into a jog to catch it, 'give me a break you lump of metal junk.'

Slamming the button with one hand I stretch out my leg to stop the doors from closing. To my surprise they remain open and don't try to trap my leg (which they have done before) in a vice-like grip. Throwing myself inside I jab the ground floor button. For a few frustrating seconds nothing happens. The thought of walking down all those stairs is nauseating. I prod the button some more. 'Do me a favour and close your doors.'

Air gets trapped in my throat as the doors slide towards each other. With a happy ping it begins its descent.

'What is going on? If this is my Christmas present, I am impressed, lift.'

When it finally reaches the ground floor and flings open its doors I walk out with a gaping mouth and a look of total disbelief. Maybe the lift is feeling festive? Even better – maybe Lady Luck is on my side today? If my plan is going to work, I bloody well need her.

Leeds station is a short walk from my city centre flat. This afternoon there's a steady flow of travellers in and out of the station. As I get nearer, I have to dodge people clutching giant bags filled with toys, people struggling with suitcases almost as big as them, excited kids chasing each other out onto the snow coated pavements and tired-looking parents trying to place screaming tiny children into pushchairs and scrabbling around for waterproofs to fit over the baby buggy.

A Spanish-looking woman wrestling with a tall Christmas tree in the doorway to the station blocks my way. I hold open the door and help her drag it through. Out of the corner of my eye I spot two figures leaving the station, a woman with shoulder length auburn hair and a smaller boy with red hair. My heart goes berserk inside my rib cage. For a few seconds I stop helping with the oversized Christmas tree and watch the woman and boy wander off with their backs to me. They do look a lot like Emily and Felix. With a heave of the tree, I tell myself it can't be them. The last place they'd be visiting is Leeds.

CHAPTER 19

EMILY

*F*elix has fallen asleep against me. Baxter is curled up in my lap, Will is busy texting someone and I am alone with my thoughts. Felix is adamant he wants to go see Rory. The thought of knocking on Rory's flat door fills me with unease. As much I want to see him, I don't think I'm strong enough to see him half-dressed with Beth peering out behind him. I've tried explaining to Felix that seeing Beth will make me sad but he doesn't seem to care. Being on this train feels surreal. I can't believe Felix ran away in St Pancras station and ended up on a train leaving for Leeds. Stroking his mop of unruly hair, I press my cheek against his head. I don't think I have fully recovered from the sheer panic of losing him.

'Not long to go,' says Will, making me turn to face him. 'An hour from now and I'll be seeing my boy.'

'Do you find it hard being so far away?'

Will nods. 'I miss him so much it hurts at times.' He looks at Felix fast asleep nestled beside me. 'That's nice of you taking your nephew on a trip to Leeds. Are you giving your sister some time off?'

I swallow back at the lump which has risen at the back of my throat. 'My sister died back in May.'

Will sits up and stares at me. His eyes widen dramatically. 'Oh, God, I'm sorry.'

'It's all right,' I say, casting him a weak smile. 'I'm Felix's legal guardian now.'

His face softens. 'How are you finding that?'

Before Felix's shock trip to Leeds, I would have deluged Will with how hard it has been with Felix. Even though I am still cross with Felix for using my card, leaving me frightened at St Pancras and for running away like that I do feel like something has changed between us. 'Well, it's not been easy, but I think today we've made a tiny bit of progress.'

Will nods. 'That's good. Who are you going to see in Leeds?'

I take a breath. 'My ex-boyfriend, Rory.'

Something flickers across Will's face. His smile loses its shine. 'Reconciliation?'

Felix is stirring beside me.

'I don't know. Rory and I split just after my sister died. Life was taking us in different directions. I'm not sure what the future holds for Rory and me.'

I turn to see Felix rubbing his eyes and sitting up. He flicks open my iPad.

'It happened to me and my other half,' Will explains. 'The love disappeared, and life parted us.'

I'm not sure my love for Rory has disappeared. Sitting here just thinking about him is making my heart flip and somersault. 'It wasn't like that between us. I didn't feel he wanted the same things as me, so I ended our relationship. Set him free.'

Felix gasps, making both Will and me stare at him. A grin takes hold of his little face, and his hazel eyes widen. What mischief is he up to now? Why do I feel so uneasy when he looks at me like this?

'Ah, this reminds me of that quote,' says Will, stroking his chin. 'Sorry, I'm a sucker for quotes. How does it go now? If you set something free and it comes back to you it's yours forever and if it doesn't…'

I finish his sentence. 'If it doesn't, it was never yours to begin with.'

He nods and holds my gaze for a few seconds longer than he should. 'That's it.'

Felix thrusts my iPad in my face. The gesture makes me jump out of my skin and Baxter wakes up with a startle and bark.

'FELIX – don't do that!'

'Rory still loves you, Aunty Emily,' he says, beaming at Will and me.

I let out an internal groan as Will turns to face the window. Is this another of Felix's predictions? Rory is probably in bed with Beth right now. 'What?'

'Look,' he says, pointing to something on Facebook messenger. 'Don't shout, Aunty Emily, but I messaged him pretending to be you.'

'WHAT?' My voice sounds like an angry roar. For goodness' sake I need to lock down all my social media accounts and make them Felix-proof.

Felix sighs. 'Sometimes a kid has to take control of things. Read his reply.'

I take the iPad and read Rory's message. It reads: *I've never stopped loving you, Emily.*

Scrolling back through the message I can see Felix messaged Rory, pretending to be me, this morning. It read, *I love u.*

The words of Rory's message dance before my eyes. My heart performs a series of somersaults. Excitement surges up my spine. It isn't long before reality kicks in and my mind starts to unpack the message. Is that what Rory sent? Where the hell was Beth when he was tapping out this message – picking up her clothes from his bedroom floor? In the shower?

'I can't believe he still…'

Felix folds his arms across his chest. 'Rory loves you, Aunty Emily.'

'Hang on a sec, Felix – why did you pretend to be me online again?'

I watch my nephew hang his head. He watches me angrily snatch the iPad away from him. 'Felix, you can't keep doing this sort of thing. I can make my own decisions.'

My phone starts to bleep. It's Lizzie.

'Are you there yet?' screeches Lizzie. 'Bill and I are beside ourselves with worry like two paranoid parents.'

Blowing the air out of my cheeks I gaze out the window and across snow-coated house roofs. 'I think we're nearly there.'

'What's the plan once you get there?' whispers Lizzie, sensing Felix might be in earshot. 'Please don't tell me you are going to drop into Rory's flat when we both know you'll be walking in on a scene from Fifty Shades.'

I hold the phone close to my lips and turn away while whispering into the speaker. 'Don't think I'm going to get a choice.'

Lizzie shouts down the phone. 'Don't let a nine-year-old rule your life, Ems. Be strong with Felix.'

I can hear Bill's voice and a tussle with Lizzie for the phone. 'Little Miss Vintage,' he booms, 'I hear you're going to drop by Rory's for a cuppa, a biccie and a cwtch.' (Welsh for cuddle.)

'Not so sure on the cwtch, Bill,' I hiss. 'More of an awkward conversation.'

Bill giggles. 'Lizzie Lupin has showed me Rory's Facebook page. I bet his new date will be over the moon to see you.'

Lizzie wrestles the phone out of his hand. 'Ignore him, Ems. I think you should explain to Felix about Rory not showing any settling down potential. Oh, Ems, I feel sick about this trip of yours.'

'So do I,' I reply, stroking Baxter's velvet-soft ears.

Lizzie takes a deep breath. 'I'm going to spend the next hour on the loo.' She sighs. 'Ems, you know how I get bad bowels when my friends are going through stressful times.'

Lizzie is being truthful. She's always suffered from an irritable bowel condition which seems to worsen when people she loves are going through hell. When Vivi died I spent a lot of time sat outside the bathroom door of our old flat while Felix played in the lounge and Lizzie sat on the loo. It sounds gross but over the years I have come to terms with Lizzie's IBS and the fact that anything horrible in my life causes her to double up in pain and race away upstairs.

'Look, I will be all right, Lizzie.'

She lets out a heavy sigh. 'Call me, I'll have my phone with me in the bathroom.'

I can hear Bill shrieking in the background. 'Lizzie Lupin, please antibac your phone when you come out.'

I hang up.

Felix lets out a whine. 'Aunty Emily, I heard all of that conversation. You've got Rory all wrong.'

Will casts me an awkward look as I erupt. All my bottled-up tension rises inside of me. 'FELIX,' I roar making him jolt. 'Rory was getting friendly with a woman called Anna before we split up. He wasn't ready to settle down and if we look at Facebook, he's currently on a third date with Beth.'

Felix shakes his head in defiance. 'He didn't love Anna, Aunty Emily. She knew...'

He stops as I stare at him. Seriously, is there anything Felix doesn't know. He's like my own secret spy. If this is what he's like at nine, there's no hope for me when he's a teenager. 'You knew about Anna?'

I watch him flick his eyes to the train floor.

'Felix, tell me.'

He holds my gaze. 'Rory will explain. Can I go to the toilet please?'

CHAPTER 20

FELIX

*L*ocking the train toilet door behind him Felix starts recording a video. 'Hello, Mummy. You'll be glad to know Aunty Emily and Baxter made it onto the train in time. I am safe. They found me. I cried when I saw Aunty Emily. We both cried for ages. She's like a mummy to me. One who doesn't smile much. I don't hate her, Mummy. She might not smile or laugh much, she might cook horrible casseroles, she might make a mess of our living room, but she makes me feel safe. She also told me back in our seats that she loves me. Even after all the trouble I have caused she still loves me.' He yanks a piece of toilet paper out of the holder and blows his nose.

Looking into the phone camera with a mischievous smile, he says, 'Aunty Emily knows I text Rory. I told her. Guess what? Rory has texted back to say he never stopped loving her.' The video carries on recording as the sound of Felix jumping and up and down and cheering can be heard.

'You always said I had good ideas, Mummy. Well, this might turn out to be one of my best ideas. Aunty Emily wants me to ask Sai what he thinks about all my future ideas before I do anything.' Felix shakes his head in disbelief and pretends he's yawning into the phone camera. 'I'll never have fun again if I have to listen to Sai.'

He takes a deep breath. 'I also used Aunty Emily's credit card to pay for my train ticket. When I am rich and famous, I will pay her back. I must go now as I need the toilet and you once told me off for videoing myself doing a wee. When you next see me, I will be with Rory and Aunty Emily will be happy again. Bye for now, Mummy.'

CHAPTER 21

EMILY

*A*s the train guard announces over the speakers that we will shortly be arriving in Leeds station, Will gets up to collect his bag.

Felix, Baxter, and I wait for Will to make his way up the carriage towards the train doors.

Turning to me, Felix asks, 'Do I really have to tell Sai all my ideas in the future?'

A smile spreads across my face. 'Yes.'

Clamping his hand over his forehead he pulls a frustrated face and I laugh.

'It was lovely to meet you, Will,' I say as we stand together on the platform and wait for Felix to tie up his trainer laces. Will smiles and places a business card in my hand. 'If things don't work out with Rory, drop me an email.'

Baxter is wriggling around in my arms so much; I can't read Will's card. 'Thanks, it was nice to meet you too. I hope you enjoy walking around the Mercedes showroom.'

He laughs and stuffs his hands in his pockets. 'Ah, yes, I can't wait. Good luck on your trip. Is your ex-boyfriend expecting you?'

Felix chips in. 'No, it will be a surprise for Rory.'

An uncomfortable feeling passes over me. Rory probably sent me that message while Beth was making him a cup of tea after a marathon sex session. He is going to get such a shock seeing us standing on his flat doorstep.

Will rubs my arm and with a smile he walks off towards the platform exit. I watch him stride away. In my mind I try to imagine Will putting his arm around me or leaning in for a kiss, but my mind refuses to replace Rory's image.

Felix scoops Baxter out of my arms. 'Come on, Aunty Emily, we have to find Rory.'

Before I have a chance to say anything he's marched away.

'Felix, can you wait for me, please?'

We hurry along through the ticket barriers and into the main station. I'm immediately distracted by a young woman wearing a stunning fifties black velvet cocktail dress with a gorgeous, pleated wrap skirt finished off with a thick gold belt. She's got her camel coat draped over one arm and is running her hand through her silky blonde hair. I am in awe of her elegance. The urge to run up to her and ask her where she bought her dress is strong.

Before I have time to take out my phone and take a pic of her for a future dress design Felix drags me away. We head for the exit. In the middle of the doors a woman is trying to manoeuvre a Christmas tree through. It's so long it's jammed on the top of the door. I can't believe she's travelled with that tree. Someone on the other side is trying to help her get it through as I can see two hands holding onto the branches. Quickly I steer Felix through the doors at the far end. Outside the afternoon light is starting to fade. The sky above has a hint of lavender to it. Before long it will turn into a rich indigo colour. There are twinkly Christmas lights everywhere and a good covering of snow. An icy wind nips at our warm cheeks. I take in a deep breath of fresh air. The sign which reads 'LEEDS STATION,' makes me gasp. Felix and I are in Leeds. What the hell are we doing here?

A busker, wrapped in a large woollen hat, a giant scarf and furry boots is stood playing a guitar near to the station. As everyone walks past on their way into the bustling centre of Leeds, he sings them Happy Christmas. I have no idea where to find Rory's flat. 'Felix, get my iPad out so we can use google maps.'

I watch Felix take it out and quickly type in my password which makes me let out a heavy sigh. Google maps is taking ages to fire up. 'Happy Christmas, lady with the smile,' shouts the busker pointing to me before bursting into his own rendition of Slade's pop classic.

I take out my phone, but it's in desperate need of a charge. It's gone red on the battery sign. Felix has passed me Baxter and is now groaning at the sight of my phone.

By the time the busker has finished his song Felix, Baxter and I are stood huddled over my iPad and phone. I am cursing new technology when the busker waves and whistles at us. 'You lost?'

'Bring back physical maps,' I say with a nervous laugh.

'Aye,' he says, strumming a few chords on his guitar. 'Shopping in Leeds for Christmas?'

'No, we have come to surprise someone,' chirps up Felix.

The busker's grin widens. 'Oh, a surprise visit for Christmas, I love the sound of it. Will this person be pleased to see you?'

Felix confidently nods and I opt to cast the busker a grimace. Rory will be entertaining Beth in the bedroom so I can't see him being pleased to see us trooping into his flat. Why did I allow myself to be dragged along by Felix?

Felix points to me. 'Rory still loves Aunty Emily.' His voice is shrill and laden with excitement.

I receive a wink from the busker. 'Well, Rory is a lucky man. Could there be some Christmas romance in the air between you and this person?'

A pink blush blossoms over my face.

Felix pipes up. 'Aunty Emily and Rory will be together again.'

'You travelled far?'

'From Brighton.'

I watch him put down his guitar and take hold of a violin case. 'You've made a quite a journey. Was the snow bad on the way up?'

'It was in places. I believe there's more to come tomorrow.'

He looks up into the wintry sky. 'Good job you're not travelling home later as I think you might have to sledge it back to Brighton.'

Felix gasps as he watches the busker take out the violin. 'You play the violin?'

The busker nods and grins. 'Special music for my new Brighton friends.' With that he places the violin under his chin and starts to play. At once the air is filled with a beautiful tune. I have no idea what the busker is playing but it's calming and at once makes me forget about what is waiting for us at Rory's flat.

Thick white snowflakes are swirling in the air around us. I turn to Felix to encourage him to put his hood up but he's dropped his rucksack and is dancing amongst the white snowflakes. He twirls effortlessly along the pavement to the beat of the busker's song. I watch his long, skinny arms and hands arc in the air. His pointed toes make complicated patterns in the snow. The music tempo increases as the busker begins to lose himself in his music. Felix leaps into the air, arms outstretched like wings and legs tucked under his body. His dance takes my breath away and makes tears prick my eyes. Lifting my face to the sky I whisper, 'Vivi, I hope you are watching your amazing boy.'

Felix finishes as the song ends and gains a powerful round of applause from travellers and commuters who have stopped to watch. He runs to me, his freckle-clad cheeks a rosy, red colour and his hazel-coloured eyes glowing. 'Can we go now please, Aunty Emily.'

My heart is pounding away inside my chest. 'Felix – that was wonderful,' I exclaim also remembering the dance he did in Brighton before we left. 'Felix, where did you learn to dance like that?'

He shrugs and slings his rucksack back over his shoulder. 'It's nothing.'

I place my hand on his shoulder. 'It's not nothing, is it?'

The busker comes over to Felix. 'Mate, that was spectacular. Do you go to a dance school?'

Felix shakes his head and takes a sleepy Baxter from me. 'I just go to an ordinary school.'

Checking my phone, I see that it's dead. Shit.

'Right, Emily and Felix, let me help you with directions,' the busker says, scratching his head underneath his woollen hat.

We show him the address. Felix printed it out. 'It's not far at all,' explains the busker. 'Under ten minutes.'

The busker points us where to go. It seems quite straightforward. I'm so cold I can no longer feel my forehead. My legs are blocks of ice and I have lost touch with my fingers. 'Right, let's grab a hot chocolate or a coffee before we go see Rory.'

To my surprise Felix nods. I did think he might kick off. The dance must have drained him of energy.

We say farewell to the busker and hurry across the main road towards a coffee shop.

Felix's dancing is still on my mind by the time I bring a cup of coffee for me, a hot chocolate for him and a saucer of water for Baxter to the table.

I empty the tray and Felix feeds Baxter using a little plastic tray and a small bag of dog biscuits, all of which were packed in his rucksack.

'Talk to me about dancing,' I say, sitting opposite Felix.

His smile starts to fade, and his eyebrows knit together. 'I don't want to.'

'Why not?'

Vivi's face appears in my mind. I watch as Felix turns away. Perhaps dancing reminds him of his mum? I think I will save the dancing questions for later. I will add them to my questions about how Felix knows about Anna — which is something I discovered on the train.

'How's Baxter doing?'

A look of relief passes over Felix's face. I have stopped talking about dancing. 'Baxter is doing fine.'

We both take sips of our drinks and savour the warmth radiating out from them.

'I'm excited about seeing Rory,' gushes Felix, his face lighting up. Baxter barks from below the table in agreement. 'Are you excited, Aunty Emily?'

Inside of me a war is raging – one half of me thinks he'll be with Beth and this trip has been a waste of time. The other half is clinging onto a tiny piece of hope that he'll be there, and Beth won't be having any more dates with him. I think that side of me might be delusional. Rory – I hope you're ready for a Christmas surprise.

CHAPTER 22

EMILY

*I*n a few seconds we're going to buzz the flat intercom so Rory can let us into the building. I just want to take some time to compose myself, take a few deep breaths and mentally prepare myself before we press the button. It's a modern building towards the Royal Armourires Museum in the centre of the city. Squeezing my trembling hands together I curse my phone for dying on me because right now I could do with a FaceTime with Lizzie and Bill to calm my nerves. In true Felix fashion, he ignores my request for a few moments to get my thoughts together, stands on his tiptoes and presses the button.

'Felix,' I hiss, making Baxter bark at me from our feet, who has recently been to the toilet on a snowy patch of grass on the way to Rory's block of flats. 'I was going to do that.'

Felix shrugs. 'I saved you a job, Aunty Emily.'

No one responds.

Felix presses the button again and still nothing.

My stomach starts to rotate. In my head I can see Rory and Beth laid in bed up there and her telling him to ignore whoever is disturbing them. I feel sick.

Before I have time to reach in my bag for peppermints Felix

nudges me and points towards a young man hurrying towards the flats carrying a toilet roll four-pack under each arm and two bulging carrier bags.

As the figure huffs and puffs towards us Felix tugs on my arm. 'He might know Rory.'

The man reaches the door and groans. 'My key fob is in my coat pocket.'

'Do you want some help?' Felix asks.

'Help would be good,' he says, 'the key fob is in my left-hand coat pocket.'

I reach inside and grab it. He gestures for me to press it against the door to the building. With a swish the electronic door opens, and the man staggers inside with his carrier bags and toilet roll packs. 'Who are you here to see?' he asks, with his back to the lift.

'Rory Wilkinson,' Felix pipes up.

He turns back to us. 'And you two are?'

I place my hand on Felix's shoulder. 'I'm Emily and this is Felix.'

With a gasp he drops his toilet roll packets and carrier bags to the floor. For a few seconds we all stand and survey the toilet roll, tinned meat and candle chaos.

'Sorry,' says the man, bending down to grab as many candles as he can. He's shorter than Rory and looks like he's in his early thirties. He's wearing a red winter jacket, a blue rugby shirt and jeans. His face is bright red and he's breathing quickly. He stops for a second. 'You're Emily as in Rory's ex-girlfriend?'

My heart starts to thump. Oh, God, why does he seem like he's in shock?

Felix leaps into action after putting Baxter into my arms. He hands the man the tins of meat which have rolled away, and the toilet roll packs.

'I'm Tom, Rory's flatmate. Well, you better come with me.'

Felix carries one of the packs of toilet roll.

'Can you press the lift button for me as well?'

Felix jams the button and frowns at all the toilet rolls. 'Why have you bought so much toilet roll and tinned meat?'

The lift button has not even lit up which doesn't bode well. I press it again.

'The snow is going to get bad, and some say there might be toilet roll and food shortages. When I was a student, I lived on tinned meat for months, so it can be done.'

Felix nods and casts him an odd look.

'Is the lift coming?' Tom is staggering around the foyer.

'The lift doesn't seem to be working,' I explain, pointing to the screen. 'There's no up or down arrows and the button is not lit up.'

A frustrated wail can be heard from behind the toilet roll mountain. 'I can't walk up six flights of steps with all of my emergency provisions.'

We've decided there is no other option but to walk up the stairs as the lift must be out of action. Tom has said this is a regular occurrence. Baxter is in my arms, and I've never appreciated him more than I do now. Thank goodness he's a tiny dog who doesn't weigh very much. I'm so exhausted walking up all these stairs. Tiredness is making my legs ache.

Tom is alongside me as we make our way up the stairs. 'It's nice to finally meet you,' he puffs, as a torrent of sweat drips off his pink face.

'Nice to meet you too, Tom.'

He gestures to his carrier bags. 'I watch a lot of survival programmes.'

I cast him a friendly smile. 'It's always good to be prepared.'

On the third floor, Tom brings us to a halt. 'Is Rory expecting you?'

'It's a surprise,' shouts Felix, from halfway up the stairs ahead. Felix's answer causes Tom to drop the packets of toilet roll from under each arm again.

'Well, this is going to be some surprise,' chuckles Tom, scratching his damp blond hair before bending down to pick up the packets of toilet roll, and bags of candles and tinned meat.

I start feeling sick again. Rory is with Beth back in the flat. A feeling of uneasiness creeps over me. I want to grab Felix, turn around and head downstairs. This is going to be embarrassing. Why did I let Felix bring me here? I should have been stronger with him. By the time we reach the sixth floor I've managed to sneak a look at my reflection in the metal lift frame. My skin has a definite greenish tinge to it.

We arrive at Rory and Tom's flat. I can't help noticing Tom, with his eyes shut, pressing his face against the toilet rolls and muttering things under his breath.

'Shall I open the door?' I ask as I am still carrying Tom's key fob.

He shakes his head. 'Open the door for me and I'll go in first.'

As we watch Tom struggle in with his toilet rolls and bags of tinned meat Felix reaches out for my arm. He leans his head against me. I ruffle his hair, close my eyes, and pray for a miracle.

Tom returns after a minute. 'Rory's not here.'

'Not here?' Felix and I say in unison.

Tom nods. 'You better come in.' He spots Baxter in my arms. 'We're not allowed pets in the flat.'

Irritation bubbles up inside of me. 'Well – Baxter's not staying out here,' I snap, holding our trembling little dog close. Felix looks up at me with a proud grin. I don't think I have seen one of those before. With a defeated nod Tom gestures for us all to come in.

We enter the spacious open-plan living area, lined with two monstrous black leather sofas and one red leather chair which lurks in the corner. On the square coffee table is a pizza box, three cans of beer, a TV controller for the giant plasma TV on the wall and a games console. Felix, Baxter, and I sit on the sofa.

Opposite us are ten empty beer bottles lined up against the wall. A giant window is on the far side.

Tom comes to stand before us. He's fumbling with his hands and shifting his weight from foot to foot. 'I don't know where Rory is. He was here with... erm...'

'Beth,' growls Felix, crossing his arms over his chest.

My stomach squelches inside of me. The sex with Beth must have been so good they've gone to christen her house. I glance at the sky out of the window. It's darkening over the snow-coated city. Given that Rory is not here, what the hell are Felix and I going to do? If the snow is going to be so bad that Tom is buying in emergency supplies how will we get home tonight? It also will take ages to get home and we wouldn't get back until the early hours. If we can't get home due to the snow we also have no accomodation booked.

My face feels hot and sweaty. Other sensible adults would have been watching over Felix in the station and would not have let him run off to board a train to another part of the country. Even if they had found themselves on a speeding train they would have been prepared for every eventuality and perhaps booked a cheap hotel room. Sensing my worry Felix tugs on my arm. 'Remember what Rory sent you, Aunty Emily, the message.'

I force out a weak smile as my belly feels like a pit of writhing snakes.

Tom flicks his eyes to the floor. 'Can I get anyone a drink?'

What are we doing here? I should be hurrying Felix away and sorting out my travel mess. 'We should probably get going, Tom,' I mumble.

Felix casts me a pained look. 'It's going to be all right, Aunty Emily. Rory is out buying us Christmas presents. Can we stay as I am thirsty?'

'One drink and then we better go.'

After we've given Tom our drink orders, we remove our coats

and let Baxter investigate the carpet. Felix curls up in the crook of my arm.

I sink back into the sofa and push my travel fears to the back of my mind. I turn to Rory-related thoughts. As much as my pessimistic side would love for me to believe Rory has gone back to Beth's house, the Facebook message he sent earlier refuses to leave my mind. The question I'm now asking myself is whether you can still love someone and have sex with someone else. I need a charger for my phone. Lizzie and Bill would know the answer to this and I'm sensing the answer is probably YES. 'Tom, do you have an Apple phone charger?'

He comes out of the kitchen carrying a a cup of tea for me and a glass of water for Felix. Swinging from his hand is a lead with a white phone charger attached. 'You are lucky,' he says, 'I took it with me into town as I knew Rory would try to pinch it.'

I take it from him and plug the charger in. My phone wakes from the dead after a minute of charge.

Tom takes the chair. 'I've tried calling Rory, but his phone is going to voicemail.'

Felix has taken out my iPad. 'Do you have a wifi code, Tom?'

I try to take the iPad away from him, but he holds on tightly. In the end I let it go and watch Tom give Felix the password.

An awkward silence descends upon Tom and me. He finds interesting things on the carpet to look at while I try to stop Baxter dragging a leather slipper from under the coffee table. 'Baxter,' I hiss, yanking the slipper from him. Felix smiles at me after gulping back his water.

'I'll drink my tea and then we will get out of your way,' I say, breaking the silence.

Tom nods. 'Sorry, I've no idea where Rory is.'

I can't help but notice Felix wiping one of his cheeks with the sleeve of his coat. He's devastated. How I wish he'd told me about his plan. Where the hell are you, Rory?

CHAPTER 23

RORY

I'm freezing my bollocks off on this platform. I've lost all sensation in my nose. I think it might have turned into a block of ice. Even though my hands are dug deep into my coat pockets there's no escape from the grip of the bone-chilling temperature. A gloomy train guard is walking up and down the platform. His face is a lifeless blue colour.

Fuck me – it's cold! The train to London King's Cross is delayed due to the snow.

This isn't the best start to my journey. A gloomy train announcer keeps reminding everyone about the hazardous conditions for train travel.

No one around me is taking any notice of what the train announcer has to say or the late running of the train; two young children holding on to their father's hands are busy singing an out of tune rendition of 'Little Donkey', a teenage couple to the left of me is locked in a passionate embrace, a noisy family from Newcastle is practically shouting what they're going to do when they get to *'Nana George's house for Christmas'*, a gang of young, giggling women, clutching huge shopping bags, are busy taking selfies of themselves and two men stood next to me are talking about what sort of meat one of their mothers is going to cook for Christmas dinner – a close call between beef and turkey, but lamb could be an outside runner.

Earlier as I raced down the steps to the platform, I did wonder whether I was going to be the only brave (some might say stupid given the weather warnings) soul daring to travel during the snowstorm. The sad-faced man behind the glass ticket booth, who kept shaking his head with disapproval, had told me I wouldn't get very far in these conditions, and he said it was unlikely I would reach Brighton. According to him everyone was cancelling and by tonight there would be no trains. I mentally prepared myself for standing on a deserted platform and attracting crazed looks from train staff.

So, you can imagine my shock when I stepped onto a bustling platform.

I've just booked a room in a Brighton Travelodge on my phone as I have no idea what time I will arrive in Brighton and Emily will not thank me for turning up on her doorstep in the early hours.

It's still snowing. The train announcer is back. A loud cheer erupts as the announcer tells us the delayed London train is approaching the station. My heart starts to pound at the bright yellow glow of the train lights coming into view.

In a few minutes I am going to board a train for London. It's the day before Christmas Eve, there is a huge snowstorm battering the country and I've no idea what Emily is going to do or say when I turn up on her doorstep clutching Vivi's locket.

Have I lost my marbles? I have just used my emergency credit card on a train ticket and hotel room, money which I don't really have, and all because of a message from Emily and a gold chain and locket. I glance down at Emily's message on Messenger. This is out of the blue and not like Emily. She's always been a fan of a lengthy message.

What if she wants to explain for the millionth time why she believes I am not good father material for Felix?

I can still back out of this. In six minutes, I can easily be in the lift from hell shooting back up to the flat for an afternoon of Xbox gaming in the warmth with Tom. No one would know I decided to go see Emily and realised on the train platform I'd made a mistake. The day could be spent playing Tom's war games and listening to him torture himself about Suzie and... slowly torturing myself with missing Emily. I wouldn't get my money back at such short notice. Why do I get the feeling there is no escape?

Emily's face appears in my mind. Her honey-dipped eyes are glinting in the light and she's casting one of her breathtaking smiles. There is a small, almost microscopic chance I could be holding her in my arms again tonight after this, and that thought has just lit a roaring fire inside of me. This is a crazy plan of mine and I must keep the faith it is going to work.

As I board the train, I help a woman with silky red hair and a lot of heavy bags onto the train. Even though she's younger than Vivi, she has a Vivi look about her. She's been Christmas shopping and the amount she's bought reminds me of Vivi too.

My goodness that woman could shop. Once I made the mistake of going shopping with Emily and Vivi. Felix had escaped by going to a friend's house. Five hours into the shopping and Vivi was still going strong. Emily and I were gasping. I liked Vivi a lot as a good friend. She always helped me out when I was late with my articles for the newspaper. No matter what time in the evening we worked to, she always had a huge smile on her face and a bubbly laugh. Her desk was always covered in photos of her, Felix, her dog Baxter, and Emily. Family was important to Vivi, her conversations always included a funny anecdote from life at home with Felix and Baxter. I could never believe a tiny dog like Baxter could cause so much chaos. Vivi adored Felix and every certificate and school report he brought home would be pinned to Vivi's office wall.

Inside the train carriage I'm greeted by rows of smiling faces, colourful bobble hats, scarves, gloves, rosy cheeks, and the sound of Slade's Christmas hit, 'Merry Christmas Everyone'.

I take the table seat next to the window and find myself opposite the two men who were discussing one of their mother's Christmas lunch meat choices.

'I'm Alfie,' says the young guy with the russet-coloured hair and an impressive beard. 'This is my husband, Michael.' The bloke with the mass of black curls sat next to him smiles. 'We might as well get to know each other as I have a feeling we could all be on this train for a very long time.' He gestures to the blizzard which has started outside.

'I'm Rory.'

Michael points at the snow. 'I hope this train has emergency shovels because I think we might have to dig our way to London.'

We all roll our eyes and return to casting desperate looks at our phone screens. According to the BBC News site, the UK's transport network is in danger of grinding to a halt tomorrow, Christmas Eve. The bookies have stopped taking bets on a white Christmas, last night temperatures plunged to minus ten degrees Celsius and thousands of children are causing their parents extra stress by making last-minute snowboard and sledge additions to their Santa lists.

'The *Mail* is now calling it the Mega Beast from the East,' exclaims Alfie, fiddling with his trendy beard and reading aloud from his phone. 'Tomorrow towns will become cut off, society will break down, there will be widespread chaos and Christmas could be cancelled.'

Michael laughs and peers over Alfie's shoulder. A sense of unease about my journey and the possible end of the world due to the snow makes me squirm in my seat. I reassure myself with the fact that the media always blow things out of proportion with the weather and society has never broken down in Scotland due to severe snow.

Alfie grins at me. 'Where are you off to, Rory?'

'Huh? Oh, erm, Brighton.'

A look of fear spreads across Michael's face. 'Oh, God, you'll never get there in this weather.'

Alfie rolls his eyes and turns to me. 'Ignore my ultra-positive husband.'

Michael casts me a deadpan expression. 'Rory, you'll be fine.' He flicks his eyes to the floor and whispers, 'You might want to buy some rope, an emergency blanket and a torch in London.'

Alfie gives Michael a playful nudge and we all start to laugh.

'You got family in Brighton, Rory?' Michael asks.

Crossing my legs under the table I shake my head. 'No. My ex-girlfriend lives there.'

Alfie's eyes widen with interest. 'Oh, I see.'

He checks his phone and nudges Michael. 'Check out that news article.'

Michael's dark eyes dart back and forth across the article. 'We need to ditch our jobs in the new year and become entrepreneurs.'

Alfie laughs. 'I'm thinking the same.' He turns to me. 'You ever had a crazy idea for a new business venture?'

A memory of Emily and me brainstorming her future online vintage clothes business while we decorated her bedroom in the flat she shared with Lizzie comes back to me. I had been encouraging her to start a dressmaking business for months after witnessing her ability to make stunning dresses for all her friends. I was confident she could make a success of it. So, we both came up with ideas for her business and battled with her fancy new wallpaper at the same time. I remember after we'd finished decorating, we went for a pizza, and she took a notebook and pen. Our business brainstorming session went on into the night and it gave us both a thrill.

Alfie grins at Michael. 'Shall we tell him our idea?'

'If we see him on *Dragon's Den* in the future selling our idea to Deborah, we will have to hunt him down,' says Michael, with a grin.

Alfie flashes his phone screen at me. I see a bold headline which reads: LOVE ON THE RIGHT TRACK – *Survey reveals increase in people meeting the love of their life at their local train station.*

They both watch my face like hawks although misread my confused look.

'I first met Michael at a train station,' explains Alfie, 'London St Pancras.'

I let out several inner groans. Why did I get myself into this conversation? I sneak a quick glance at the bloke a few seats along the train aisle who is sat in his own little world listening to headphones. He had the right idea.

Michael takes over their story. 'Before we got together Alfie lived in Wolverhampton and I was based in Lincoln. It was a Saturday, and we were both in London for the rugby. I dropped my ticket and handsome stranger, Alfie, picked it up and handed it to me.'

'I knew I was in love from the moment he smiled at me,' says Alfie, winking at his husband. 'An unforgettable smile.'

Emily had an unforgettable smile when Vivi introduced us in a pub. I couldn't take my eyes off her. When she smiled, I felt light-headed and for the first time in my life I felt nervous in front of a woman. It took me until the fourth date to pluck up the courage to kiss her.

'We swapped numbers,' says Alfie, 'and he called me later from a bar in Richmond to invite me over to join him for a post-match drink.'

Michael nods. 'London St Pancras will always be a magical place for us.'

Alfie's face lights up. 'We later discovered that, within our respective friendship networks, quite a few people had met the love of their life at... London St Pancras.'

Scratching my head, I try to remain looking vaguely interested.

Michael holds up his fingers on his right hand. 'Kylie, who I met when I was backpacking around China, got talking to her future husband while buying her ticket there. Alfie's mate Kevin met his future hubby while boarding a train to Lincoln.'

'Kevin dropped his bag which wasn't zipped up,' Alfie adds. 'His toiletries bag fell out and hit the platform floor. This I can believe with Kevin as he's the most disorganised person I have ever met. He never packs his stuff. Just grabs what he can lay his hands on and chucks it into a bag. As he's always late for everything there's no time for him to zip up his luggage. Anyway, his soap bag exploded and according to him the platform looked like he'd been on a pharmacy shoplifting spree. Luckily, handsome stranger, Gareth, was there to rescue his hair wax pot and deodorant. They got married last year.'

Michael continues. 'Fran from my office. She met her boyfriend there, although they've split up now, but I know they are still secretly seeing each other so they'll be back together soon. Also, Maddie from work met her girlfriend in St Pancras as they were queuing for coffee.'

'Station love is a thing,' interjects Alfie.

Michael runs his hand through hair and excites all his dark curls. 'London St Pancras is probably the best station for love.'

'I haven't heard anyone meet at King's Cross,' says Alfie, with a frown. 'Or Paddington for that matter.'

'So, what's the business idea?' I ask.

Alfie's eyes flash with excitement and in a low voice says, 'A station dating app.'

This is going to be a long trip listening to these two and their station dating app. I've always disliked train stations. When I left university, I endured years of exhausting and frustrating commuting across London. Trains never ran to time, they were always crammed, stuffy and I always ended up being squashed next to someone who smelt like they ate nothing but raw garlic. All the jobs I had back then were for sales companies who promised meteoric careers but in return demanded twelve-hour days of wearing an uncomfortable telephony headset, being eager to take a call even when sat on the office loo, and fake smiles always plastered across faces.

My hatred of train stations intensified when Emily and I spent the first year of our relationship living apart, me in Clapham and she in Brighton. Neither of us had a car so we had to rely on public transport. Sunday evenings would always leave me with an aching chest and a headache. She'd come with me to the station and watch me reluctantly walk away through the barrier. Five painful days without her in my life would stretch ahead of me. On a Friday evening the excitement of seeing her rushing into my arms at Brighton station would make me scoop her up and suggest we get a taxi back to her flat and stay in bed for the entire weekend. Time would rush by and before I knew it I would be getting the train back to Clapham with a heavy heart.

I can't see me liking train stations anytime soon.

My phone bleeps. It's a text from Anna. It reads: *I hear my mother has contacted you. She says I'm being childish for not speaking to you for months and I should apologise. According to her life is too short. I'm sorry for thinking our friendship was something else and the reason I have been ignoring you is that I have been embarrassed over what happened.*

The night where everything went wrong comes rushing back. I was supposed to be going with Emily to Vivi's to babysit Felix, but I ended up getting into a long conversation with Anna after work in a bar and that seemed to carry on into the night. Soon

153

we were back at her flat and I was sat on her sofa draining a bottle of beer. A drunken Anna had gone to get something from her bedroom before entering her living room in just a black bra and thong. I did hide my eyes as all I kept thinking was what would Emily think if she knew where I was. My stomach started to knot. All I could do was guide Anna back to her clothes and tell her I wanted to remain friends. While all this was going on, Vivi was dying on her bathroom floor and Emily was in pieces.

'Here's your coffee, Rory.' Alfie places a large takeaway cup in front of me. He's just returned from the buffet car bringing a coffee for me, Michael's cup of tea and his own can of Diet Coke. Michael moves out of his seat to let his husband in.

Alfie stares out of the train window. 'The blizzarding has stopped. It doesn't look too bad wherever we are. I can see cars moving freely on the road over there.'

Michael nods as he uncovers his tea. 'I think the media have blown it out of proportion, like I said before.'

Alfie takes a swig from his can of Diet Coke. 'What did you think of our business idea then, Rory?'

My head is stuck in the past so I don't hear him. The memory of Anna joining the company I was working for, a few months before Vivi died, has glued itself to the inside of my mind. At first, I had no idea she had links to my past. We were on an office night out when we became friends. There were six of us left at the end of the night, including Anna and me. We'd all had far too many drinks, shots and cocktails and were slumped in a bar. One of our workmates, Ravi, was asleep under the table. We'd all promised to take him with us when we left to get taxis. Our track record of remembering Ravi being unconscious under the table was not great. On the four previous nights out we'd forgotten about him, and he'd been woken up by two hefty bouncers who'd carried him through the doors and practically launched him into the sky at closing time. On this occasion we'd all sworn on the lives of our loved ones that we wouldn't forget Ravi. Everyone had reached that final stage on an office outing where each person starts talking about deep stuff combined with a bit of drunken nonsense. In my experience these are usually the conversations you end up living to regret the next day in the office.

Things became complex when Anna turned to me and said, 'Don't you remember me? I remember you.'

CHAPTER 24

EMILY

'We better go,' I say, placing down my empty cup and feeling sick at the thought of the late journey ahead back home with Felix, Baxter and the snow.

To my surprise Tom shakes his head. 'Stay for some food.'

Felix has clasped his hands together in a prayer-like pose. 'Please can we have some food, Aunty Emily?'

'Felix, it's late and we somehow need to get home.'

'Why don't you all sleep in Rory's bedroom?' Tom suggests, pointing to the door off the living area. 'The weather report is not great and I would feel bad sending you out into the snow late at night,' Felix jumps up with a huge grin on his face and Baxter wriggles so much with excitement I wonder whether his little body might explode.

'Really?' I stare at Tom. 'Are you sure?'

He smiles. 'I'm sure.'

Tom's busy on his phone ordering us all a pizza. He told us he wanted to save his tinned meat for when the snow gets bad, and he can't get to the shops. Felix asked whether we should buy tinned meat, candles, and toilet roll on the way home. Tom looked shocked when I told him I had not bought any emergency food provisions for the snow.

Felix, Baxter and I are going to be sleeping in Rory's bed. This fills me with unease for several reasons; I have no idea when Rory last changed his bedsheets, whether he has a stash of clean bedsheets, whether he's brought any women back into his bed and will he come barging into his bedroom in the early hours with a girl in tow.

Following the familiar smell of Rory's citrus aftershave, we push the door open, flick on the light and step inside. The walls are painted a tranquil grey. The floor is a dark hardwood and is littered with shoes and trainers. His bed is a tangled mess of white sheets and a stylish black duvet. I notice that his wardrobe doors have been flung open as if he was in a rush to get away. With a shiver I peer into his wardrobe and to my dismay his jumper and fleece are gone. Felix walks over to the package on the bedside cabinet. 'What's this, Aunty Emily?'

'Leave it alone,' I say, bending down to remove Rory's boxer shorts from Baxter's jaws.

Lifting my head up I see Felix is holding a framed photo. 'Aunty Emily – check this out.'

I gasp as my eyes settle on the two faces smiling from the photo. It's a photo of me and Felix in an elegant gold frame. My heart goes crazy at the thought of Rory going to sleep every night with a photo of us two by his bed. 'Where did you find that?'

Felix points to Rory's bedside cabinet. 'It was on top of here. Rory does still care about us, Aunty Emily.'

'That's such a nice thing to have by his bed,' I say, frowning at the messy sheets. I will have to change them. 'Where would he keep his clean bedsheets?'

Felix points to Rory's chest of drawers. An uncomfortable feeling crawls over me. Rory is my ex-boyfriend; I have no idea where he is and here am I going through his drawers in search of clean bedding.

'Do we have to change the sheets?' Felix whines.

'Yes, we do,' I say, yanking open the bottom drawer. There's no bedding. Instead, the drawer is filled with lots of photographs and albums which are scattered across the bottom. Felix comes to peer over my shoulder. 'Boring photos.'

I run my hand over the photos. There are lots of family photos showing a couple and their two young boys. I study a few of them. One of the boys is Rory. There's no mistaking his mop of black curly hair, his skinny frame, and his giant grasshopper legs. I don't recognise the smaller boy with his sandy blonde hair and cheeky smile. Rory told me he didn't have any siblings so the boy could be a childhood friend. Putting it down I spot a pile of postcards. They're all from his mum, Tina, who I've never met as she's been busy spending her retirement sailing around the Caribbean with her new husband. I pick up one postcard. She's telling Rory how happy she is with his stepdad, Phil and how wonderful it is to be fulfilling a life dream. At the end she finishes with, *I raised a toast to him last week. I am still waiting for you to pick up the phone and talk, Rory. Maybe one day – eh? Take care, love Mum xx*

I flick my eyes to the postcard's date stamp. It's from last year when we were still dating. I wonder who she's referring to?

Baxter has gone underneath Rory's bed. I do hope he's not going to the toilet under there. Felix is on his hands and knees trying to encourage him to come out. 'Aunty Emily, he's got something in his mouth.'

'Get him out of there.'

Felix grabs the little dog and brings him out. In his jaws is a cream-coloured jewellery box. Baxter drops it into my hands. I stare at the logo on the front. It's from the little jewellers in Brighton. The one Rory and I used to walk past when we were together. I became obsessed with a little gold locket on one of the velvet trays. Rory kept promising me he'd buy me it.

Carefully, I open the box to see it's empty. Everything goes blurry. Rory must have given Beth a Christmas present while she was here earlier.

What a git! Buying Beth the locket I have had my eye on for months. Maybe I am better off without Rory?

'Pizzas are here,' shouts Tom. I place the box on his bed and guide Felix and Baxter out of Rory's room.

Once we've finished and cleared away the boxes Tom goes into the kitchen to make a cup of tea for me. I follow him as Felix is busy playing on Tom's Xbox.

'I've no idea where he is,' Tom says, frantically stuffing pizza boxes into a recycling bag. His arms are trembling and sweat beads are forming on his brow.

'I understand.' As he's struggling to fit the box into the bag, I hold one end for him.

Tom wipes his brow. 'Look, when I last saw Rory, he was with...'

'Beth, I know, Tom.'

He casts me an awkward look. 'Really?'

'I saw Facebook.' I take a deep breath. 'You're not going to believe this, but I was tricked into coming all this way by my nephew in there.'

Tom's eyebrows rise his pink forehead. 'That little lad in there tricked you?'

I nod. 'He used my credit card without telling me and he ran off to board a train to Leeds at Kings Cross.'

Tom's eyebrows shoot up his forehead. 'Jeez. How old is he?'

'Nine.'

His mouth falls ajar in shock. 'Are kids that sneaky at nine?'

'Yes.'

Judging by Tom's bewildered face I can tell I am not promoting having children.

He grabs a sheet of kitchen roll and wipes his brow. 'My ex-girlfriend, the one I have just split up with, well... she finished with me actually… anyway she wanted kids. Now that I've heard your experience, I think I might have had a lucky escape.'

Feeling guilty for talking about Felix I follow up with, 'He misses Rory.'

Tom grabs a second piece of kitchen roll. 'Wow – that kid will go to any lengths to see Rory. So, you're not missing Rory then?'

I go silent and tie up the recycling bag.

'He talks about you both a lot.'

My head shoots up at lightning speed. 'Really?'

Tom nods. 'Yes, he does. I get the feeling he thinks he's messed up his chances of getting back with you.'

'Why do you say that?'

Tom props himself up against the kitchen counter. 'When he's pissed, he always goes on about you and how you misunderstood him. He then starts to talk about what an idiot he was.'

I try to suppress a smile. It appears for a few seconds as my mind pushes the subject of Beth to the front of my thoughts. 'And Beth?'

Tom folds his arms across his chest. 'I think Beth is more into Rory that he is her.'

'Why do you say that?'

Tom chuckles. 'On their second date they went to a restaurant, and she spent the whole meal lecturing him on her trip to America. He met me in a club later and said he didn't get a chance to talk the entire evening.'

'Do you think he's with her, Tom?'

An awkward silence descends upon the kitchen. He keeps his eyes on the recycling bag and mumbles, 'I think he might be.'

With Felix engrossed in a video game I grab my phone and go out into the flat hallway to phone Lizzie. She answers straight away.

'Why am I here, Lizzie?' My voice is thick with emotion.

She sighs. 'You were manipulated by a nine-year-old. What's happened?'

'Rory's not here.'

I can hear her knock something over in surprise. 'What?'

'His flatmate Tom has no idea where he is.'

Lizzie relays the message back to Bill in the background. 'What are you going to do?'

'The weather is bad,' shouts Bill.

'Yes, the snow is bad, Ems,' agrees Lizzie. 'I wouldn't travel back tonight. Can you stay over in his flat?'

'We are going to stay over in Rory's bedroom.' The thought of Rory coming back later hand in hand with Beth makes me clamp my hand over my forehead and groan. 'What happens if he and Beth come back here later and find us in his bed?'

'Well, you will get to see the real Rory – won't you?' replies Lizzie. 'If he staggers in drunk with that woman, you'll know he's moved on with his life.'

Felix's face appears in my mind and my heart aches. 'That will break Felix's heart.'

Lizzie sighs for a second time. 'Felix masterminded this entire thing. This could teach him a valuable lesson about the consequences of his actions. Bill wants to know how Felix got on a train to Leeds without a ticket?'

I take a deep breath. 'He used my credit card without me knowing.'

Lizzie's screech is so loud I pull my phone away from my ear. 'HE DID WHAT? OMG he used your credit card without you knowing?'

'Yes, he's nine years old and is showing an early talent for credit card fraud.'

Lizzie has gone quiet which is unusual for my best friend. I can hear Bill laughing in the background.

'Ems, you need to change your tack with Felix. You have to take control.'

I let out a wail of frustration. 'I've tried, Lizzie, you know that.'

My best mate lets out the heaviest of sighs. 'Ems, Rory is not coming home, Rory has moved on. Let's all face facts. You need to stay over tonight and, in the morning, take Felix home. Once home you need to have a conversation with that young man about his behaviour.'

Exhaustion washes over me. Lizzie is right. It's time to move on.

'Ems, you made the right decision about letting Rory go. It's now time to sort out Felix.'

CHAPTER 25

FELIX

'Hello, it's me again. I'm in Rory's bed with Baxter. Aunty Emily is in the shower. My plan hasn't worked out and I'm a bit sad. Rory isn't here. Tom, his flatmate, doesn't know where Rory is.' He removes his socks, squashes them into a ball and chucks them across the bedroom in frustration while Baxter licks the phone screen. 'BAXTER.' He wipes the phone screen with his T-shirt.

'Rory's bedroom is cool. I will show you.' Flipping the camera, he scans the room's grey walls and Rory's black industrial-style wall shelves opposite the bed with the phone. 'He hasn't got a yucky purple carpet like I have. Sorry, Mummy, I know you love my carpet.' Turning the phone to himself he grins at the camera.

Placing Baxter on a pillow he takes the phone and, standing on the bed, shows his mum the shelves. 'If you were here, you would tell me not to touch Rory's shelves. I promise I will not drop or break anything. Check out his orange clock which looks like an old TV with an aerial and buttons for the channels. That is so cool. He has some bottles of aftershave too, but they smell like that stuff you used to use to clean the bathroom. I have smelt them all.' He turns the camera on himself and wiggles his eyebrows while grinning mischievously. 'Rory also has a cactus, and it looks like a big fork.' He points the phone camera at the green cactus and touches it before yelping. 'I don't like that plant.'

Sitting back down he pulls the sheets over him. 'Aunty Emily has been looking in Rory's drawers for clean bedsheets. I keep telling her I like the ones which are already on the bed. They smell nice and are warm. When I sniff them, I think of Rory, which makes me feel nice.' He rubs the sheet against his cheek, closes his eyes and pulls what only can be described as a cheesy smile for the camera.

'I hope Rory comes home soon. Maybe he's gone out to buy extra Christmas presents?' Wiggling his eyebrows at the phone camera he grins. 'Any present from Rory will be cool. There's a present on the bedside cabinet.' Holding up the phone he points the camera at the red and gold wrapped gift. 'I think he bought one for me and forgot one for Aunty Emily, so he had to rush back out to the shops.'

'Amelie has sent me an iMessage to say she's secretly opened the corner of one of her presents under the tree. It's not from Santa. Amelie thinks it's from her mum's friend who always buys her cuddly toys. Amelie doesn't want cuddly toys. She wants rollerskates and a longer skipping rope. In the summer she says we are going to tie her new rope to the back of my bike and she's going to pretend she's water skiing on her rollerskates. She wants me to cycle very fast so she can lean back and do tricks like holding on with just one hand or sticking one leg out. I like Amelie, she's exciting.' He chuckles away to himself. 'Do you remember, Mummy, when she cut her own hair? You were so shocked when you saw what she had done your mouth fell open and you didn't say anything for ages. Amelie got in so much trouble. Her new haircut is what you call a *mullet*. Aunty Emily told me everyone wore mullets long ago. I asked you for a mullet haircut and you said no very quickly. Amelie wants to cut my hair like hers, but I think Aunty Emily would shout a lot. I also think I need to be a good boy for a bit after all the trouble I have caused.'

His smile disappears. 'Jade has emailed me. My new friend from the train. The one who was in the video when I was in the train toilet. She wanted an update on my plan. Her mum is nervous about what Sidney is going to say when she asks him to marry her. Jade is not worried. Sidney works in the hospital at night, so Jade is staying in the bedroom he's decorated for her when she stays at his flat. She has sent me a photo. The wallpaper has loads of footballs on it. Jade loves playing football. She's in her school football team. Her mum has told her that if she asks her one more time about whether they can get a dog like Baxter she's going to explode. Jade says she's only asked her sixty-four times since we left them in London.' Felix smiles and Baxter licks the phone screen again.

Scratching his head, Felix screws up his face at the camera. 'Jade wants to know whether I will be her boyfriend. She says when we are both back home, we can meet up on the beach and take Baxter for walks.' He sighs. 'I like Jade, but I get the feeling she likes me because I have Baxter. The only girl I do like is Amelie. Sai knows I like her but has told me girlfriends get you into trouble. He thinks I should have a girlfriend when I am older. What do you think, Mummy? If Rory was here, I would ask him. When he turns up, I will ask him. I will also ask what he thinks of a *mullet* haircut. Amelie says it's easy to cut as you just chop the sides very short and leave the back long. Aunty Emily is coming. Bye.'

CHAPTER 26

RORY

A young boy with golden hair and a blue stripey top is making his way along the train carriage. My mind is trying to suppress the little inner voice which is whispering, *'he looks like a young Lawrence.'* In a flash I am back to the same train journey we used to make every Saturday morning. I used to take him to ballet practice which was always a train stop away. We'd board the train with pockets stuffed with packets of sugary sweets and cans of fizzy drinks. All the things our parents banned us from eating. On the train we'd stretch our legs over two seats each and empty bags of sickly-sweet sherbet into our mouths. Lawrence would then move on to lollipops, and I would hit the tangy jelly sweets that glued themselves to my teeth for hours.

From an early age Lawrence danced. He used to say it started because of Mum and Dad shouting at each other. He'd get so upset at hearing them yell obscenities he'd race out of the back door and up the street. In the disused car park of the old ice cream factory, he'd start to dance amongst the litter left behind by the older boys after one of their nights out drinking cider. As the caring older brother I'd always chase after him. When I found him, he'd be twirling across the car park or leaping into the air, with arms outstretched like an elegant bird. Dad never wanted Lawrence to go to ballet. He said the thought made him feel uncomfortable. I spent years trying to persuade Dad to secretly watch Lawrence in the car park. If he'd seen Lawrence's dancing ability, he would have changed his mind. When Dad walked out and left us for the woman who had a mobile burger van, Mum and I decided to get Lawrence some proper dance training.

To my relief Alfie carries on talking. 'On our app you would meet your date at the station of your choice.'

'We think it would work well for time constrained commuters,' adds Michael.

Alfie twirls his phone around the shiny train table. 'We would pilot it at London St Pancras as we think that's the best station for finding love.'

'It's a special place,' Michael is scrolling through his phone.

I need to steer the conversation away from station romance. 'So, what do you two do when you're not designing phone apps?'

Alfie smiles. 'We both have dull office jobs by day but after work we are musicians.'

'Oh – what do you play?'

Michael lifts his head up from his phone. 'We both play the piano, but I also love the drums.'

Alfie laughs. 'Our neighbours are not so keen on his drums.'

Michael starts pointing to something on his phone. I don't want to return to the dating app conversation.

To my relief Michael and Alfie take out their headphones and start listening to something on Michael's phone. I take out mine and press play on the first playlist without looking at which one it is. I soon realise that it's the playlist titled Emily and has all of our favourite songs on there. We were both huge fans of Amy Winehouse. On a Friday evening in the summer we'd lift up the sash window of Emily's flat bedroom, put on the Back to Black album, sip wine, talk and relax on her bed. Amy's insanely soulful voice starts to fill my ears and I find myself wishing I was lying with Emily in my arms.

Michael initiates a lively conversation about football which lasts for a good hour or so and includes a lot of sharing of football video clips on our phones.

When the football discussion comes to an end, I can see Alfie has taken a notebook out and is scribbling notes inside it. The fear of another lengthy discussion about their dating app forces me to control the conversation.

'I'm assuming you both are going to London – are you there over Christmas?'

Alfie shakes his head. 'We're only there for a night and tomorrow through the day. This is our annual celebration.'

'Nice,' I say, nodding my head and picturing them both at a fancy restaurant, drinking fancy wine and posh food.

Michael puts his phone down. 'Christmas is an odd time for us. This journey that we make every year is our way of handling this difficult time.'

Alfie shifts uncomfortably in his seat and closes his notebook.

Michael continues. 'We have both lost a family member at this time of year, so we make the same journey to celebrate them.'

'Oh... I see.'

Alfie nods. 'Our respective loved ones died at different times, but both had a strong connection to music like us.'

Michael stares wistfully out of the window while Alfie continues. 'We plan to make this same trip for the rest of our lives. People think we're mad but we both think it's important to remember our loved ones. Have you ever lost someone close, Rory?'

The night I lost Lawrence comes rushing back to me. A wave of emotion rises inside of me as I remember a paramedic trying to steer me away from the wrecked car. Lawrence had already gone by this point. He was still in the driver's seat and a fireman was trying to cut him out. I wanted to stay with him, but the paramedic was insistent I step away. Blinking tears away I turn to the window.

Alfie senses it is a subject I don't want to discuss. 'Michael has been my rock.'

Michael pulls Alfie into a hug. 'You're mine and that's why we work.'

When I close my eyes all I can see is a crumpled Emily sitting on a plastic chair in the hospital after losing Vivi. She had assumed I was her rock. My good friend, guilt, is busy wrapping itself around my body like a powerful boa constrictor, compressing me to the point of breathlessness.

My brain and mouth lose connection and from nowhere words start to pour out of me.

'I'm going to see my ex-girlfriend. She lost her sister earlier this year. It was an aneurysm, so it was sudden and unexpected. I let my ex-girlfriend down the night her sister passed away. I let her down when she really needed me.'

Alfie and Michael remain silent.

My phone buzzes with a text. It's from Anna. *Just to let you know I'm staying in London for Christmas so if you're about let me know, it would be good to catch up.*

I turn to look at the blizzard outside the train window. Doubt and confusion creep into my head. My words echo in my head. I let Emily down at a time she really needed me. In the weeks before Vivi died I caused Emily unnecessary worry about my friendship with Anna. I remember Emily asking me why I was going on another night out with Anna when I'd been out with her a few days before. Emily deserves someone better than me.

'Mate, I'm so sorry,' says Alfie.

Michael nods. 'Me too. Listen, mate, you can't change the past, but you can change the future.'

'I don't know why I let her down,' I say, running my hand through my hair. 'She's the best thing that ever happened to me.'

'Rory, I think you need some thinking time,' says Alfie.

'There's a reason why you let your ex-girlfriend down and I think you need to find that out. It won't be easy but that's the only way to deal with it.'

Anna's text messages are catching my attention. She also deserves an apology. I sent her the wrong signals. Maybe Alfie is right? Maybe I need to go back to where my life went off track before I see Emily. Without hesitation I type a reply to Anna. *It's okay. Everything got a bit chaotic back then. It's nice to hear from you. I'm on way to London on the train and I think I am going to get stranded due to the snow. Where are you?*

CHAPTER 27

EMILY

*I*t's nearly midnight. Felix is sat up and leaning against my shoulder in Rory's bed. His tears are soaking into one of Rory's T-shirts which I borrowed to sleep in. Baxter is asleep on a cushion on the floor beside the bed. 'I thought Rory would be here,' sobs Felix. 'I wanted him to be here, Aunty Emily.' Throwing my arms around him I pull him closer. 'Come on, don't cry, Felix. This was a surprise trip and Rory had obviously made other plans for tonight.'

He nods and sobs some more. Hearing his distress is cutting me up inside. I nestle my face in his hair. My heart has been aching all evening with the realisation that Rory and I are finally over. Now I ache so much I could do with some painkillers. 'We're going to be all right – me and you.'

Wiping his face with the back of his hand, he looks up me with watery pink eyes. 'Are we, Aunty Emily?' he croaks.

Why do I detect doubt in the tone of his voice? If I'm honest I am doubtful about looking after Felix. He's certainly not the younger version of his mother.

I push a bunch of hair behind his ear. 'There are going to be some changes, I promise.'

Felix hangs his head. 'Yes, you said earlier about tidying up the living room.' The gloominess in his voice says a lot about how he's feeling at the prospect of the future consisting of just me and no Rory. Once again, I find myself wanting to give up being his legal guardian. I made the child depressed and turn to financial crime.

Staring up at the ceiling I hope Vivi is not looking down on us. What a bloody mess, Ems, she'd say.

Felix has started crying again about Rory. 'I wanted him to be here.'

'Let's get some sleep. No more tears.'

He shakes his head.

For fuck's sake Rory – why couldn't you have been here tonight?

Felix sits up and wipes his tear-stained face. He looks at me and something flickers across his face. 'Rory was the only one who didn't think I was weird.'

I cast Felix a puzzled look. 'What do you mean? I don't think you're weird.'

He waves his hand at me. 'I meant before Mum went to write for God's newspaper.'

A little ball of warm tingles shoots across my chest. That was my analogy. When he was bereft hours after his mum had died and kept asking me why his mum had left him, I had to think on my feet and that was what I'd come up with. It pacified him for a while. He hasn't brought it up since she died. I can't believe he's used my analogy. He must have buried it deep inside him. My heart is swelling with pride.

'Talk to me, Felix,' I say, squeezing his hand.

Felix rubs his puffy eyes. 'Rory helped me do something. When Mum was telling people on the phone I was weird and making me sad, Rory made me happy again.'

I gesture for him to carry on.

He plays with the duvet corner. 'Mum saw me dancing once.'

My heartbeat has quickened. I think back to what I saw outside Leeds station. 'Did she say how amazing you were at dancing?'

Felix shakes his head. 'I was in my bedroom and wearing...' His voice evaporates.

'What were you wearing?'

He sits up straighter. 'I wanted to be like them.'

'Who?'

He takes in a huge breath. 'The ballet dancers.'

'Right – doing ballet, that's not weird.'

Batting away my hand he hides his face in the duvet. 'Mum said it was weird.'

I glance up at the ceiling. Vivi – why didn't you tell me that evening I came over? You should have prepared me for stuff like this. 'Felix – tell me.'

He says something into the duvet, but I can't hear him as its muffled. 'I can't hear if you are going to do that.'

He sighs and removes the pillow. 'I was wearing a girl's pink ballet outfit. Amelie gave me it. Her mum tried to make her go to ballet, but Amelie hated it. Amelie knows how I love to dance. She gave me her outfit and told me to have fun.' He pauses to fiddle with his T-shirt. 'Mum said she thought I was practising rugby tackles on my bed.'

In my mind I can hear Vivi saying something like that. I love my sister dearly, but she had strong views at times, particularly on what sort of life she wanted Felix to have. She'd even planned out his future on a spreadsheet with tabs on it. I found it when sorting out her laptop. I think Felix should find his own way in life.

'Felix, that's not weird to me. If you want my honest opinion, I think it's great you were seeing how it felt to be a ballet dancer.'

He studies my face with his button-shaped hazel eyes. 'You mean that, don't you, Aunty Emily? I can tell when you're lying and that's not your lying face.'

I pull him in for a hug. 'So, how did it make you feel?'

He breaks away with a goofy smile on his face. 'It was great and made my chest feel like there was a ballet performance happening inside it. I told Amelie the next day about it. She said my smile gets wider when I dance.'

I give him a squeeze. 'Can we forget the weird thing? I'm sure your mum didn't mean what she said to someone on the phone.'

'She did mean it. I knew when she was telling the truth. Amelie said her mum thinks she's weird for wearing boys' T-shirts. That made me feel a bit better.'

I need to steer him away from this conversation. The last thing I want to do is create bad feeling for Vivi. She was an amazing mother to Felix. 'Tell me about Rory?'

Felix sniffs. 'I told him about what had happened.' He wipes his pink nose. 'He was like you, Aunty Emily, he didn't think it was weird.'

'What did Rory do?'

I watch my nephew's face light up. 'Rory took me to ballet classes.'

His words ping around the corners of my mind like mini ball bearings in a pinball machine, Rory did that for Felix. Gasping, I stare at Felix. 'When?'

A grin spreads over his face. 'We never went to football. We went to ballet.'

'Actual ballet classes?'

Felix nods with a huge smile. 'Every Saturday.'

A memory of Felix dancing in the snow earlier comes rushing back to me. 'Did you enjoy them?'

'Yes, they were cool. I miss them.'

I take his hand. 'Hang on – why haven't you told me about this?'

He shrugs. 'I thought you would say I was weird.'

'Oh, Felix!' I exclaim, pulling him into a hug. 'I would never say that. Don't ever think that again – okay?'

He nods.

'Has not going to classes made you sad?'

I can feel him nod against my chest. 'Very sad. I've had to practice in my bedroom. When I am out with Amelie, she lets me dance in her dad's garage, but we must stop doing that as I was doing a leap and crashed into the family tent. Amelie had to tell her mum that she'd ripped a hole in the tent.'

Even though I think Amelie is a little wild with her mullet-like haircut, her love of boys' basketball T-shirts and her giant trainers, I do like her friendship with Felix.

My mind is busy making sense of Felix's revelation. All the bangs and crashes I've been hearing were him practising his ballet. It all makes sense. 'After arguments you often go upstairs – do you dance in your room?'

He nods again. 'Ballet makes me feel happy again.' With an elegant swing of his arm, he leaps off the bed, accidentally knocking the package off Rory's bedside cabinet, and twirls around the room.

'I thought ballet made you think of your mum and her ballet DVDs.'

After a jump into the air, he comes to a shuddering halt. 'Only one was her DVD. The rest were mine.'

'Oh, I see,' I say, pulling up my knees, thinking about Rory and Felix's revelation. 'I can't believe Rory took you to ballet classes.'

Felix comes to sit by me. 'He knew of a ballet school in Brighton.'

'Did your mum ever know about this?'

He shakes his head. 'Mum thought we were going to see the football. The money she gave Rory for the football was used to pay for my classes. Amelie lent me her black shorts and her ballet shoes.'

'Did Rory leave you at the ballet classes and pop to the pub?' I can see Rory doing that. He was always on his way to or back from a pub.

'He sat and watched me at every class.'

Sitting back against Rory's headboard I stare at Felix. Before tonight I thought I knew my ex-boyfriend. I also believed we didn't have any secrets. Vivi and I used to talk about the transformation in Felix when he came back from seeing the football. He would have an ear-to-ear smile on his face and, as Vivi always said, he wouldn't lock himself away and bang about in his bedroom. I can't believe Rory has been such a good friend to Felix.

Blowing the air out of my cheeks I glance over at his bedside cabinet and see that the package has disappeared. 'Where's his package gone?'

Felix follows my gaze and dives off the bed. I hear a loud gasp. Felix emerges from the side of the bed holding the opened package. His eyes are wide, and his face has gone pale. 'It had opened on the floor.'

'What is it?'

Felix places the tissue paper package on the bed. Peeling back the red and gold paper I see two black leather ballet shoes lying toe to toe in the centre. 'Oh, Felix,' I whisper in shock.

He points to a gift label tucked inside one of the shoes. 'You should read that.'

I peer over. It reads: *To Felix, I'm so proud of you, Rory.*

Tears begin to bubble inside my eyes. 'Oh, wow.'

Felix wipes away a trickle of a tear. 'He bought them for me, Aunty Emily.'

I can't stop my tears.

CHAPTER 28

RORY

A long queue of relieved people behind us snakes all the way back up the carriage. Everyone is eager to get off this train. It's a miracle we've arrived in King's Cross, especially after we sat for an hour in a blizzard. All the harassed guard could do was reassure us the emergency services would find us in the dark and snow if the worst happened. He also explained it might take several hours, but eventually the train would be located.

'Have a good Christmas, Alfie and Michael. Enjoy your celebration.'

Michael gives me huge hugs. 'Take care, Rory, mate.'

Alfie grins. 'Yes, take care, Rory. Hope Brighton goes okay. It's enjoyable once we get into our celebration but a bit stressful beforehand.'

I cast him a puzzled look. Michael laughs and pats his husband on the shoulder. He turns to me. 'Alfie says that our loved ones are with us in spirit when we do our performance and if you knew them, you'd know they had very high standards for playing music.'

'Are you in a band or on the stage?'

They both chuckle to themselves. Alfie shrugs. 'We don't like to talk about our celebration. It's a personal thing.'

The urge to find out more about their celebration is strong but I sense they are keen to get away. We shake hands. 'Good luck with the station dating app.'

Michael casts me a deadpan expression. 'If we see you on *Dragons' Den* nicking our idea, we will hunt you down.'

Alfie and I laugh.

'Your idea is safe; I can assure you.' They wave as I set off.

I head for the ticket barriers. Inside, a war is waging between my head and my heart. My head is telling me that trying to get to Brighton by train in this snow tonight will be futile. It would be better to persuade Anna to let me stay over with her in London. Tomorrow I can assess the weather situation and head back to Leeds if need be. It will also give me a chance to sort my head out and, as Alfie said, I do need to think about why my relationship ended.

My heart on the other hand is telling me my love for both Emily and Felix is still strong. I think about both every day, and trying to forget them seems to make my suffering worse. No matter what it takes, I should try to get to Brighton tonight.

Refusing to concede, my head is reminding me how I messed things up with Emily and to do that again to her would break my heart. What if she was right about me not wanting to settle down? What if she was correct about not wanting the pressure of being a father figure to Felix? Felix is a great kid, but I think my head is right, he deserves someone better than me. Someone who has a job, someone who is sensible and someone who doesn't get carried away with a female friend who turned up unexpectedly in his life.

Weaving my way past groups of travellers disembarking from the train I think about how life was before everything changed. Anna came into my life, and I became distracted. I need to understand why. The thought of meeting up again with Anna doesn't sit well with my gut and I am going to have to buy some mints. Even though I am technically single, I still feel guilty for arranging to meet Anna. Why do I feel like I am letting both Emily and Felix down?

As I get close to the ticket barriers and the crowd of frantic Christmas travellers all trying to jam their tickets into the machines or tap their travel cards, I can see Anna waving at me. It's hard to miss her mass of black hair and bright pink lipstick.

A queue has formed for the ticket barrier. I'm staring down at my ticket getting ready for my turn to go through the barrier and wondering whether I am making the right decision about meeting Anna. Everything feels wrong. This was a quick decision I made in a moment of madness on a train which was about to get stuck in a blizzard. Shouts behind me make me jolt. Someone slams into me from behind. A piercing scream fills my ears. Time slows down as I see the side of the ticket barrier come rushing towards my head. I try to put my arms up but it's too late. The world around me goes black.

'He's opening his eyes,' shrieks a familiar female voice. 'Rory, it's me, Anna.'

Everything is blurry. Where the hell am I? Blinking as fast as I can I wait for the world to become clearer. Hang on, the blinking is making my head hurt. Oh, God, my head has a ring of hot, searing pain around it. The voice of the station announcer telling me about the delayed train on platform seven is making me wince. Can someone please tell them to stop talking? Am I in a train station?

'Rory – can you hear me?' Anna is bending over me. Her long black hair tentacles are brushing my face. 'The paramedics are on their way.'

Paramedics? Am I injured? 'No,' I mutter and try to lift my head off the cold surface.

A male voice from behind me is talking fast. 'Stop him from moving.'

Anna is towering over me. 'Rory, stay still. You've hit your head.'

'What?'

A second familiar voice breaks my confused state. 'Alfie, look its Rory from the train. What's he doing on the floor?'

Everything is flooding back to me. I am at King's Cross station. I was waiting to get through the ticket barrier when someone rugby tackled me from behind and rammed my head against the metal stand.

Coldness is starting to engulf my body. The pain from my head is making me feel sick. I need to get up.

'Lay back down, Rory,' says Anna, pinning me down while looking over her shoulder. 'The paramedics are here for you.'

'Where?' I croak.

She cranes her head. 'Oh... they look like they're seeing to a pregnant lady.'

'What?'

I struggle again and once more I am restrained. 'A little bit longer,' sighs Anna.

'Seriously?' I can't lie here any longer. It's uncomfortable and I need some painkillers.

Anna nods. 'Rory, you need to get checked out.'

'How long was I out for?' It felt like a long time to me.

Anna shrugs. 'A few seconds.'

'Oh, is there any blood?'

She grins. 'Nope, just a huge egg shape on the side of your head.'

The searing pain in my head is getting intense. 'Any sign of the paramedics?'

My heart sinks as she shakes her head.

With a gloved hand she holds back some of her black hair, preventing it from falling on my face. 'I'm so glad we've met each other again, Rory.'

This is not the time for casual conversation. My head feels

like it's about to break in half like the way Emily cracks open her Easter eggs.

'Look, I know this is not the best time to talk to you...'

She can say that again. Clamping my lips tight shut I grimace and try to suppress the vomit which is waiting to shoot out of my mouth.

'I've been wanting to tell you something. It's important, Rory, and I need to say it.'

For goodness' sake – Anna's timing for a deep conversation is not great. I'm freezing cold lying on this chilly platform, I'm in so much pain with my head and she now wants to tell me something important.

Someone taps her on the shoulder, and she steps out of the way. To my relief a paramedic is kneeling beside me. 'Hi, I'm Kevin, a paramedic – can you tell me your name?' he says, surveying my head.

Why do I get the feeling this is going to hurt?

CHAPTER 29

RORY

*T*he green curtain of the A&E cubicle swishes open. In walks a tall man carrying a sheet of white paper and a pen. He's wearing a knitted grey jumper, beige cords, and an impressive pair of sandy coloured Timberlands. In a commanding voice which rises above the cacophony of sounds from outside the green curtain (phones ringing, machines bleeping, trolleys being pushed along the corridor, nurses talking cheerfully to patients and a small child crying), he says, 'My name is Doctor Sidney Wilson, I'm an A&E doctor. What's your name and date of birth?'

As I say my name, he checks what's printed out on his piece of paper.

'Do you want to tell me what happened to your head?'

Sitting up in the cubicle chair makes my forehead lump scream with pain. It prefers no movement whatsoever. With trembling hands I try to reach up and touch the bandage but the thought of making the stabbing pain any worse makes me nauseous all over again. So I opt to talk instead. 'Someone ran into me, and I hit my head on a ticket barrier.'

The doctor nods before perching at the end of the bed. His

dark brown fingers grip the pen, and he scribbles something down onto the form. 'Were you unconscious?'

'Yes, but only for a few seconds.'

'You live in London?'

I shake my head. 'Leeds.'

His pale green eyes study my face. 'Are you down here for Christmas?'

'No, I am supposed to be giving my ex-girlfriend something… a piece of jewellery.'

He stands up and walks over to where I am sat, kneeling to inspect my lump. As I watch him study my head I have a horrible thought. What if the chain and locket flew out of my shirt pocket when I collided with the barrier? Panic and fear takes hold of me. My trembling hand goes to my shirt pocket. A wave of relief floods through me as I can feel the locket through my shirt.

My joy is short-lived as I have to grit my teeth as the doctor's long fingers gently peel back the bandage. 'Does she live in London?'

'No, Brighton.'

A wide smile breaks across his face. 'My girlfriend lives near there. Whenever I'm not working up here, I am down there playing football on the beach with her daughter and looking at all the fancy shops in the Lanes.'

Gripping onto the wooden arms of the chair, I pray for him to stop staring at my swollen head.

'We'll need to get your head scanned. That's quite a lump you've got there. Do you have any blurred vision?'

'Nope.'

He holds up his finger. 'Follow my finger to the left and to the right. After the accident did you experience memory loss?'

'Briefly but only for a few seconds.'

Afterwards he gets back to his feet. 'You have a concussion. We need to check properly there has been no significant damage. I am going to see if we can get you a CT scan but it depends on how busy we are. The results will take about a week to come through so you'll need to contact your GP. I'd also like to take some blood just as a precautionary measure.'

I watch him scribble something down. 'My girlfriend and her daughter have come to visit me for Christmas. It was a nice surprise to see them earlier, but I had to go to work.'

'You'll have a nice Christmas then?'

He nods. 'The best yet. I have a feeling my girlfriend is up to something. She's got this mischievous look about her.'

'Oh?'

'I think she's going to propose.' His grin returns as he writes something else on his form.

'Wow, will you say yes.'

His face has lit up. 'Guaranteed. My girlfriend is an amazing woman. She's right when she tells me she's a rare edition. She's my best friend too.'

I recall Emily telling me after a few months of us dating that she felt like we were becoming best friends. My heart tries to compete with my head and lets out a series of aches.

'Right, let's get a scan of your head to see what damage you've done. You seem coherent and there's no blurred vision, which is good. I will get you some more paracetamol.'

With a swish of the curtain, he leaves and enters the cubicle next door.

I am left with a mind awash with thoughts about my relationship with Emily, our late-night chats about our life dreams over a bottle of wine, her longing to have her own fashion business and my dream of writing a novel; our mutual love of board games, especially Monopoly, where we'd both try to bankrupt the other in record time, our long walks along Brighton beach when one of us was worried about something and we'd talk it out while throwing stones into the sea and swearing into the waves. The crazy parties at her flat where we'd sneak off with a bottle of champagne to go kiss in the empty bath; the adult roller discos we went to; helping her to gift wrap one of her amazing dresses, which she'd made for one of her mates, and the fun we had ice skating when we used to take Felix out with us. We were good at being best friends. Actually… we were bloody amazing at it.

My phone bleeps. Taking it out of my pocket, I see it is a text from Anna. *'Any news on your head? I am in the hospital concourse enjoying a late-night coffee. Let me know if you think you will be discharged tonight.'*

Anna. Guilt takes hold of my chest and sets off a tightening sensation. What the hell am I doing in London with Anna?

My mind goes back to the first work night where we got talking. She claimed she knew me. I recall some bloke from the office overhearing and slapping me on the back like I was some prize-winning animal. Ignoring everyone staring at us, I studied her face for any signs of familiarity. Was she someone from school? Was she someone I'd got off with when I was a spotty, greasy-haired, cider-fuelled teenager? Was she someone I'd worked with?

'You don't remember me – do you?' She smiled and stirred her colourful cocktail. 'I'm cool with that.'

After taking a mouthful of cocktail I gestured for her to tell me.

'You used to take your little brother to my mum's ballet school.'

To say I choked on my sidecar cocktail was an understatement. By the time I had composed myself and wiped my streaming eyes, everyone around me was asking whether I needed an ambulance.

Anna twirled a long lock of black hair around a manicured finger. 'Lawrence.'

I took in a large gulp of air and gripped onto my bar stool.

'You must remember me from back then. I was the plump

ballerina who was always being shouted at by the teacher.' She rolled her eyes. 'Her own frigging mother.'

Shrugging my shoulders, I cast her a puzzled look. 'I don't really remember much from back then.' My eyes were only on Lawrence. I wasn't into ballet or any other dancing. Back then I preferred football, heavy metal music and playing war video games in my best friend's bedroom. Lawrence and I were at different ends of the interest scale. However, I knew ballet made him happy and back then that was a big thing for me.

For a while Anna and I both went silent. I'd thought she'd dropped the subject of Lawrence. I was wrong.

'Lawrence and I were at Brighton uni together.'

The words seem to hang helplessly in the air after they'd left her lips.

She drained her cocktail. 'We were close friends at uni.' I watched as she swirled the ice around the glass. 'I miss him a lot, Rory. Lawrence was a good guy.'

The feeling I experienced while sitting opposite her and hearing all this was strange and surreal. For so long I'd locked away all my memories of Lawrence at the back of my head and thrown away the key. Anna had the key. In a flash, she'd opened it. Within a few seconds my head was filled with thoughts and memories of Lawrence.

'You knew him?' I croaked.

She nodded. 'Yes, I remember him from ballet when I met him during freshers' week. He made me promise not to tell any of his uni mates about his ballet days.'

My heart has started to thump away inside my chest.

'Mum told me that you have started taking a boy called Felix to her ballet classes – is he your son?'

Felix's cheeky face popped into my mind. We were great friends. He was my little buddy who used to come and sit with me when I accompanied Emily to Vivi's house. Whenever he came over to the sofa, he'd always bring his latest school project or a certificate he'd received. I would give him a high five, sit him beside me and ask him to tell me about his achievement. We shared the same sense of humour and, after we'd talked about school projects, I would get out my phone and we'd play a game on it. I could tell he was a smart kid. He was quick to pick up games on my phone and would always end up beating me. I never told him or Emily about Lawrence. As far as they knew I didn't have a younger brother who died in a car crash years ago. When Felix took me aside once and explained his mum thought he was weird, it was like history repeating itself. As he told me about his love of dance, I could see Lawrence in his eyes. He hugged me when I told him he wasn't weird and how I'd once known a great ballet school and I would see if it was still doing classes. The following week Felix and I went along to his first proper class. I cried into my hoodie watching him and told him I had an eye allergy when he finished.

'He's my ex-girlfriend's nephew.'

Anna nodded. 'He must remind you of Lawrence.'

'He does, and Lawrence would hate me for saying this, Felix is a better dancer.'

Anna laughed. 'Lawrence is probably loading up the lightning bolts for you right now. He was so competitive at university. He always had to be the best.'

That was how it started with Anna. We'd go drinking after work and then on for a meal, talking nonstop about her memories of Lawrence from university. Anna had this knack of bringing Lawrence back to life. The more time I spent with her and the more stories she told me about Lawrence's first year university antics, the easier the pain became.

CHAPTER 30

EMILY

A slam of the flat door makes me sit bolt upright in Rory's bed. Curled up to the right of me and hugging his new black ballet shoes, Felix murmurs and falls back asleep. My phone says it's nearly two in the morning. Baxter is on a cushion from the lounge and hasn't stirred, which is a miracle. Footsteps are outside the bedroom door. Rory is back. It must be him. My heart has broken into a mad gallop. I wonder what he'll say when he sees us all camped in his bed. Felix will go berserk when he sees Rory and so too will Baxter who was also a loyal member of the Rory fan club.

My hopes sink when I hear Tom muttering to himself. His footsteps pass Rory's bedroom and drift into the living area. It wasn't Rory. Tom must have gone out when Felix, Baxter and I crept to bed. The slurry tone of Tom's voice drifts into our room. Craning my neck, I try to make out what he's saying, but it's difficult to hear what he's saying to himself. I have picked up on one word – *challenge*. Maybe he's been doing a drinking challenge with some mates? Maybe he's spent the night in search of Rory?

I leave the bedroom in a pair of Rory's shorts and one of his

T-shirts. Tom is sat on the sofa with his head in his hands. On the coffee table is a piece of paper and a glass tumbler filled with what looks like Scotch.

'Are you feeling all right, Tom?' I whisper, walking past him and settling myself down on the chair.

He lifts his head and throws me a wobbly, drunken smile. 'Never felt better. Is he back?'

'Rory? No, he isn't.'

Tom rubs his eyes. 'Seriously – he's still out?'

'Yes.'

After a burp and a glug of his Scotch, Tom leans back on the sofa. 'I didn't like to say earlier but Beth looked A-M-A-Z-I-N-G.'

I didn't think my heart could sink any lower in my chest, but it has just reached a new depth. 'Oh, good for Beth,' I say, with an air of disappointment.

Tom nods and holds up the piece of paper. 'Rory's probably doing his part of our challenge.'

'Oh, I see. What sort of challenge is it?'

A drunken grin slides across Tom's round face. 'If you complete the challenge you're guaranteed to forget about your ex-girlfriend.'

'Sounds interesting, Tom.'

He drains his tumbler and wipes his mouth with the back of his hand. 'My brother came up with the challenge after he went through hell following his break up with Marie from Huddersfield.'

'Was Marie from Huddersfield special to him?'

Tom's eyes widen. 'Marie from Huddersfield was very special to my brother. Anyway, she dumped him, and he got sad. We'd never seen him so down.'

'Oh, I see.' Looking around I question why I am sat here with this drunken fool. I could be back in bed snuggled up to Felix and thinking about how things are going to change when we get home. Nothing good will come from sitting here listening to Tom.

Tom shakes the sheet of paper in my direction. 'This challenge saved my brother. You must sleep with ten women and once you've done all that you will be over your ex-girlfriend. After sleeping with ten different women my brother is back on form and hasn't thought about Marie from Huddersfield for weeks.' Sliding the piece of paper towards me he grins. 'Rory and I took up the challenge a few weeks ago.'

My entire body tenses. 'Really?'

He nods. 'Check out the performance table.'

With a trembling hand I pull the paper towards me. It had a pen drawn table on it. I can see faint rows for both their names and across the top columns for ten women. Shutting my eyes before I can see how they're both performing on their challenge, I push it away. 'I don't want to read it,' I say, shooting out my seat. This is the proof I needed; Rory has moved on.

Tom's grin fades to my surprise. He lets out a heavy sigh and scratches his head. 'It's so hard missing your ex-girlfriend. I have been in agony for weeks over Suzie.'

'Is she your ex-girlfriend?'

He rubs his cheeks with both hands. 'I was an idiot, Emily. It was my fault Suzie broke up with me and I've been in a form of hell ever since. She goes to the same clubs and bars as me so every time I go out, I bump into her. It's torture to see her looking so beautiful. There's no escape for me at work either as she works in the law firm across the road. I can't get her out of my head. The challenge is my only hope.'

'What about Rory?' I say through gritted teeth, preparing myself for the worst, which is for Tom to say that Rory has outperformed on the challenge and Beth is number ten.

Tom shakes his head. 'He's doing better than me.'

Shit. My legs have turned to jelly. Reaching out I try to steady myself on the arm of the chair. Oh, God, what the hell does that mean? Rory has outperformed the challenge and is now onto his fifteenth shag. I don't need to hear this. Putting my hands over my ears I pull a grimace at Tom and make my way towards the bedroom. The last thing I need to know is that my ex-boyfriend has turned into a sex maniac.

Once inside the bedroom I shut the door and crouch at the end of the bed. My heart is thumping away inside my rib cage. Why did I let Felix manipulate me? If I'd stayed in Brighton, I would be none the wiser about Rory's crusade to shag as many women as physically possible. I also wouldn't have met Tom with his stressful topics of conversation. My fingers are itching. It's at times like these I wish I carried around something with me to sew. Although judging by how I am feeling it would probably be another version of angry sewing. A little whimper at my feet makes me spot a small dark shape. It's Baxter. Lifting him onto my lap I stroke his head. To my surprise he lovingly licks my chin before snuggling into me. A warm feeling spreads over my chest as I smile down at Baxter. If I hadn't come all this way Baxter and I would still be enemies. I do need to discuss the Rory situation with someone. Taking out my phone I text Lizzie to see if she is still awake. *Help!*

Lizzie replies almost immediately. *Rory's come back with two women instead of one?*

Rolling my eyes, I type back. *No.*

Rory's come back with a man?

I let out a heavy sigh. *Still no sign of Rory, but his flatmate has just told me about their Sleep with Ten Women Challenge, and he says Rory is doing the best.*

There's a pause. Lizzie replies. *Bill wants to know whether Rory and his flatmate are having a thirty something crisis and have gone back to behaving like irresponsible students because this sort of challenge was something he did when he was in university.*

Apparently it is a way to get over your ex-girlfriend. After sleeping with ten different women, you forget about your ex-girlfriend.

Lizzie pauses with her reply. I get the feeling all my answers are being relayed to Bill.

Bill says you should find out Rory's score. I think you should forget about it and come home on the earliest train.

The thought of seeing Rory's score makes me feel sick. *I don't want to know how many girls he's slept with.* Felix is stirring. He's rolled over and is now hugging his ballet shoes on his other side. I have an urge to tell Lizzie about Felix's dancing. *Felix told me earlier that he has a secret love of ballet and I have seen him dance. OMG – he's amazing. He told me tonight RORY used to take him to BALLET lessons instead of football. Can you believe that?*

There is a lengthy wait for Lizzie's reply. *OMG* and a series of shocked faced emojis.

When I heard all this, I started to believe in Rory again. He's even bought Felix some beautiful ballet shoes for Christmas and there's an adorable tag which says that he's so proud of him. That's the sort of partner I want in my life. Someone who loves and supports Felix as much as I do. All my trust has been destroyed by his stupid challenge.

Her response is quick. *Bill is emotional now after hearing about the ballet shoes gift. He says if Rory's score is less than five shags you should make an exception and take him back.*

I send back a series of eye-roll emojis.

Bill also says the fact Rory is doing the challenge means you are still on his mind.

Crawling back into bed, clutching Baxter and my phone, I sigh at Bill's opinion.

Lizzie texts to say, *Bill says you are both technically still single. Sorry, Ems, I think I might evict Bill from this flat for his controversial views – just say the word.*

With a sigh I text back, *Bill can stay. Speak in the morning x*

Baxter has curled up on my pillow, so I decide to follow his lead and do the same. Before I close my eyes, I send a little prayer into the darkness. 'Please God, can Rory's challenge score not be more than ten women as I don't think I am strong enough to hear that sort of news.'

CHAPTER 31

RORY

a porter is wheeling me down for a CT scan. According to the nurse who came to take my blood pressure and take some blood it has been a busy night in A&E. The porter parks my chair in a corridor facing a row of closed doors with flashing yellow and red lights on them. I am behind another wheelchair. 'Wait here and they'll come and get you. Once you are finished they will buzz me and I'll wheel you back.'

The guy in the chair in front of me turns around to say hello. He looks of a similar age to me with brown curly hair and a matching beard. 'You look like you're having as much fun as me tonight,' he says, with a grin.

'Yep, you can say that again.'

We both give each other knowing nods. 'What are you getting scanned?' I ask.

'My knee.' The man rolls his eyes. 'Me and my boy were playing football in the living room, and he did a phenomenal tackle which sent my knee one way and the rest of my leg the other.'

'Ouch.'

The man grimaces. 'I fell through the coffee table too, which my partner wasn't happy about. She was more concerned about her broken coffee table than my injured state.' He raises his bandaged hand.

'Crikey you've been in the wars.'

The man chuckles. 'That head bandage you've got is impressive.'

'I got pushed into a ticket barrier headfirst. By accident, I'm pretty sure – I don't think anyone did it on purpose.'

I watch the man's eyes widen with horror as he stares at my head.

'Did you give your son the red card for that nasty tackle?'

The man laughs. 'No, he's a great kid and, like I say, it was a bloody good tackle. If only my old knee had not decided to throw a hissy fit. He's just got back into his football after not playing for ages. Last year he lost his confidence and decided to give it up. I struggled seeing him so down. Last couple of weeks I have been made up seeing him play in matches and score goals.'

He carries on talking about how his boy has turned around the fortunes of his local club. All I can think about is the time before Felix confided me about his ballet. Vivi had been worried about him. She'd invited both me and Emily over for dinner to try to work out why Felix was so glum. Emily suggested she contact his schoolteacher. Vivi put her head in her hands and said she was at the end of her tether. She believed someone was bullying Felix and had started collecting him from the school gate so that she could survey the other boys around him. Felix's sad state continued, and I remember me and Emily became concerned too. I hated seeing his little sad face and the sight made me want to reach out and hug him. I can still remember the day Felix told me about his secret. Watching his troubled facial expression evaporate as I told him I would sort him out some ballet lessons made me feel amazing. He smiled for the first time in months. Seeing it made me lift him into the air and let out a cheer.

'You don't think I'm weird,' Felix asked me once I had put him back down on the floor.

'No, I think you are amazing for wanting to follow your dreams.' Those were the words I wished I'd said to Lawrence when he was younger and started dancing. When someone close to you dies, you find yourself wanting to go back in a time machine and make more of their key moments in their life. Even now, I still find myself wishing I'd told Lawrence I loved him. Back then I had teenage coolness to maintain. You didn't gush over your siblings back then and I also had to make sure no one saw me entering a ballet school with my younger brother. Back then being spotted going into a ballet school would have been social suicide for me. I think all Lawrence got from me was an encouraging nod and a shove into the building when it was time for his lessons.

Felix wrapped his skinny arms around me. 'I like you, Rory.'

Gradually we all started to see a new Felix emerge. One with a huge ear-to-ear smile and one who told everyone how great it was to go and watch the football every Saturday with Rory.

Taking out my phone I tap into the photos I have of Felix. There are so many and, when I'm sad, I often take them out and smile at his mischievous grin. My chest aches as I flick through the photos of him having a piggyback on my shoulders along the beach, us two outside the ballet school eating packets of Quavers after his lesson and us two laughing at the camera, against a brilliant blue sea and a golden beach. I miss you, Felix. I have missed you as much as I have missed Emily. Towards the end of the album, I come across a photo I took of him leaping into the air during one of his ballet lessons. I'm not even sure he'd been taught to leap like a gazelle, but he did it anyway. Luckily, I'd had my phone ready as he launched himself into the air. A tingling sensation is travelling up my spine as I stare at the photo. Felix has a dreamy, goofy smile on his face as he reaches for the ceiling, his legs stretched out behind him. In the background I can see

Denise, the ballet teacher, stood open mouthed and staring wide eyed at Felix. We all knew Felix had something special back then. I know he won't have returned to his ballet classes. He won't have told Emily about his love of dance either. The thought of all his talent going to waste brings tears to my eyes.

Lawrence gave up ballet six months after taking it up. He loved to dance, but hated performing in front of others. I also got the feeling that being the only boy ballet dancer amongst all those girls made him the centre of attention, which he'd have despised as it showed just how shallow they were. Lawrence was happier dancing away to himself in an old car park where no one was watching him. My little brother could really dance. He was nimble on his feet and could stretch his legs above his head while laughing at me. However, he was a quiet, shy kid and preferred his own company.

Felix is different and I know, if Lawrence were still alive, he would agree with me. With Felix its more than just dancing. It's like magic happens when he dances. Felix makes you go into a trance-like state when he glides across the floor. He doesn't seem to mind who is watching him when he dances.

My phone buzzes in my pocket and bringing me out of my head. It's Anna. *Do you think you'll be kept in or discharged?*

I reply that I am about to have a scan and hopefully will confirm soon.

She texts back. *I do need to talk to you*

What am I doing here in London with Anna? Before today the last time I spoke to Anna was the day after Emily had told me she wanted us to split up. I was hungover and a mess after embarking on an all-night drinking binge to soothe my broken heart. Anna was shocked to learn that Emily and I had broken up. She commiserated with me in a bar booth, bought a few drinks and then she said a few things which irritated me so much, I ended up leaving her in the bar and storming off to Leeds. Anna had leaned over and said, 'Maybe it's for the best you and Emily have split

up, Rory, as you have never struck me as the settling down type.'
She stroked the edge of her wine glass and followed it up with, 'I
know our timing has not been great but maybe this is a chance
for us… to… you know.'

Emily had said the same thing in her break up speech, about
how I wasn't the settling down type and how I might want to
consider starting a relationship with Anna in view of the amount
of time I was spending with her. Those comments made me
angry for months. They still echo in my head. Even now I can feel
irritation and frustration bubbling away inside of me.

'We could be waiting here all night,' sighs the man in front of
me. 'Penny for your thoughts.'

I forget he's a stranger and talk out loud. 'You know when
people assume something about you which is wrong, and it really
pisses you off.'

The man laughs. 'All the time. Last Christmas my partner
wrongly assumed I had issues with her booking a girlie holiday
to Spain. I have no idea why she thought I was some arsehole of a
partner who would try to tell her what she could and couldn't do.
I mean, the thought of her going away for seven days, leaving me
and the kids to relax and make the house a mess, was my idea of
bliss. She opened her Christmas gift from me, saw that I'd paid
for her ticket and accommodation. She had to spend the rest of
the day eating humble pie. This Christmas she thinks I don't
know about her being pregnant again with our third child and
that if I did know I would apparently be cross as we can't really
afford another kid. Once again, she's assumed wrong. The eldest
child can't keep a secret and told me. I was over the moon. Once
again, my partner will see the error of her ways when she opens
up her Christmas gift.' He grins. 'You have to prove them wrong.
Merry Christmas.'

I look up to see a cheerful nurse at my side. 'Hello, Rory – let's
get you scanned.'

As she wheels me towards the scan room I shout to the man

with the swollen knee, 'Same to you. What are you getting for her Christmas then?'

I hear him chuckle. 'A silver heart-shaped framed photo of her secret scan picture and a new cot for the little one.'

'That's so nice,' says the nurse as I try to dismiss the warm, tingling feeling which is engulfing me.

CHAPTER 32

RORY

I'm back in my cubicle and bored out of my brain. The last time I asked a nurse for the time it was three in the morning. I have been here hours.

Sidney, the A&E doctor, enters the cubicle with an impressive swish of the green curtain. He comes to stand by my chair. 'The scan results will be with your GP in about a week or so. You need to rest after a knock to the head like that and can take paracetamol for the pain. Use an ice pack regularly for the next few hours, it will help reduce the swelling.'

He hands me a leaflet on head injuries. 'Watch out for any sudden changes like problems with your vision and worsening of pain. I'm happy to discharge you, but you will need someone to keep an eye on you for the next forty-eight hours. Have a nice Christmas,' says Sidney, giving the stethoscope around his neck a squeeze.

'Good luck with the proposal,' I say, with a wink.

He nods. 'It will be amazing. I'm a very lucky man.'

'You are.'

It must have been the way I said it because he casts me an odd expression.

'Ignore me – I am just envious of you. Six months ago, my girlfriend and I split up. I've been missing her like crazy. She was my best friend too.'

Sidney nods. 'It sounds like you need to get her back... although get some rest first.'

Anna shoots out of her seat as I stagger into the hospital concourse. It's nice to see a familiar face after several hours in my cubicle. She rushes towards me. I let her place her arm over my shoulders. 'Oh, God, Rory, you look dreadful.'

'Thanks.'

She laughs. 'Right, have you got somewhere to stay?'

I try to shake my head but end up wincing at the pain. 'No as I need to get to Brighton.'

'Brighton?' Her smile begins to fade. 'Didn't the doctor say you need someone with you? When Mum banged her head after falling in the garden, I had to stay with her for the first twenty-four hours. Let's go back to my hotel room, you can lie down, and we can talk when you're not tired. There's a lot to catch up on and I need to tell you something.'

I hesitate and touch the outside of my shirt pocket to feel the gold chain and locket. My heart reminds me that this trip was about seeing Emily and Felix, not Anna. 'What do you need to tell me?'

She slips her hand into my arm. 'Come on, let's grab a cab and talk in my hotel room.'

I stop her. 'Anna, I could do with a coffee which has not come from a hospital machine.'

'Well, there's a late-night café down the road so we could go there. Since you went into A&E I have been a regular takeaway customer.'

We trudge down the road carpeted with snow and enter the café with coats adorned with white flakes. I take the seat by the window, decorated with colourful Christmas lights, as she goes to order us coffee. Looking around the café I smile at all the tinsel and decorations. I bet Felix will have covered Vivi's house in decorations and it will be like entering Santa's grotto. Last year Vivi let him loose with a box of decorations and me as his human ladder. We had so much fun hanging ribbons of cards, sticking up bunches of mistletoe, placing as many baubles as physically possible on the tree without any thought about a colour scheme and placing a Spiderman figure on the top.

'How's your head?' Anna asks while placing the tray on the table. 'What did the doctor say about it?'

'Concussion. I have to take paracetamol, rest and put an ice pack on it.'

'Did you have a CT scan? Head injuries can be nasty.'

I nod and watch her slide in opposite me.

'How's your mum doing? Is she still living the life in the Caribbean?'

Taking a sip of my coffee I savour the warmth. 'She's busy sailing around it in my stepfather's new boat. I don't hear from her much.'

From a young age I can remember Mum getting out colourful travel brochures and telling me and Lawrence that one day she would be sailing her own boat around the crystal-blue waters of the Caribbean. After Lawrence died and Dad married the woman with the mobile burger van, Mum met Phil, who has always had more money than sense. A few years ago, they decided to pack up their life in the UK and go sail around the Caribbean.

Anna raises a perfectly sculptured eyebrow at me. 'Is that because she's busy sailing or are you avoiding talking to her about him?'

Grimacing, I turn away.

'I thought so,' says Anna with a heavy sigh. 'Does Emily know about Lawrence?'

I forget about my head wound and shake my head, then let out a yelp at the pain. 'I never told her about him. I didn't want to burden our amazing relationship with my dark feelings. Before

Vivi died I wanted to tell her as she kept thinking I was being unfaithful with you, but then Vivi died, and everything got messy.'

'So, am I the only person you talk to about Lawrence?'

I nod. 'Yes, you are. You knew him so well, Anna. You even managed to drag him out of his introverted shell at uni.' With a chuckle I raise a toast to her.

Lawrence died in such a horrible way, lying in Mum's crumpled car, with me screaming beside him, that it has been comforting to hear he had such an amazing couple of months leading up to his death. A reassuring feeling takes hold of me as I recall Anna's wild and wacky tales about her friendship with my little brother in their university halls of residence.

'Who would have thought my little brother, who rarely left his bedroom as a teenager, would turn into a party animal. I'm so pleased you were in his life. Cheers. Mum gets too emotional when I talk about him. I tried to tell her a few months ago about some of your tales but she got upset. Emily would freak out if she knew I was in the passenger seat of the car when Lawrence lost control of the car.' Guilt wraps itself around my chest and squeezes. 'I should have taken control of the car and stopped us from flipping into that field.'

Anna leans across the table. 'Rory – stop it! We've talked about this. The crash happened so fast. You couldn't have done anything.'

We both take a sip of our drinks and find interesting marks on the wooden table to stare at. I sense there's something on Anna's mind as she keeps avoiding my gaze. 'Are you all right?'

She stares at me. 'Rory, there's something I need to tell you.'

With a chuckle I ask, 'Do you have any more memories of Lawrence, because right now I could do with a giggle?'

In a second my mind whisks me back to our first meal after work where Anna talked nonstop about her friendship with Lawrence. I remember sitting in a Thai restaurant laughing at her tale of the university pub crawl where she and Lawrence dressed up as pirates and both got so pissed by the end of the night, they kept having drunken pretend sword fights on top of pub tables. When Lawrence and I were kids, he was crap at any kind of play fighting. I would always win. Both Anna and Lawrence got thrown out by the bouncers. Feeling mischievous, they convinced a mermaid and a merman to swap outfits with them. Lawrence needed someone like Anna in his life. She claims they were only best friends and there was no romantic connection between them. I can't believe my little brother didn't make a move on Anna. He loved girls with long, dark hair.

I watch her put her hands on either side of her face. 'Rory, I don't know how to say this.'

'What?' Anna has probably come to tell me that she and Lawrence had a relationship. Yes, that's it. I would be proud of Lawrence if he managed to pull Anna. Lawrence didn't have many girlfriends before he went to university. We all put it down to his shyness.

Her eyes are pink and watery. 'I had such a crush on you when you brought Lawrence to ballet. Every Saturday I would ignore Mum's ballet lesson and stand by the barre watching you.'

I grip onto the table until my knuckles turn white.

'When I went to university, I saw you and your mum come to visit Lawrence. You were even more handsome than when I saw you at Mum's ballet classes.'

My shoulders and neck have tensed. I'm not sure I want to hear this.

'So, when Mum said earlier this year that you'd started coming again with a young lad I tracked you down on Facebook and as luck would have it, I got a job where you worked.'

My gut has just rotated one way and is now performing the same manoeuvre in the other direction, leaving me with a horrible queasy sensation.

Anna lowers her head and stares at the table. 'Rory, I want you to know that I did what I did because I have been in love with you for so many years.'

'Anna, we've talked about this. I only want to be your friend.'

She nods, still looking down into her drink. 'I have to tell you. Mum says I have to be honest with you.'

'About what?'

'I did go to the same university as Lawrence but...' Her voice fades. She takes out a ball of tissues and dabs at her cheeks. 'Lawrence and I were never close.'

My heart is pounding against my rib cage. 'What do you mean?'

Lifting her head, she stares at me with a tear-stained face. 'I made up all those stories about me and Lawrence. He said hello to me once or twice, that was it.'

Time has come to a shuddering halt. All the air in my lungs has just evaporated. A crushing sensation has taken over my chest.

With a sniff she says, 'I thought by telling you the stories you'd want to be with me instead of Emily.'

'Why would you do that?' I croak, feeling like a prize-winning idiot for believing her stories about Lawrence, for spending so much time listening to her fictional memories that Emily had to endure her sister dying on her own and ended our relationship because she thought I was a two-timing wanker. For goodness' sake, why didn't I question what was coming out of Anna's mouth? When Lawrence and I went out to the pub we sat right at the back and almost out of view because he didn't want to bump into anyone and make small talk. My brother hated talking trivia with strangers. What was I thinking? Why didn't I query whether Lawrence had somehow had a personality transplant the second he stepped into his university halls of residence. He also never mentioned a close friend called Anna. The only people he ever talked about were his Dungeon & Dragons club members.

'Rory, I'm so sorry. When you texted me earlier about being in

London, I knew I had to tell you. Mum said it was the right thing to do.'

I shoot up, knocking my chair over. 'Sorry, but I have to leave.'

She grabs my arm. 'Rory – please stay, you've got a nasty bump to your head.'

I bat her away. 'Sorry, Anna, I have heard enough. Please don't ever contact me again.'

She follows me out of the café and onto the street. 'Rory, I love you.'

A spurt of anger shoots up inside of me. Turning around I glare at her. 'I trusted you. Hearing all those stories made me feel happy that my little brother had found some enjoyment, that he'd been happy before he died. I spent so much time listening to your lies that I allowed the person I loved to walk out of my life. Goodbye, Anna.'

'I'm sorry,' she wails. 'I never meant to hurt you.'

I keep on walking until I come to a taxi rank.

CHAPTER 33

EMILY

To my surprise, Tom is sat on the sofa when I creep out of Rory's bedroom carrying Baxter, who is desperate for the toilet, at seven. Tom looks up as I pull on my coat and grab Baxter. 'I'm just taking him outside to the toilet.'

Tom gets to his feet. 'Do you want me to take him?'

As he comes over, I notice he's still in his clothes from last night. His hair is messy and his plump face the colour of chalk. 'Let me do that for you, Emily. It's the least I can do.'

I cast him a puzzled look. He hangs his head. 'I was drunk and angry last night. Some of the things I said were not very nice. It's Christmas Eve and I don't want you and Felix going home thinking I am an arsehole.'

He takes Baxter, my dog poo bags and his coat. 'Come, little fella, let's go find somewhere for you to have a festive crap.'

'Be careful,' I say, as Baxter throws me a frightened glance and a new sense of protectiveness for the little dog takes hold of me. 'He's tiny.'

Tom smiles. 'I'll take good care of him, promise.'

They're gone for a long and arduous eight minutes. I can't

believe I am sat here timing them on my phone. What has Baxter done to me on this trip?

Tom opens the door and Baxter races towards me. His little tail is wagging so much I think it might fall off. Scooping him into my arms I give him a cuddle.

'He did his business, as soon as we were out of the door. I bagged it up and popped it in the bin. We came straight back as it was cold.'

I watch Tom hurry out to the kitchen. With Baxter in my arms, I follow Tom.

'Coffee?' He's stood by the sink washing his hands.

'I stand by the work surface. 'Yes please.'

After drying his hands, Tom grabs two coffee mugs from a cupboard. 'Yesterday I was jealous you had come to see Rory. You wouldn't believe how much I wish Suzie would come to visit me.'

'Oh, I see.'

He flicks on the silver coffee machine. 'I was an idiot with Suzie. It's all my fault we split up. It's been eating me up for months.'

As he launches into a rambling explanation about how they split up, which involved a drunken night where he and Suzie both told each other about their inner secrets over a bottle of strong Scotch and he told her something about having a one-night stand with a sexually frustrated forty-year-old woman from Norwich, I glance at the sheet of paper pinned to the freezer and gasp. It's that bloody challenge. Before my brain can stop my eyes, they follow Rory's row along the ten columns. Three columns have been marked with a cross. My heart sinks. Rory has slept with three women. I try to remind myself what Bill said via Lizzie, that technically Rory is a single man. Rory has no idea Felix, and I are here.

I hug Baxter a little bit tighter, and he licks my face. Well, I suppose it's better than ten women. Rory is moving on with his life and now I must do the same. A heaviness in me makes me bend over and stare at the socks I was wearing yesterday.

'He's always talking about your dress business,' says Tom, making me lift my face.

'Really?'

Tom nods. 'He made me share your Instagram site with everyone where I work. A few of the women were amazed at the dresses you make and sell.'

I cast Tom a look of surprise. 'Really?'

Tom smiles. 'He's really proud of you, Emily. You do know that, don't you?'

'Yes.' I am flooded with warm tingling feelings. 'It was Rory who urged me to start my own business when we first began dating. He and my sister practically ganged up on me to persuade me to jack in my marketing job and start my own business.'

Felix is calling me so I hurry out of the kitchen and into the living area. Felix grins and comes to hug me and Baxter. 'Wow – Felix, you don't normally hug me.' I feel light-headed, this is new territory for me and Felix – morning hugs.

He gazes up at me with a familiar intensity. In a flash I'm whisked back to the night he was born and while Vivi was being cleaned up, I got to hold my little nephew, Felix, and whisper how I already loved him so much. His hazel eyes stared back at me in the same way.

Since Vivi died I've lost sight of Felix being that same precious baby who Vivi brought into the world. The little baby who restored our faith in life and love.

Mum had been dead over a year when Felix arrived in the world. She'd died alone after a huge drinking and drug-taking binge in a hotel room. It was the day after she'd screamed at Vivi and me, telling us she'd never loved us and wished we'd died in the woods all those years ago. Vivi and I held hands as she tried to hurt us once more. After her outburst we walked away, still holding hands, and it was then we made a pact that we would do whatever it took to make sure our future children's lives would always be filled with love.

Gulping back a wave of emotion and guilt, I think back to how I threw myself into dressmaking when Vivi died, leaving Felix to fend for himself. I was so wrapped up in my grief and my lack of confidence in being able to raise Felix.

He tugs on my arm. 'You don't think I'm weird.'

I shake my head. 'No, I think you're great.'

'Aunty Emily,' he says, as I pop Baxter down and return Felix's hug. 'Can I just call you Emily from now on?'

Well, that's a surprise. But he's hugging me, so it's not because he hates me.

He rests his head on me. 'You're more than an aunty to me.'

Bending down to his level I blink away juicy tears. 'Felix, I know I've not been present since I moved in with you. It was easy to lose myself in my dressmaking. Your mummy was the best sister anyone could have had and losing her felt like a piece of me had been removed. I want you to know that from now on I will be here for you. You will be my priority and I will do what it takes to make our home a happy one.'

Felix smiles. 'I'm going to try and be a good boy when we get home.'

I pull him against me again, and we rock back and forth until he starts giggling and his T-shirt has soaked up my tears. 'Felix, we're going to make a good team,' I sob. This boy is going to be shocked at how much change I am going to make to his little life.

'I know,' he says. 'Please don't cry, Emily.'

Wiping my damp cheeks, I smile at him. 'I might not be as good at child-rearing as your mummy, but I am going to try my best.'

Felix giggles. 'Take some cooking lessons?'

I playfully wrestle him onto the sofa until he's roaring with laughter.

We sit back up and hold hands. With his thumb Felix catches a stray tear of mine. 'Rory's not coming back – is he?'

Releasing him I gaze into his round hazel eyes and smooth his hair down. 'No, he isn't, and that's all right.'

Felix nods. 'I'll always love him.'

'I know,' I say, kissing him on the cheek. 'I'll always love Rory too.'

Tom comes over with a bag of croissants. 'Sit down both of you – let's eat.'

We all sit down and bite into fluffy croissants. Tom tears a piece of his and before he puts it in his mouth, he holds my gaze. 'Rory told me about how you and your sister were in the newspaper. Something about surviving two days in a forest as little children.'

My cheeks are growing warm. Felix is staring in amazement at me. Vivi clearly never told him. 'Yes, that's right.'

'Wow,' exclaims Tom, 'were you playing in the forest and get lost?'

I shake my head. 'One day our mother decided she didn't want us, so she took us to the forest and left us there.'

Tom's mouth has fallen open in shock. 'How old were you?'

In my head a memory is playing. It's of our mother taking Vivi out of her car seat and popping her down next to me. I remember grabbing hold of Vivi's tiny hand as we watched our drunken mother stagger back into the car and drive away. A part of me back then was relieved we were free of her. Vivi looked up at me with a terrified expression and I smoothed down her red hair and told her we were going on an adventure. 'I was seven and Vivi was four.'

'That must have been scary. How did you survive?'

Felix has gone quiet. Maybe I shouldn't have told him?

'I made us a den inside an old tree which had fallen over. It had a hollow inside and was perfect for us to use as shelter. Before we were dropped off at the forest, I had stolen a packet of biscuits from the cupboard, they were shoved up my sleeve. I also collected berries for us to eat and found a little stream we could drink from.'

'Were you and Mummy scared?' Felix whispers.

I turn to him. 'I made sure your Mummy wasn't scared by telling her stories about runaway princesses and magical forests.'

'You must be very brave,' says Felix before resting his head on my shoulder.

Tom takes a sip of his coffee. 'So how long was it before you were found?'

'Two days. Some ramblers found us. By that stage we were hungry and dirty, and the whole adventure idea was starting to lose its appeal.'

Felix lifts his head. 'Why did your mother not want you?' The question Vivi and I asked her almost every day after we were returned to her care after the woods incident. Mum would be busy putting on a show for the social worker who was assigned to us after that. Making sure that when the social worker visited we looked like a happy little family and Mum's addictions were a thing of the past. Once the social worker left, Mum would return to her old uncaring self and tell us she didn't want to be a mother.

Tom scratches his stubble-clad chin. 'That's some story. Rory was right, Emily, you were amazing for keeping yourself and your little sister safe.'

The living area goes blurry. 'I couldn't keep her safe when it mattered though.' Felix wraps his arm around my neck, and I try to block out the memory of Vivi being carried out of the house by paramedics.

Tom passes me a little pack of tissues. 'Yes, Rory told me about your sister. I'm so sorry.'

We all go silent, and Felix hugs me a bit tighter.

'So, what's your plan?' Tom asks, changing the subject.

'Everything is going to be all right. We're going home,' announces Felix. He looks up at me and I notice how he's sitting up a little taller.

Tom's face breaks into a smile. 'Well, I hope you both have a nice Christmas.'

I grab Felix's hand and give it a squeeze. 'We're going to have a lovely Christmas. We just need to get a move on, so we have time to get to Brighton, buy some decorations and some good food, and get home. I also want to buy some emergency provisions for the journey home. We are going to be prepared this time.'

Felix smiles at me before jumping up. 'I'm going to get ready and pack up my stuff.'

He and Baxter race away.

Tom sits back in the sofa and crosses his leg over his knee. 'Sorry about Rory not showing up.'

'It's all right. This trip has proved to me Rory has moved on with his life.'

Tom stays silent.

I get up from my chair and with a heavy heart go to see what Felix is up to.

We both emerge twenty minutes later ready for our trip back home. Tom is sat waiting for us. 'It was nice to meet you both,' he says. 'At last I can put faces to the names I hear such a lot.'

Felix nudges me but I hurry us towards the flat door. I've seen enough of Leeds. 'It was good to meet you, Tom. Do you have any plans for Christmas?'

His face lights up. 'I've decided to see if I can persuade Suzie to give us another go.'

'Really?'

He nods. 'I've texted her and invited her over for a chat. Wish me luck.'

We step outside the door. Felix picks up Baxter and I sling my bag over my shoulder. 'Thanks for giving us somewhere to stay, Tom, I appreciate it.'

He nods. 'Shall I tell Rory you were here?'

'Wish him a happy Christmas,' I say, steering Felix in the direction of the lift.

With a sigh Tom waves and heads back into his flat.

Felix, Baxter, and I make our way towards the stairs, as the lift is still out of action.

As we start our descent, Felix puts his arm through mine. I think he can sense my sadness at not seeing Rory. Those three damn crosses won't get out of mind either. 'It's going to be all right, Emily.'

As we make our way down a few steps there's a noise from above. It's Tom. Felix pulls us to a stop. Tom appears at the top of the stairs carrying a piece of paper. 'Emily,' he tries to get his breath. 'Look what I said last night about Rory doing better than me on the challenge – well that was a lie.'

'What do you mean?'

He holds up the chart. 'Rory hasn't…' He stops, noticing Felix staring intently at him. 'Rory hasn't had *afternoon tea* with anyone.'

'What?'

Tom gestures at Felix. '*Afternoon tea.*'

I am assuming that this is his code word for sex. He points to the crosses. 'The crosses mean fail. Rory keeps calling the women he dates Emily. Every date he's had has ended abruptly after he's called them Emily.'

I gasp and stare up at the chart as fireworks shoot across my chest.

There are four crosses against Tom's name too. 'You also have crosses.'

Tom nods. 'Every woman I meet seems to bump into Suzie, then listens to what she has to say about me. Rory and I are crap at dating. We can't stop thinking about our ex-girlfriends.'

My brain reminds me of Beth and my excitement sinks. 'I guess Beth was different.'

Tom screws up his face and stares at the chart.

'Goodbye, Tom,' I say, as he goes blurry. Felix, Baxter and I carry on making our way down the stairs.

CHAPTER 34

FELIX

'Mummy, it's me again. I'm waiting for... Emily. She's in the café behind me buying a coffee for her, sandwiches for us both, a bottle of water and an iced bun for me for the journey. We've just been into a clothes shop and she's bought me a new jumper in case the train gets stuck in a snow drift.' Flipping the camera on the phone he scans the thick layer of sparkling snow coating the pavements. 'As you can see there is a lot of snow up here in Leeds. I'm not allowed to put Baxter down as Emily says he might sink into a snow drift. Last night Rory didn't come home which has made us both sad. I don't think my idea about coming to Leeds was a good one.' He stares gloomily at the phone camera.

The peals of laughter from two children having fun with their mum in the snow across the road distracts him. He continues to talk but keeps his eyes on the children. 'I have asked Emily whether I can call her Emily and not use the *Aunty* word. We talked last night. I told her my secret. Please don't be cross, Mummy, about me telling Emily, Rory, and Amelie before you. I have been worried about what you'll think. Emily was nice and told me she was proud of me. Last night she changed into the old

Aunty Emily that I knew before you went to work on God's newspaper in heaven. This morning we have laughed a lot and we had a play fight which I won. I hope the old Emily stays. I will tell you my secret when I am ready, Mummy.'

Gently, he presses Baxter's face against the phone screen. 'Baxter says hello. He liked Rory's bedroom and chewed on one of Rory's trainers. Emily says she will apologise to Rory when she sees him again.' He sighs and kicks some snow. 'Where is Rory, Mummy?'

Peering into the shop window to check where Emily is he spots her by the till. 'She is still in the queue. I can talk for a bit longer. Jade emailed me again this morning to ask whether I want to be her boyfriend. I don't know what to say to her. She doesn't know about my secret, and she might not like me when I tell her. I might talk to Emily. Right, I need to go as Emily is coming back outside. Bye, Mummy.'

CHAPTER 35

EMILY

*F*elix and I trudge through the snow towards the station. I've been worried about Baxter and the cold weather. When I came out of the café, I asked Felix what he thought about opening the top of his rucksack and making a little warm bed for Baxter. Felix's face lit up. I'm now smiling at the sight of Felix walking beside me with Baxter, wrapped in a jumper, peering out of his rucksack throne.

I recall the conversation we had last night about the ballet classes Rory took him to every Saturday and Felix's passion for dancing. 'Thank you for telling me about your ballet secret last night.'

Felix smiles. 'I love dancing.'

'I hope you are going to dance more around the house, and not just in your bedroom.'

He looks up at me with such affection I can feel myself melting inside. 'I will if that's allowed?'

'You have my approval to dance whenever you feel like it. Do all your friends know about your ballet secret?'

'Only Amelie.'

'Why only Amelie?'

He shrugs. 'Ronnie would laugh at me and Sai would worry about me breaking my leg.'

We both go silent and listen to the crunch of our feet on fresh snow.

'Emily.' Felix taps me on the arm. 'When you first met Rory how did you know he was going to be your boyfriend?'

Every day some of the things Felix comes out with manages to shock me. He sounds like nine going on thirty-five at times, I shoot him a puzzled expression. 'Wow – that's a big question. Why do you ask?'

He casts me a blank expression like it's just a random question, but I can't help noticing two spots of pink blossoming on his cheeks. 'I was just wondering.'

My mind whisks me back to the first couple of dates with Rory; the surfing lesson, the rock-climbing wall and the nineties roller disco. Everything with Rory felt different. There was no urgency to kiss or hold hands. I don't think he kissed me until our fourth date. We talked a lot on our dates although probably too much during the surfing lesson and on the rock-climbing wall, and we got told off by the instructors. Rory was the first man I'd met who wanted to get know me as a person before the romance started. 'Well, our dates didn't feel like dates. More like two good friends having a laugh.'

'Really?' I can see Felix's furrowed brow through his coppery hair.

'Yes. Friendship is really important to me.' I take Felix's hand. 'Why do I sense there is something on your mind?'

He blows out the air inside his cheeks. 'Jade, the girl on the train yesterday, wants to know whether I want to be her boyfriend. She emailed me last night to ask me and again this morning to see whether I had made a decision.'

I try to stifle my gasp and suppress my look of horror. They're both nine years of age and only met on a train to London for an hour or so. My goodness, Jade is a fast mover. I'm not sure I had the confidence at nine to even talk to a boy on a train let alone email him that evening and ask him out. Children are growing up fast these days. Panic courses through my veins – if this is what kids are like at nine, what will they be like in the teenage years? 'Well, what do you think?' I say, forcing out a fake smile.

Felix points at my face. 'You're not really smiling, Emily.'

'Tell me what's on your mind?'

He casts me a worried look. 'I think Jade only wants me to be her boyfriend just so that she can see Baxter a lot.'

'Yes,' I nod. 'She was obsessed with Baxter. It was a bit awkward when her mother had to order her to hand Baxter to us. You know what Felix, I agree. She does want to see more of Baxter but... she could still be a good friend to you. Why don't you ask her if she wants to be friends? We could invite her over and you can go play football with her on the beach.'

A look of relief passes over Felix's face. 'She does make me laugh.'

'So, what are you going to do?'

He lets out a little cheer. 'I'm going to tell Jade we will have more fun being friends.'

The station has come into view. I can't see many people hurrying towards it. Maybe the snow has caused trains to be cancelled? The thought of being stuck in Leeds over Christmas with Tom and his gigantic mound of toilet roll and no Rory fills me with dread.

I return to the conversation. 'Do you want a girlfriend?'

'Amelie is the one girl I would want as my girlfriend but...' His voice trails off.

'But what?'

He exhales. 'Amelie and I have stuff to do as friends. Next year when she has an extra-long skipping rope, she wants me to tie one end to my bike so I can pull her along on her new rollerskates. She wants to be a water skier, but without being on the water.'

Every muscle inside me clenches with fear. I recall Vivi asking me to do the same when we were kids, and that game did not end well. I hurtled down our old steep driveway on my bike with her tied behind on roller skates. Neither of us predicted the neighbour's cat, Twinkle Toes, would step out in front of my bike causing me to make a sharp left turn. To my horror Vivi sailed past my bike and went smack into the wall of the house. She had to be peeled off the wall by me and put on the sofa for the rest of the day, covered in antiseptic cream. Guilt for agreeing to that silly and reckless game consumed me for weeks. Vivi didn't care and wanted to do it again once the cuts on her face, chest and legs healed. 'Don't agree to that game, Felix. I played it with your mum, and it still gives me nightmares.'

'You sound like Sai,' chuckles Felix.

I pull us to a stop. 'Felix, you've got the rest of your life to find someone special. Why don't you enjoy being friends with Amelie and Jade?'

He smiles. 'Relationships are stressful – aren't they?'

With a laugh I ruffle his head. 'Yes, relationships are stressful. You know you can talk to me about anything – don't you?'

'I know.' He hangs his head.

I pull him into a hug, making sure I don't knock Baxter off his blanket throne. 'No more secrets. I am going to make sure I'm not so busy when we get home so we can talk more.'

When we break apart, he takes out his phone. 'There's something else I haven't told you.'

I take a lungful of chilly wintry air and brace myself for another of Felix's revelations. In my head I pray this secret does not entail buying something on my credit card or running away again.

He lifts his face to mine and I can see his hazel eyes are swimming in tears. 'What is it?'

I watch him switch on the phone. 'This is Mummy's old phone.'

'Yes,' I say, kneeling into the snow so I can talk to him at his level. Taking out a ball of tissues I dab away the tears which are streaming down his pink cheeks. 'Talk to me.'

He sniffs and starts to sob. 'I've been talking to Mummy using her phone.'

Instinctively I pull him into me. His tears trickle down my neck.

When he's stopped crying, he takes the phone and with me watching taps onto photos and videos. With his finger he scrolls through a lot of video clips of him talking into the camera.

'Oh, Felix,' I gasp. 'Did you make all of these?'

Nodding he wipes his eyes with the back of his hand. 'It feels like she's watching them from heaven. I talk to her about things which have been happening to me. We used to talk a lot.'

Guilt takes hold of me. While I was getting obsessed with dressmaking this poor lad was in desperate need of talking to his mum.

I close his fingers around the phone, and I place mine over the top. 'Your mum would be so proud of you and I'm sure she's looking down and watching you record them.'

He offers me the phone. 'Don't you want to watch them?'

His offer is tempting but I shake my head. His eyes widen and his mouth falls open. 'Really?'

'Those videos are for you and your mum. They're private. You should keep them and carry on recording her video clips.' With a wink I say, 'I bet you are moaning about me on a lot of them.'

The speed at which his little face reddens tells me what I need to know. In view of how obsessed I have been with my dress business and grieving for Vivi, I don't blame him. With a smile I kiss the top of his head. 'I don't blame you for moaning about me. I admit I haven't been great to live with and I need to take better care of you.' Placing my hands on his cold cheeks I stare deeply into his hazel eyes. 'When your Mummy died, I lost my sister. She was my best friend in the whole world. At home I was never sad about looking after you. I was missing your mum. Do you understand me? Felix, you are my family now. I love you with all my heart.'

To my surprise he opens his arms and hugs me. 'I love you, Emily,' he says and plants a kiss on my cheek.

By the time we enter the station we are both smiling, holding hands, and singing Christmas songs.

CHAPTER 36

RORY

'Hey, buddy,' I say, scraping a layer of soft snow from Lawrence's gravestone and crouching down in front of it. 'It's been a long time. I'm sorry.'

With a finger I trace the italic lettering across the front. *Loved and missed by all the family.*

Casting my eyes across the little white-coated cemetery I gulp back a wave of emotion. The last time I came here was a few years ago with Mum. She claimed I was avoiding going to see Lawrence's grave, so she practically dragged me here. Shame and guilt wrestle together inside of me.

After leaving Anna and her dreadful revelations, I got the last train to Brighton and stayed in the Travelodge. The woman on reception took pity on me as I struggled into the hotel at seven A.M. with a swollen face. She handed over a makeshift ice pack for my head (a bag of ice from the bar wrapped in a large white serviette). I tried to sleep but was woken up by the young children in the hotel room next door singing Christmas songs and shouting at their mum and dad to wake up. The throbbing pain is not too bad although purplish bruising has started to blossom.

Before I go to see Emily and Felix, I've decided to come here.

'I've been a complete idiot. You wouldn't believe the mess I have got myself into.'

It's eerily quiet here today with the only noises being me whispering to Lawrence, a whistling icy wind racing around the snow-capped gravestones, and the sound an old man trudging through the snow and along the same gravestone row as me. He comes to gaze down at the stone next to Lawrence's. His balding head is pink with cold but his ears are covered in thick patches of white hair. 'It's a good time to visit,' he says and gestures towards the stone. 'That's my wife, Sheila, down there. Who is she next to?'

I stand up and nod towards Lawrence's granite stone. 'That's my brother.'

The man chuckles. 'Sheila can talk a lot. I feel sorry for your brother.'

'I'm sure she's keeping him company.'

Blowing warm air into his hands the man turns to me. 'You been in a boxing match?'

I smile. 'Someone pushed me into a station ticket barrier.'

He chuckles. 'Are you a regular visitor here?'

Shaking my head, I stuff my hands into my coat pockets. 'First time in ages. Haven't been here for a few years.'

The man nods. 'The early years are the hardest. It takes a long time for you to accept they are somewhere else. Can I ask what's brought you here today?'

'He's been on my mind a lot this year. Not sure why as he's been gone nearly ten years.'

We both go silent and listen to the wind chasing its tail around the cemetery.

'Maybe you needed to do some more grieving for him?'

'Is that how it works?'

He casts me a knowing smile. 'Grief is an odd thing. It is like a distant friend you don't see very often and who one day turns up

225

out of the blue bringing with them a box filled with painful memories.'

Nudging a pile of snow with my boot I think back to those days after the car accident when Lawrence had died, and I'd survived with barely a scratch. All I could think about was how God chose the wrong brother.

'The thing is,' explains the old man, 'you have to look through the box of painful memories. There's no point in trying to avoid it because this friend will keep turning up unexpected and unannounced.'

Scratching the back of neck, I fight the urge to walk away. 'I was with my brother in the car when he died. He was driving and lost control.'

The old man nods and stares at Lawrence's grave. 'I bet you still blame yourself – don't you?'

I nod. 'I'm his older brother. That's what older siblings are meant to do – protect the younger ones.'

'You have to accept that it was out of your control. I bet it happened in the blink of an eye.'

Lawrence's gravestone has gone blurry. 'I've tried my hardest not to think about him for years, to block out the pain, but then my girlfriend's nephew told me he was interested in going to ballet classes. Lawrence went to ballet when he was young too and...' My voice grows weak.

'Your distant friend called grief turned up on your door – eh?' the man asks.

'Yes,' I say, blinking away hot tears. 'So did the anger, the frustration and the sadness. I also allowed myself to be tricked by someone who I thought was a friend. As a result, my girlfriend, who I love very much, split up with me and I've been a mess ever since.'

I feel him pat me on the back. 'I'm sorry, I really am. Grief can get you into all sorts of trouble.'

Kicking the snow away from the grave I let out a sigh. 'I

believed the lies this friend told me about my brother. They were all lies.'

'You're the only person who knew your brother.'

We both stand and watch the wind play with the snowflakes which are starting to fall.

'Stop beating yourself up,' says the old man. 'It's not worth it. We all make mistakes. Your brother wouldn't want you to live a life of sadness.' He pats me on the shoulder again. 'As I said before, when your friend grief turns up unannounced and without warning, you have to invite it inside and look through the memories it has brought you. Closing the door on it will only make things worse. It sounds like you've been shutting the door on grief for a long time. Don't be afraid of it or the uncomfortable memories it wants you to experience.'

I remember my first visit back to Lawrence's old ballet school with Felix. I honestly thought that, as it has been so long since Lawrence died, being back at the ballet school would not affect me. All I wanted to do was see Felix happy again.

'Your girlfriend's nephew – did he enjoy the ballet classes?'

With a smile I nod. 'Felix claimed it was the best thing he'd ever done. He's stopped dancing now.'

'Oh, why's that?' The old man casts me a look of concern.

'My girlfriend's sister died suddenly. His mum. Ballet reminded him of her.'

I watch the old man bend down to clear snow away from his wife's stone. 'Grief isn't always bad, you know. A few months before Sheila passed away, she took over an allotment. Nice little patch it was, overlooking the sea. Sheila planted all sorts of vegetable seeds. Sadly, she died before all her hard work came to fruition. I hadn't been a gardener up until that point. When grief kept coming to my door in the months that passed, I found solace on Sheila's allotment. That patch of ground has become my pride and joy. It got me through some tough times, and I met my partner, Jill, there too.'

'Wow – that's great.'

He straightens up and knocks his gloved hands together to rid them of snow. 'Perhaps grief is trying to show you a new direction in your life. One which will help you reconnect with your brother.'

For a few minutes I stand and reflect on what he's said. He's right. Whenever grief has come to me, I have refused to let it in. My fascination with Anna's fabricated stories about Lawrence was a distraction. If I lost myself in her tales about her close friendship with Lawrence I didn't have to think about the night he died, the suffocating guilt I experienced as I listened to the paramedics telling me they'd done all they could to save Lawrence but it was too late, and the sounds of my parents weeping downstairs as I lay upstairs in my old bedroom wondering what the hell had happened to my little brother.

Talking to Emily about Lawrence would have been like opening the door to my grief. I chose not to as I didn't want to think about Lawrence. How I wish now I had told her about Lawrence. She is the best thing that's happened to me in a long time. The last two years with her have been amazing. We had so much fun, and I got to know Vivi and Felix as well.

The old man points to my chest. 'Your brother lives on inside of you. That's something you haven't come to understand yet.'

'What do you mean?'

'The people we love take up residence inside of us. They never leave us. Your brother is inside of you and it's clear he's trying to make you see things. Perhaps you should start to listen to what your brother is telling you. He wants you to reconnect with your girlfriend.'

The thought of Emily makes my fingers locate the golden locket deep inside the pocket of my shirt and a warm feeling races up my spine.

'Is there any chance you and your girlfriend could work things out?'

I take out the locket and it glistens in the pale, early morning light. 'This locket belongs to my girlfriend. I have made this trip from Leeds to give it to her. It was a birthday gift her sister had bought for her before she died. This journey I have been on has made me realise how much I love her.'

A huge smile breaks across the man's face. 'Well, what are you waiting for?'

Carefully I place the locket back inside my pocket. 'Thank you.'

An ache radiates out from my chest, and it hits me. Both Emily and Felix are my future. I know I have been a prize-winning idiot over Anna, and I know I let Emily down, but I now know Emily is the only woman I will ever love and being a father figure to Felix will bring me so much happiness.

He extends his hand. 'It was great to meet and talk to you. Good luck on your journey and don't forget, the next time grief comes to your door, invite it in and look at what it's brought you.'

'Merry Christmas.'

He gives me a wave as I hurry through the cemetery towards the exit. As I am about to step out onto the road I stop. Vivi is in that cemetery. Turning around I hurry back inside. Her stone is over to the far left near the large oak tree.

'Hey, Vivi,' I say, bending down to clear the snow away. Standing up I take out the locket. 'I did what you asked. I bought Emily the locket you wanted her to have. Today I am going to give it to her, and I know it will bring back that beautiful smile of hers which disappeared the day you left us.' Snowflakes dance and twirl before my eyes. 'Vivi, I am going to repair the damage I caused before you died.'

I manage to flag down a taxi. As the taxi crawls through the slushy, snow-lined Brighton streets, I rub my chest to try to slow down the feeling of excitement inside of me,

It's brilliant to be back in this fabulous city and even better that I am a few minutes away from seeing Emily again. The taxi turns onto the seafront. On one side of the road, I can see the dark strip of sea hemmed in by a snow-covered beach and on the other side twinkly Christmas lights, glowing hotel entrances and shops lit up by colourful festive decorations. This time last year Emily and I walked hand in hand looking out across the wintry seafront and made plans; we talked about all the countries we wanted to visit, the places in the world we wanted to live, the life goals we wanted to achieve and our career opportunities, and when we were tired of sounding like adults, we giggled like school kids over our excitement for Christmas. Oh, Emily, I can't wait to take you in my arms and tell you how much I love you. I want to apologise to you for making you think I was being unfaithful to you. I want to sit you down and tell you about Lawrence. When I am finished, I want to hug Felix and persuade him to dance for us. I want to promise to make his ballet dream come true.

Vivi's house is a red-brick Victorian house a few streets away from the seafront. With a pounding heart I pay the taxi driver and walk up the path. Raising my hand, I knock on the door and hold my breath.

CHAPTER 37

EMILY

Felix, Baxter, and I are on the train to London. It left Leeds over an hour ago. We have managed to get a window seat which I know is going to be both a blessing and curse. It will provide a distraction from the Christmas party atmosphere in our carriage, due to the raucous family opposite, all dressed in loud Christmas jumpers and singing carols... badly, at the tops of their voices. However, the dramatic scenes of the snow blizzard outside will also fill us with horror.

I am busy unpacking the contents of my handbag onto the plastic table. Baxter is watching me from the table with what looks like an irritated expression. I get the feeling he liked his rucksack throne. My phone has disappeared. 'Felix, have you seen my mobile?'

He shakes his head and opens his rucksack. 'I'll check my bag.'

Anxiety makes my hands tremble as I check all the pockets of my handbag. I can't lose my phone. Nausea churns inside my tummy. All the pockets are empty. 'Oh, God, I've lost my phone, Felix.'

Baxter barks from his seat on top of the table as I stand up to check my coat and the seat. Felix looks at me with dismay. 'It's not in my bag either. Where did you last have it?'

Sitting back down and screwing up my face I try to remember last having my phone. 'Well, I sat and timed Tom taking Baxter out to the toilet earlier.'

Felix giggles. 'Why did you time them both?'

'Before our journey I didn't really get on with Baxter but over the last twenty-four hours I think we've bonded. Anyway, this morning Tom offered to take him outside for his morning poo. Can you believe I was so worried about tiny Baxter getting stuck in a snow drift I sat and timed Tom. If he was longer than ten minutes with Baxter I was going to go out and search for them.' Clamping my forehead, I let out a wail. 'I left my phone on Tom's coffee table. That's where it is.'

I can feel the train slowing down. Anxiety courses through my veins. We can't even see out of the window now as the snow is so bad. 'Why did I leave my phone in Leeds when the weather is dire, I won't be able to call anyone to tell them we are stuck. Lizzie and Bill will worry, and customers might be trying to contact me if their dress doesn't fit or hasn't arrived.'

'Rory will send it back,' sighs Felix. 'Don't worry, we have your iPad.'

The mention of Rory's name makes my heart flip a few times with delight. In a flash I am inundated by memories of Felix telling me how much help Rory had given him with his dance passion, Tom telling me all about the support he's given my business and Tom's admission Rory was struggling to date women because of me. I know what I said about us having to move on because Rory has, but I still love him. You wouldn't believe how much my love intensified for him when I saw those ballet shoes and the note. I wished we had seen him in Leeds.

Felix glances at me before taking out my iPad from his rucksack. 'We can message people from the iPad, and you can access your emails from it too.'

I stroke his hair. 'Felix, have I told you lately how fab I think you are?'

He chuckles and opens Facebook.

'What are you doing?' I whisper.

'Having a look at what Rory is up to.'

I try to take the iPad away from Felix but he's too quick. 'Give me that back. We're not going to torture ourselves anymore about Rory. He's moved on.'

Felix eyes narrow. 'Trust me, Emily, I know what I am doing.'

'You're nine years old and you shouldn't be on Facebook.'

He sighs. 'I have been on Facebook for years. Mum never knew about me going through her Facebook albums and secretly deleting all the embarrassing photos of me which she had uploaded. She didn't understand that the mums of my school friends were on Facebook too and used to show their children those photos of me dressed as an Easter chick and a garden gnome.' Vivi's choice of dressing-up outfits for Felix when he was young always made me smile. I watch him tap onto Beth's profile.

Placing my hands over my eyes I turn away. 'Please don't tell me what Rory and Beth have been up to. I don't want to know or see any romantic photos of them in matching Christmas jumpers sitting by a log fire.'

Felix gasps and I jump out of my skin. Removing my hands, I stare down at the iPad screen. Felix points to Beth's post which consists of a quote about how good it feels to be single again. We both scan the comments like hawks watching for small, furry prey.

'Their date ended in disaster,' says Felix, pointing to Beth's reply to one of her friends. He gasps for a second time. 'Look, Emily, Beth went out on her own last night which means she wasn't with Rory.'

I stare at the photo she's been tagged into. It is a photo of her and her girlfriends from last night all wearing minuscule Santa dresses and stilettos, and holding up champagne flutes. My heart breaks into a wild gallop. 'Rory and Beth's date ended in disaster.'

Felix punches the air above his head. 'I knew everything would be all right.'

'Well, if he's not with Beth – where is he?'

'Can I have a hot chocolate?' Felix tugs me on the arm.

The queue for the buffet carriage gives me a chance to gather my thoughts. Felix is guarding our seats, our belongings and Baxter.

With regard to Rory, so far I have managed to ascertain he has been on three dates but not slept with any of them – and in large part that seems to be because he keeps calling them by my name. Fireworks shoot across my chest in celebration. Through Facebook and Felix, I now know that Rory and Beth's date ended badly yesterday and by the sounds of it, things didn't go to plan. If Rory isn't with Beth – then where the hell is he?

Maybe he's gone to see his mum in the Caribbean? Although Tom would have mentioned something like that, and I sensed Tom had no idea where Rory was either. Perhaps he's gone to visit his dad who he doesn't talk about much? The one who lives with his wife in a travelling burger van. Rory hates burgers so I can't see that happening and he has never had a good word to say about his father.

The woman in front of me shakes her long, raven coloured hair and Anna's face appears in my mind. Perhaps he's gone to be with Anna? That must be it. He and Anna were so close in the weeks leading up to Vivi dying. I remember listening to Rory talking about the great time he had with Anna one evening over dinner. His face seemed to light up when he spoke about her. There were also all the shared memories they had from someone they both knew at university. Maybe Rory has realised he has feelings for Anna and has gone to tell her. My stomach gets ready to perform a nausea-inducing swan dive for the train carriage floor when I remember Felix's comment from yesterday about

Anna. I am sure Felix mentioned something about Rory and Anna only being friends. Why do all roads seem to lead to Felix?

I manage to carry Felix's hot chocolate, my latte and two Twix bars back to our seats without spilling anything.

'Yesterday you said something about Anna, Felix.'

Baxter has climbed onto Felix's lap and is being cuddled. Felix looks up at me and smiles. 'Yep.'

'Once again, Felix, I'm sensing you know more about Anna than I do.'

Stroking Baxter's velvety ears Felix shoots me a mischievous grin. 'Anna's mum was my ballet teacher. Rory's brother was taught by her too.'

'Rory has a brother?' My voice has a loud shrillness to it which makes the family opposite stop singing their dire version of Little Donkey and stare at me. Ignoring them I turn to Felix. 'I thought Rory was an only child. He's never mentioned a brother to me.'

Felix shrugs. 'He never told me either. I only know because my ballet teacher told me when I first joined her class.'

'Do you know his brother's name?'

'Lawrence, that's what she told me.'

Sitting back in my seat I let Baxter hop onto my lap for his second cuddling session of the journey. 'So, that's the link to Anna then.'

Felix nods. 'I was at ballet once and Anna turned up to see her mum. Rory told her mum that he and Anna were just friends and you were the one he loves.'

All this new information is overwhelming. I hungrily take a huge bite of a Twix. Vivi always swore that scoffing a Twix in stressful situations was one of the best things you could do to calm down. I recall looking inside Rory's drawer and seeing the photos of a young Rory holding the hand of a small, blond-haired boy. That must be his brother. Why did Rory not tell me about his brother?

'Maybe Rory's gone to visit his brother?'

Felix hands me the iPad. 'We should FaceTime your phone to see if Tom or, even better, Rory picks up.'

'Really?'

Felix nods. 'Even if Rory is not there we can see if Tom picks up. We need him to send it back to you.'

'I do need my phone.'

Felix touches on the FaceTime icon. 'Go on, do it.' He peers over my shoulder.

I wait for the FaceTime to connect with my phone all the way back in Leeds.

We both gasp as an attractive woman with curly, long brown hair answers.

Her perfectly sculptured eyebrows travel up her make-up clad forehead. 'Who the hell are you?' she snaps.

'Is Tom there?' My voice is crackly.

She lets out a heavy sigh and rolling her mascara-clad eyes. 'Tom – there's ANOTHER woman on FaceTime for you. I'm out of here. There's no chance of us getting back together.'

I can hear Tom in the background. 'Suzie, stop, you don't understand. That's not my phone. I have told you this.'

'Forget it,' she says, rising from the sofa. 'Too many women calling. It's like managing a dating hotline here. Goodbye, Tom.'

The door slams and Tom's groan drifts across the wifi airwaves.

Felix nudges me and whispers. 'Wasn't Suzie the woman of Tom's dreams?'

I nod and rub my aching chest. How I wished Rory had come home and had answered my phone instead.

'Tom's sad isn't he, Emily?'

I nod and let Felix rest his head against my shoulder. 'Suzie thought I was another of his girlfriends.'

'Did she think you were one of his four crosses on his chart?'

Placing my hands over his ears I make the 'shhhhh' sound. 'Let's not talk about that chart and those crosses.'

Felix removes my hands and smirks. 'Was it a chart to see who had kissed the most girls?'

'No,' I say, with a nervous laugh. In my head I say silently, 'If only it was just a kissing contest.'

Felix shakes his head. 'I didn't believe the afternoon tea bit. Why do adults try to trick children?'

'The crosses meant meeting up for afternoon tea.'

Felix rolls his eyes. 'It was a kissing contest. Rory was losing because he kept calling the girls he had to kiss your name.'

'Can we change the subject?'

Felix giggles, placing his hand over his mouth. 'Brett at school tried to kiss Amelie at school and she hit him.'

'Good for Amelie,' I murmur as a sense of dread engulfs me. At some point I am going to have to explain the birds and the bees to Felix. I remember Vivi coming to me to ask what the word sex meant as some boys had been laughing about it in lessons. It was terrifying for me back then at fourteen. In the end I marched her to our local library, sat her down at an empty table and urged her to read the book I was shoving in her direction. While she sat and stared in horror at the illustrated diagrams of people having sex, I ate a packet of cola bottles and prayed for a sudden earthquake. Perhaps that book is still in print?

CHAPTER 38

RORY

here's no sign of Emily and Felix inside Vivi's. The house is dark and locked up. I've come all this way and they're not here. Sadness engulfs me. My bruised forehead and face let out a series of depressing aches and painful twinges. Snowflakes stick to my face as I turn to look up and down the tree-lined street for sight of Emily and Felix trudging back through the snow. They could have nipped out for a pint of milk or some teabags. Something on the ground by the front door catches my eye. Bending down I can see a tiny Christmas tree sticking out of a white carrier bag. There's a note attached to the bag. In scrawly writing it reads: *Felix – happy Christmas, Amelie. Remember nine-and-a-half-year-olds can change the world.*

'They've not been back home since yesterday,' says an anxious voice, from over the fence, taking my attention away from the bag. 'You look familiar. Where have I seen you before?'

Turning around I see the owner of the voice. It's Vivi's neighbour. Well, she's Emily's neighbour now I guess. The one who used to complain about the noise of Vivi's parties. She's dressed in a hand-knitted purple cardigan, a blue blouse, a grey woollen calf-length skirt, thick tights, and brown leather shoes.

On the collar of her cardigan is an elegant brooch. Her pale blue eyes are inquisitive and are currently surveying every part of me. She reminds me of my old headmistress when I was in junior school, the one who used to patrol the playground and could spot a child being naughty within a hundred feet. She takes one look at the state of me and gasps. I must look something out of a horror movie.'

'I'm Rory, Emily's ex-boyfriend,' I say holding up my hands. 'You used to complain to Vivi, Emily's sister about the noise of her music.'

She nods. 'Yes, I remember you, Rory and the lovely bunch of flowers you bought me once after Vivi's party had gone on until three in the morning. You were so thoughtful. Have you had some sort of accident?'

'Yes. It's a long story and I will save you from the gory details.'

She smiles. 'I can see why Felix talks nonstop about you.'

I cast her a puzzled look.

'Felix always talks about you whenever I chat to him on his way home from school.'

A warm feeling floods through my veins.

She rubs her arms. 'Have you got time for a chat? I am very worried about Emily and Felix. You might be able to help.'

My heart breaks into a panic as I enter her living room. It's warm and meticulously tidy. There are two large bookcases covering two of the walls and an old dresser on the third. By the window there are two high-backed armchairs and a nest of small coffee tables.

She hands me a hot cup of tea five minutes later. I'm slumped in her armchair by the window praying for my head to stop throbbing. 'Drink this. You look like you should be resting. Have you come a long way?'

'Leeds.'

Her eyes widen with surprise. 'Well, that must have been quite a journey. I'm Miss Hemingway by the way. Now, I have been worried about Emily and Felix. They didn't mention to me last night they were going to be away overnight.'

Sickness and fear form an alliance in my gut. 'Where were they going?'

She takes a sip of her tea. 'This is what worries me. They were going to London to see the lights, but I know Felix was planning a secret trip of his own.'

'Maybe they stayed over in a hotel or something?'

I watch shadows race across Miss Hemingway's face. 'Felix told me the other day he was planning to carry out some secret mission in St Pancras station.'

'Oh, I see.'

The chink and nervous rattle of her cup make me sit up straighter.

'I should have said something to Emily. When they didn't come home last night I panicked.'

'I'm sure there's a simple explanation.'

Miss Hemingway puts down her cup. 'Rory, I shouldn't tell tales, but things have not been great next door.'

'What do you mean?'

She glances out of the window and turns back to me. 'Felix and Emily shout a lot at each other. Some days morning, noon, and night. The other week Felix told me...' Her voice trails off.

'Told you what?'

She stares at me with watery pink eyes. 'He wanted to run away.'

My heart starts to thump inside my chest. 'Really?'

She nods. 'He thought his Aunty Emily had made a mistake about looking after him.'

The hairs on my neck stand on end. 'Do you think he was planning to run away?'

Miss Hemingway nods. 'Yesterday I saw he had taken his little rucksack with him.'

Sweat beads have gathered on my forehead. 'I'm sure Felix

would not have done anything silly. He's quite switched on for his age.'

We both go silent and drink our tea. My mind is awash with thoughts about Emily and Felix. It was never going to be easy for Emily becoming Felix's main carer. As she said herself the day we split up, her life had been turned upside down. Overnight she had been thrust into the chaotic world of a grieving nine-year-old. In the space of a week, she'd moved out of Lizzie's flat and into Vivi's house. She thought Felix needed stability in the aftermath of his mum dying. Emily had also been to see to his schoolteachers to talk to them about what had happened, and she'd also managed to get Felix some weekly sessions with a child bereavement counsellor.

When Lawrence died, I was a mess, so I can relate to what Emily and Felix have been through. It can't have been easy for either of them trying to fill the giant-sized crater in their lives that Vivi left.

'Felix is a sensible kid,' I say, trying to reassure myself. 'His schoolteachers used to say he was one of the smartest kids they'd ever taught. I used to read his school reports pinned up on Vivi's kitchen wall.'

Miss Hemingway nods. 'You're right. I am sure they have decided to stay over in a nice London hotel or something. I need to stop being an old busybody.' She points the black TV controller at the screen. A newsreader is busy talking to the camera. As the volume is on mute, I can't hear what he's saying however the red banner at the bottom brings my heart to a shuddering halt. *Search for missing child in London St Pancras continues. Police appeal for information.*

My heart grinds to a halt. Felix. Please, God, not Felix.

Miss Hemingway gasps and then lets out a frightened wail.

Shooting to my feet I grab my phone and try to FaceTime Emily's number. For some reason it won't allow me to FaceTime so I am forced to call her. To my horror a muffled male voice answers and then... my phone dies. The thirty per cent battery charge from yesterday has finally run out. Who the hell was the male voice? Perhaps it was a police officer?

'Shit. I have to get to London.'

Miss Hemingway gets to her feet. 'Do you think Felix is the missing child?'

Glancing back at the TV screen I see the words, *'nine-year-old boy'* flash up. Sickness rushes up my throat. 'I've got to go.'

Charging out of Miss Hemingway's house I struggle through the snow with my sore legs which feel like jelly. Once down to the seafront, I frantically hail a cab.

CHAPTER 39

*P*lucking up courage, Felix taps Emily on the shoulder. 'Would you film this video for Mummy with me?'

She glances at the phone. 'Yes, of course – what, now, on the train?'

Nodding he holds up the phone between them and presses the record button. 'Mummy, it's me, and look, Emily has agreed to join us.'

'Hello, Vivi.' Emily waves and blows a kiss. Felix copies her.

'Mummy, Emily and I have been talking a lot and we've agreed to no more secrets. Haven't we?' He turns to Emily with an ear-to-ear smile.

Emily beams. 'Yes, we have, Felix. All secrets are banned.'

'Ronnie says his older brother who is at university has lots of secrets.'

Emily lets out a nervous laugh. 'I'm sure he doesn't, Felix.'

'Ronnie says when you get older you have lots of secrets.'

Patting Felix on the arm she grins at the camera. 'Let's not think about when you are older, Felix.'

'Can we still have secrets about birthday presents?'

With a wry smile Emily leans over and puts her chin on his

shoulder. 'As long as they don't involve running away, train journeys and my credit card. Oh, Vivi, when we get home, I am going to sort Felix out a new carpet.'

Felix giggles and puts his hand over his mouth. 'Mummy, Emily doesn't like your purple carpet either.'

'Vivi, I love you but your choice of carpet for Felix is questionable.'

'Mummy, Rory never came home so we are on our way back to Brighton.'

Hugging Felix, Emily presses her lips into his hair. 'We're okay, you and me, and that's what matters. Things are going to be different when we get home.'

Felix cups his hand and whispers, 'Shall I tell Mummy my secret?'

Emily smooths down his chaotic hair. 'Felix, tell her in your own time. There's no rush. I know how much it means to you. Anyway, she might be looking down on you so she may know already.'

'What's your funniest memory of Mummy, Emily?'

With a chuckle Emily secures a piece of her hair behind her ear. 'Vivi, I'm sorry about what I am going to say but the funniest memory has to be when you liked a lad from this farm. Felix, your mother must have been about sixteen, seventeen maybe and she had a crush on a young lad who worked on his family farm. She would make me drive her up to this farm on a Saturday so she could work alongside this lad. One Saturday she persuaded me to come with her and help muck out the pigs.' Emily starts to giggle. 'We were mucking out the pigs when this lad came past in a tractor. Your mum started waving frantically to him and in her excitement, she fell over backwards and landed in a huge pile of pig poo.' Felix erupts into hysterics.

'There was pig poo in her hair and on her jeans. I laughed so hard I couldn't breathe.'

He turns to the camera. 'That's funny, Mummy. You must have needed a bath.'

'No matter how many times she washed her hair she couldn't get the smell out.'

He looks up at Emily. 'Did the farm boy ask Mummy to be his girlfriend?'

Emily shakes her head. 'Sadly not, as your mum admitted she hated working on a farm because it ruined her glittery nails. Sorry, Vivi, you must be getting ready to fire lightning bolts at me now. It was very funny at the time.'

Felix holds up the camera to his face. 'Mummy, while we were eating breakfast Emily told me and Tom all about the time when you both had to live in a forest. It must have been very scary.' He rests his head back against Emily. 'Luckily you had Emily to look after you.'

Emily sighs and blinks away hot, stinging tears. 'It was a long time ago.'

'Did you watch *Bear Grylls* before you went to the forest?'

She shakes her head. 'No, Bear Grylls wasn't on TV back then. I used to read a lot of books about children having adventures when I was little.'

'You kept Mummy safe,' says Felix quietly. He looks up at her. 'Yesterday when I was on my own on the train and feeling scared, I thought about how you make me feel safe.'

Hugging him she kisses his head. 'I will always keep you safe.'

'Mummy, we're going to go now. Bye for now.'

'Bye, Vivi. Love you.' Emily blows her sister a kiss and Felix kisses the phone screen.

CHAPTER 40

EMILY

A red-haired woman wearing an eye-catching, elven green dress with silver bead embroidery walks down the carriage. I am drawn to its pleated skirt and the intricate floral bead design. My heart beats faster and I fight the urge to stop this woman and ask her who made her delightful dress. It is handmade and pieced together with remarkable precision.

Felix cuddles Baxter in his lap and taps me on the arm. 'How are things going to be different at home?'

A cloud of heavy sadness floats over me and chases away all my excitement over dressmaking. I can't continue with Forever Vintage when we get home. I got so obsessed with it that I neglected Felix. With a gulp I grip onto the table and try to resist a hot tidal wave of emotion building inside of me. I can still carry on making dresses but perhaps return to sewing in my spare time. Even though I got carried away with my business and ended up working day and night, the whole process gave me so much pleasure: sewing hems and diamond seams, giving sleeves their puff back, cutting up different fabrics, pinning garment shapes, listening to the steady whirr of my sewing machine, mending waist ties, belts, delicate lace wrap tops, and adding buttons, beaded bow pocket details and tiny ribbons. I even loved the planning stage, deciding how a dress was meant to look and what work was needed to restore it.

A memory of Vivi and me dressing up in our mother's old cocktail dresses comes back to me. Vivi would have a school disco to go to and we would go through a lengthy process of creating something fabulous for her. With our mother over at her lover's house we would climb deep into her vast wardrobe and take out the many cocktail dresses she'd stuffed at the back.

Before she met our father, she worked on the cruise ships as a jazz and cabaret singer. Her days were spent travelling the world on luxurious cruise ships and entertaining hundreds of passengers with her expressive smoky voice. Everything changed for her when she met Dad while singing and fell pregnant with me. Her singing days ended, and she found herself living in a two-bedroomed terraced house on the outskirts of Brighton, penniless, with two small children, a husband who had left her to find himself in India and little hope of ever returning to her glitzy cruise days.

Her old evening dresses used to render me speechless when we dragged them out into the light. Vivi used to say I would slip into a trance as we would parade around in beautiful, fancy dresses. Once Vivi had decided which dress she wanted to use for her disco outfit I would get to work with my old sewing machine which the old lady down the street had given me after I'd told her about my love of making dresses. She also gave me a few lessons in return for me sweeping up the leaves in her garden.

Vivi's requests for my custom-designed dresses continued into her adult life. When Felix was two Vivi started dating a museum curator called John who was fascinated by the 1940s. His obsession with the era resulted in him wearing 1940s double-breasted jackets, wide trousers, waistcoats and white shirts rolled up at the elbows. Vivi fell in love with the era too and everything she ordered had padded shoulders, puffed sleeves, nipped-in high waists and A line skirts.

My mind finds a memory of Rory taking me out for dinner on our fourth date and encouraging me to talk about my business idea for Forever Vintage. It was the first time I felt a man was interested in me as a person.

It's time to return to normality and back to a marketing job which is confined only to a laptop and strict office hours. It's time to give Felix the life he deserves. When I get home, I'll finish any outstanding dress orders in the kitchen, close my online site and bring back Vivi's violet living room.

Taking Felix's hand, I give it a squeeze. 'Completely different.'

He returns the squeeze. 'It will be nice to have a normal living room. Where will you do your dressmaking?'

'I'm going to close my business.'

His hazel eyes grow wide, and he gasps. 'But you love making dresses.'

Stroking his face, I smile. 'I do but it takes over my life and the house, and stops me caring for you.'

'Mummy loved your dresses,' he says, gazing out at the snow-coated world outside the window. 'She'll be sad to hear you're stopping making dresses.'

'It's for the best, Felix.'

He shakes his head. 'If you don't sew you get grumpy.' After a pause he grins. 'If I don't dance, I get grumpy too.'

'I can't believe that's what all the banging upstairs was – you practising your dancing. I used to think you were throwing things.'

Felix laughs and then his smile disappears. 'I don't want you to get sad, Emily. Our house needs to be a happy one.'

Throwing my arms around him I pull him close and nearly squash poor Baxter who yelps. A stray tear begins its solitary journey down my cheek as Baxter crawls up onto the table and shakes himself back into shape. Deciding to shut my business feels like a part of me is dying. 'I promise it will be a happy house.'

Felix picks up my iPad. 'I need to send my friends a message to tell them about my plan.'

'You should invite them over after Christmas,' I say, remembering how teenage Vivi used to fill our tiny house with all her friends. I would be instructed to make a lot of party food, so I spent most of my time in the kitchen cooking endless pizzas.

Felix turns to me. 'I would like that, Emily.'

I gently squeeze his arm. 'We'll make sure they have somewhere to sit in the living room.'

Hearing him laugh lights me up inside. I watch him tap out a message to Amelie, Ronnie, and Sai.

I lean back in my seat, stroke a sleeping Baxter, and reflect on the last twenty-four hours. This trip to Leeds has changed my relationship with Felix. I will return to Vivi's house a different person to the one who left yesterday. 'Felix, even though I was very cross yesterday I'm glad you went through with your plan.'

He nods. 'Me too. Mummy always said I had good ideas.'

'I feel like we're closer now.'

'The old Emily is back with me.'

He's said that phrase a few times over the last twenty-four hours. 'What do you mean by the old Emily?'

'Before we went to Leeds you were different. Now, you are acting like the old Emily who came over to take me to the park or the arcades.'

The raucous family opposite us have stopped singing. They are silent and engrossed with their phones. The wife and mother notices me staring at her. She raises her phone. 'Have you seen the news?'

'No – why?' Panic floods through me. Whatever she is going to tell me must be connected to the snow.

'A little kid has gone missing in London. Can you believe he's still missing on Christmas Eve?'

Felix sits up and fires up my iPad.

'Where did he go missing?'

The woman shakes her head. 'They reckon he ran away from his parents in St Pancras station yesterday.'

I recall the emotional couple with the police officers yesterday.

'Although the press is saying he might have been snatched.'

Felix is avoiding my glare. He's busy bringing up the BBC News online page on my iPad. Leaning closer to him I whisper, 'I know another boy who ran away yesterday in London St Pancras – don't I?'

He carries on staring at the iPad screen. 'I felt bad, so I phoned you.'

'It could have been you, Felix. Those poor parents must be beside themselves.'

Felix points to the photo of the missing boy. 'He's called Jack and is the same age as me.'

My eyes take in the photo of the little lad, wearing a yellow bobble hat and grinning mischievously at the camera. That could have been Felix. My heart thumps away inside my rib cage. Even though he ran away at St Pancras station, got on a train to Leeds using my credit card and made me feel sick with worry, I love him so much.

CHAPTER 41

RORY

The taxi driver dropped me at Brighton station five minutes ago. He spent the entire journey moaning about the lack of gritters, the amount of snow on the roads and the treacherous conditions for taxi drivers. I spent the entire time gripping onto the seat in the back and firing off several silent prayers about Felix being found safe and well.

I'm sprinting through Brighton station, clutching my throbbing forehead and a ticket to London. Emily must be so distraught. She'll be blaming herself. Bloody hell, Felix, why did you run away? I let Emily down once before, I am not going to do it again. She needs me by her side.

There's a train ready to depart on platform four. Dashing onto the platform I smile at the female guard in the hope she'll take pity on me and let me onto the train. To my relief she does, and I leap on board.

The train is packed, which is a surprise given that the snow is getting worse and it's Christmas Eve. As I make my way through the carriages the only seating option is a window seat opposite a young woman and her son.

After sliding into my seat, I take out my phone and silently curse it for running out of battery on me. I need to speak to Emily. I want to tell her I am on my way and reassure her that Felix will be found. He's probably tried to recreate *Home Alone 2* where the kid gets the wrong plane and ends up in New York by himself at Christmas. Felix is probably seeing the sights of London and having a whale of a time. We both sat and watched it last Christmas while Vivi and Emily were giggling over a bottle of wine in the kitchen. Felix thought it was a cool film and afterwards we talked about what we'd both do if we found ourselves stuck in New York at Christmas.

I remind myself he's been missing for over twenty-four hours and an uneasy feeling passes over me. Where the hell would he have slept last night? My bowels loosen with fear. Please God, can Felix be found safe and well?

The train has left Brighton station. It's crawling and not going as fast as I would like it to. For some reason, the woman opposite me is making an odd facial expression at me. She's yanked her dark eyebrows all the way up her forehead and keeps tilting her head in the direction of her son. I think she's mouthing something at me. What the hell is she trying to communicate to me? Maybe it's my bruised forehead? It did look ghastly when I peered into the bathroom mirror in the Travelodge early this morning.

Ignoring her I gaze out of the train window.

The woman coughs and catches my attention. Once again, the woman's eyebrows travel up her forehead, she does the same tilting gesture and she's mouthing the word HIM. I let out a heavy sigh and catch sight of her son who has one eye shut and the other eye is sneakily looking at his mother. He reminds me of Lawrence who used to pretend to be asleep to avoid being asked to do household chores. Maybe I should pretend to be asleep too?

Seeing me return my attention to the window makes the woman let out what can only be described as a little squeak of frustration. I cast her a puzzled look followed by a shrug.

Her jade-green eyes perform a dramatic roll, she exhales loudly and folds her arms across her chest. I'm clearly missing something.

To my horror she starts to squeak at me and as I lower my eyes, I see that her right hand is pointing at her son.

I don't want to give the boy's game away. 'He's asleep,' I whisper back to her which causes her to squeak even louder and shuffle about on her seat.

'Are you in pain?' I whisper, which causes her face to go from beige to an angry raspberry in a few seconds. More squeaking follows.

Again, she starts pointing at her sleeping son.

'Is he sick?'

She shakes her head in bewilderment. 'THE BOY,' she mouths to me.

The boy? Is she referring to her son? 'Is he your boy?'

Her squeak is getting louder, and her eyes are narrowing. 'MISSING BOY,' she mouths.

'Where?' I say, looking up and down the train aisle.

I can hear her muttering things about me under her breath. She points again to the sleeping boy beside her. His yellow bobble hat has been pulled down over his face and he's curled himself up beside her. The sight makes me think of Felix. 'IS HE THE MISSING BOY?' she mouths.

'I thought he was your son?'

She lets out what can only be described as a frustrated wail. 'HE IS NOT MY SON.'

'Oh, I see.'

My response makes her cast me a deadpan expression.

Hang on, Felix is supposed to be the missing boy. 'I think my girlfriend's nephew is the missing boy.'

She lets out a heavy sigh at me. 'HE LOOKS LIKE THE MISSING BOY.' I watch her take out her phone. After tapping something into it she lets out another wail of frustration. 'No bloody signal,' she hisses. 'Do you have a phone?'

I hold it up. 'Out of battery.'

The woman plunges her face into her hands and mutters more things under her breath.

It's a long anxious wait before her phone has signal again. Luckily for us the boy now looks like he's fallen asleep.

Her face lights up as she taps something into her phone. 'LOOK,' she mouths and points at the photo of the missing boy. 'THAT'S HIM.'

A huge wave of relief crashes over me as I scan the news article and see that it's not Felix who ran away at St Pancras station, but another nine-year-old boy called Jack. The woman is right as the sleeping boy does have the same yellow bobble hat as the lad in the photo and she claims he has luminous yellow laces on his boots which the article refers to when describing him.

'Do you think we should call someone?' she whispers.

I nod. His poor parents must be distraught.

The woman carefully gets up from the seat. 'I am going to phone someone. Keep him here,' she whispers.

I watch her walk away and to my surprise the boy opens both eyes. Sitting bolt upright he casts me a frightened look. 'Where is she going?'

'It's all right, don't look so worried.' His face is ashen white and eyes are small.

He lifts his bobble hat. 'Have you been in a fight?'

I shake my head. 'I had an accident.'

As the boy studies my head I recognise him from the photo. 'Does it hurt?'

'It aches a bit.'

The boy nods and looks out of the window. 'I don't want to go home.'

'Why not?'

I watch him cover his face with his hands. 'My grandpa is sick in hospital. I don't want him to die.' His voice is thick with emotion. I watch tears roll down his pink cheeks.

'Is that why you ran away?'

He nods, still behind his hands. 'I tried to visit him in hospital but I got scared the nurses might call my mum. He's going to die and I will miss him.'

Lawrence's face is in my mind. The urge to do something new in my life and speak about Lawrence is strong. The old man in the graveyard was right. When grief has showed up at my door, I have tried to suppress my memories and thoughts about Lawrence. I remember the warm feeling I experienced in the graveyard after the old man explained Lawrence still lives on inside of me.

This little lad needs my help. 'My little brother died.'

The boy removes his hands from his face. His cheeks are damp, and his eyes are pink. 'Really?'

I nod. 'Do you want to know something amazing?'

'What?' he says.

I touch my heart. 'When people you love die, they still live on inside of you.'

The boy's dark eyes widen.

'My little brother is in here.' I point to my chest. 'He's a part of me.'

'But I won't be able to talk to Grandpa anymore.'

I smile at him. 'Yes, you will. You just talk to him inside your head.'

The boy stares at me. 'Did you get sad about your brother?'

'I did get sad and the biggest mistake I made was not talking about my sadness.'

We look at each and I spot the faint outline of a smile on his face. 'Grandpa will always be with me,' he murmurs.

'Always. I promise.'

CHAPTER 42

EMILY

*T*he train has been delayed for over an hour and a half due to the snow. We've been diverted a few times and are finally now going in the right direction and coming into London. It's been six hours since we boarded the train in Leeds. The threat of Baxter doing a wee on the table again is worrying Felix and me but there's nothing we can do.

I've just returned from a trip to the buffet carriage. Felix is busy drinking a can of lemonade, unwrapping a sandwich, and feeding Baxter. I have a coffee and a ham and cheese toastie. The family opposite must have burst into song while I was gone as the carriage is filled with their loud version of 'Away in a Manger'. As I take a bite out of my toastie the woman stops singing and reaches over to tap me on the arm. 'They've found the missing boy, he's safe and well.'

Both Felix and I let out a cheer of delight at her news. 'Where was he found?'

The woman casts us an ear-to-ear smile. 'A couple found him on a train.'

'That's so good to hear,' I find myself gushing and pulling Felix into an unexpected hug.

The woman goes back to her singing and Felix brings up a photo of Vivi on my iPad. She's stood in her kitchen modelling one of my restored dresses; it was a second-hand embroidered powder-blue dress adorned with tiny pink flowers and bows. 'You can't give up your dressmaking,' he says, pointing at Vivi. 'Mum would not be pleased. She always talked about you starting your own dress company.' A ball of warmth and tingles travels up my spine. I can't believe Felix is now trying to persuade me to change my mind.

'But it makes such a mess, and it covers up your Mum's living room.'

Felix carries on talking about the day the photo was taken as Vivi had been to the school's summer fete in that dress and all the other school mums kept telling her how fancy she looked. Felix said he was very embarrassed but thought his mum looked pretty.

In my head my words, *'it covers up your Mum's living room,'* are being replayed back to me. My dressmaking did cover up Vivi's living room. It exploded the day I decided to start my own fashion business, six days after she'd died, and I had become Felix's guardian. In a matter of days there were dresses hanging on the walls, fabric laid out on the dinner table, patterns and books scattered over Vivi's rug, and sewing boxes on the sofas. I remember looking around the living room a few weeks later and experiencing a moment of relief as when I surveyed the room, I no longer thought of Vivi. Restoring old dresses and making my own dresses was all I wanted to think about. The more mess I created with my business the less I thought of Vivi.

Had I intentionally turned the house into a scene from a dressmaking disaster movie to help block out painful memories?

A WhatsApp video call is coming through on my iPad. It's Lizzie. In a few seconds we can see her silky black bobbed hair. She's without make-up which is unusual, and purple circles are looping around her eyes. 'Where the hell have you two been?' she barks, making Felix turn down the volume so no one else on the train has to listen to our call. 'Bill and I have been frantic all morning. Every time I called your mobile I either got some strange woman asking me who the hell I was or an emotional guy who shouted at me for making his ex-girlfriend think I was his bit on the side.'

'That's Tom,' I say, 'Rory's flatmate. I left my phone on his coffee table.'

'Oh, God, that's one of my worst nightmares, leaving my phone in another part of the country and even worse the home of an ex-boyfriend,' says Lizzie, making a frightened face.

'Thanks,' I say, with an air of sarcasm which makes her giggle. 'What's Tom's problem?'

Felix grins. 'Tom only had four crosses on his kissing chart.'

Bill wanders behind Lizzie and waves at us. His curly brown hair looks like he's been plugged into the electricity mains overnight. The trouble with Bill is that sometimes his mouth works faster than his brain. 'Kissing chart – I thought it was a sleeping...'

One of the many things I love about Lizzie is that she's quick to react to Bill. Before I can raise my hands to remind Bill to watch what he's about to say in front of a nine-year-old, Lizzie has grabbed a cushion and put it in Bill's face which muffles what he is about to say. She turns to a chuckling Felix. 'A sleep-over challenge. Bill was trying to tell you that before I rudely shoved a cushion in his face.'

Felix looks up at me. 'I thought you said it was a kissing challenge.'

Lizzie seizes the moment. 'Well, it's a quick kiss challenge before they go to separate bedrooms when they stay over at each other's houses.'

Felix scratches his head. 'So, Rory has had three sleepovers but called the women by your name, Emily, before they all went to bed?'

'In separate bedrooms,' adds Lizzie. 'At separate ends of the house. In their own pyjamas.'

I nod and pray for a change of conversation while Bill is trying not to laugh.

Felix gets bored and turns to Lizzie. 'Emily's going to give up her dressmaking.'

In unison both Lizzie and Bill shout, 'NO.'

Lizzie grabs the screen and glares at me, her face close to the camera. 'DO NOT GIVE IT UP.'

Bill peers over Lizzie's shoulder. 'I think you should broaden your range and go into men and women's sleepover nightwear.' He winks before Lizzie pushes him away.

'Ems, what's made you think about giving up your business?' shouts Bill.

I let out a heavy sigh. 'The house is always in chaos. Felix hasn't got a normal living room.'

'There is the other bedroom,' Felix says. 'With all your boxes of stuff from your flat.'

Lizzie claps in agreement. 'Exactly, Felix, there is another room.'

'I haven't been inside those boxes for months.'

He looks up at me. 'Mummy used to throw out my toys if she hadn't seen me play with them for six months.' I watch him scratch his head and I can't help thinking about how he's been scratching a lot in the last twenty-four hours. The last thing I need right now is head lice.

'She claimed it was every six months but some of my toys went missing a few weeks after I had got them for Christmas. Remember when you bought me that toy trumpet? That vanished.'

A smile spreads across my face as I recall getting bombarded with texts from Vivi after I had given Felix a huge toy trumpet for Christmas. She jokingly claimed I was an evil sister, and she even recorded the dreadful sound a young Felix was making as he marched around with his trumpet.

'Anyway,' says Felix, 'Mummy said if you hadn't played with something for six months then it was time for that toy to move on to someone else. You haven't touched all those boxes so maybe it's time for someone else to use your stuff.'

I think about the small room upstairs.

Lizzie shouts with glee. 'Felix – brilliant idea. Ems, sort out the room and move your business in there. You can't close Forever Vintage as I won't have the world's best dating conversation starter.'

'Which is?'

She pouts at the camera. 'Did you know I am a model in my spare time?'

'Emily,' says Felix. 'I know you said I wasn't to look inside the boxes...'

In the last twenty-four hours it has become really clear to me that nothing is sacred with Felix. 'But you decided to look anyway?'

He nods and Lizzie giggles.

'Yes. Every single one. It's a shame all that brand new kitchen stuff including the cool toaster are not being used.'

'I bought the new stuff because before your Mummy died, I was thinking about getting a flat with Rory.'

Before Anna appeared in our life, Rory and I had talked about renting a place together. We had looked at a few flats to rent but didn't like any of them and I was still unsure about whether I wanted to move out of Lizzie's place. That didn't stop Rory and me going to IKEA one Sunday, getting excited and buying a lot of house stuff.

Lizzie laughs. 'You kept saying you were not sure, Ems, but kept coming home with more stuff.'

Rory's face appears in my mind and my heart aches. 'I wonder where he is.'

Bill is engrossed at something on his phone behind Lizzie and suddenly lets out a shriek. 'Rory is on the news.'

'What?' Both Felix and I gasp.

Bill shoves his phone in front of Lizzie. I watch her mouth fall open in shock.

'Tell us, please,' pleads Felix.

Lizzie looks up with wide eyes and an odd trance-like expression. Bill talks for her. 'You know a couple found that missing boy on a train this morning?'

I nod.

'Well, he's the bloke. Check out his new girlfriend.' Bill snatches the phone away from Lizzie and holds it up at the camera. There on the BBC online news page is a video of Rory and a woman with short, black hair talking to the camera about how they found the missing boy.

Before I have a chance to watch the video the train manager informs the passengers that we are arriving at London King's Cross.

CHAPTER 43

RORY

'We're NOT a couple,' I snap at the journalist, who is talking fast to someone on his mobile phone about his possible story of the year. When I bought the train ticket, I didn't realise I would be sitting in front of a career hungry and determined young journalist.

The journalist bats my hand away. 'Picture this, Graham. It's Christmas Eve and across the United Kingdom people have been anxiously sat on the edge of their sofa waiting for news on the whereabouts of the missing young boy. Everyone will sit down tonight to wrap presents and at the same time watch the news where I interview the couple, who were on their way to a romantic date in London, about how they found the missing boy on Christmas Eve, alone and scared on a train. Once I have talked to them, I will then interview the parents and the boy. Viewers will want to hear how he'd slept in a bus stop overnight and a homeless man lent him his sleeping bag. It will be heartfelt and magical.'

The woman opposite me growls at the journalist.

'I'll ask them... hang on.' He grins at both of us. 'Can I count you both in for the interview?'

Before I have time to tell the journalist that I don't want to take part in an interview, Jack's sobs fill the carriage. He's talking to a police officer who boarded the train at Gatwick a few seats up towards the carriage door. 'I don't want to go without Rory,' Jack wails before pushing past the police officer and charging down the aisle to where I am sat.

'Please stay with me, Rory,' sobs Jack, standing before me by the window seat table. 'I don't want to go with them.' He points to the Transport Police stood in the train carriage door. Rubbing my face, I close my eyes and wish Emily and Felix had been in Brighton when I knocked on Vivi's door. As Felix wasn't the missing boy, I am still not closer to finding them both. They've obviously stayed over in London after enjoying the sights. The memory of the emotional male voice answering Emily's phone comes back to me. Who the hell was that? Maybe she has got a boyfriend? A wave of sadness rises inside me. I'm too late. They must have met up with her boyfriend in London.

I take Jack's hand and give it a gentle squeeze.

The journalist ends his call. He gets up and lets Jack sit next to me. 'This is going to make such a good interview.'

Irritation and frustration at the journalist join forces inside of me. I don't want to take part in his interview and if he refers to me and the woman opposite me being part of a couple again, I will struggle not to lamp him.

A female police officer strides down the aisle and hands Jack a phone. 'It's your mum on the phone.'

Jack shakes his head and bats the phone away.

I lean over and take the phone from the police officer. 'Jack, come on and talk to your mum. She's been very worried about you.'

He hides his tear-stained face in my arm. 'She'll tell me off for running away and causing all this mess.'

I let out a heavy sigh. 'Yes, Jack, she will probably shout but she'll also be terribly upset. Come on, be a good lad and talk to her.'

The journalist has taken out his phone and is busy tapping away into it. 'Just making some notes.' He looks up and smiles at the woman still sat opposite us. 'Your boyfriend is such a hero.'

I made the decision to follow Jack and the two Transport Police officers to London Bridge station and watch him reunite with his parents.

Jack is in the middle of a tearful group of his relatives and friends who are all over the moon to have him back safe and well. He's currently being kissed, hugged, and cried over. It's a great sight to see and I'm so relieved he's back with his family. The look on his face when I told him I would accompany him to London Bridge to see his mum and dad was priceless and something I will always treasure. Everyone has thanked me for talking to Jack and I even got a tearful hug from his father.

London Bridge is busy and is buzzing with commuters and Christmas shoppers. Out of the corner of my eye I can see a couple, who have clearly been separated until Christmas and are reuniting, running into each other's arms. My heart aches as I would give anything to spot Emily and Felix alighting from the underground and I picture myself running towards them, arms outstretched, with a goofy happy smile plastered across my face.

I am stood with the woman who was sat opposite me and alerted the police about Jack. Her arms are folded tightly across her chest and her lips are clamped shut. I'm sensing she doesn't want to be interviewed either. The journalist is busy chatting to a sweaty-faced camera man who has just turned up. I don't want to be here much longer. There's no point in returning to Brighton as Emily is probably enjoying herself in London with Felix and the man who answered her phone. Stuffing my hands into my pockets I rock back and forth on the balls of my feet. My fingertips find the gold locket and disappointment overwhelms me. Damn – I forgot to post her locket through her door. I have come all this way to deliver the locket and now it's still in my pocket.

'Right,' says the journalist, 'let's get this interview started.'

The man with the camera points it at us while the journalist gestures for us to stand closer together.

'Ready,' says the man with camera as a few London Bridge commuters stop and watch the interview.

The journalist flashes us a sickly sweet smile. 'I'm stood with the couple who found missing Jack Gardener on the train from Brighton to London this morning.'

Before the journalist has a chance to say another word, I tap him on the shoulder. 'We're not a couple.'

The woman lets out a loud sigh. 'We have told you a hundred times – he and I are not together.'

Ignoring us, the journalist beams at the camera. 'This is the good news story we all want to hear on Christmas Eve. A missing nine-year-old boy is found safe and well on a train by this couple, Rory Wilkinson, and Zoe Frederick. Tell us what it was like to find young Jack?'

Zoe opens her mouth, but I am quicker. 'Jack was asleep on the seat next to us when we boarded. Can I just say that Zoe and I are *not* a couple?'

Zoe pushes me aside and looks directly at the camera. 'I was the one who noticed Jack first. It was me who contacted the police, not this man, who didn't have a clue what I was talking about when I clocked it was the missing boy,' she says, pointing at me.

Irritation at this situation prickles up my neck. 'I couldn't hear what you were saying.'

She rolls her eyes and looks away.

The journalist switches his attention to me. Out of the corner of my eye I notice the group of commuters now stood watching the interview has grown larger.

'Jack told me you helped him on the train. Jack ran away because he was upset about his dying grandfather. Apparently, you spoke to him about your experiences with grief.'

To say I am stunned at what this journalist has just said is an understatement. I've gone from not talking about Lawrence for nearly ten years to potentially talking about him on the news in twenty-four hours. All I can do is nod.

The journalist gestures for Jack to come over. Jack rushes over dragging his mum by the hand.

'Jack, are you pleased to be back?' The camera points to Jack who is still wearing his yellow bobble hat.

Jack gazes up at his mum, who smiles. 'Yes, I am.'

'Can you tell the people at home how Rory helped you on the train?'

Jack smiles. 'Rory told me Grandpa will live on inside of me when he dies. That makes me happy.'

Everyone around us breaks into a round of applause and Jack's mum bursts into tears.

The journalist senses he's creating the most emotional and heartfelt news interview of his career and turns quickly back to me. 'Rory, Jack tells me your younger brother died and you believe he's living on inside of you.'

The face of the old man from the graveyard appears in my mind. 'I can't take the credit for it. I met a gentleman this morning who told me loved ones who die live on inside of us. This morning I needed to hear it and I am glad I got the chance to pass it on to Jack.'

I watch the journalist nod and turn to interview Jack's parents. Now is my time to escape. Turning on my heel I am stopped by Jack. 'Merry Christmas, Rory.'

'Happy Christmas, Jack. Remember what I said about your grandpa and no more running away.'

He grins. 'Mum says I am not allowed to go near St Pancras station for the rest of my life, although I did lose my favourite yellow scarf there so we might have to return.'

'You lost your scarf in St Pancras station?'

Jack nods. 'My grandpa bought it for me last year.'

I detect the tinge of sadness in his voice.

'Didn't the police have it?'

He shakes his head. 'No, Mummy never told them about my scarf as I was wearing it under my coat. It doesn't matter now.'

'Why did you take it off?'

Jack shrugs. 'I was hot, and I was hiding from Mum. I shouldn't have tied it to one of the seats.'

'You tied it to a seat?'

He nods. 'Near one of the pianos. Grandpa won't be happy.'

CHAPTER 44

RORY

*A*s I walk away from the group of Jack's relatives and friends, the journalist, Zoe and the audience of Christmas commuters I turn around to see Jack watching me go. From a distance he looks like Felix, and he makes me act the way I would with Felix. I just want to see them both smile. I'd also walk to the ends of the earth for both boys. As I get to the ticket machines, I know what I must do, go to St Pancras, and see if Jack's yellow scarf has been handed in to Lost Property.

I wait for the Northern Line tube and find myself distracted by a man and his little son. They're sat on the plastic seat talking and pointing at things on the adverts covering the underground walls. It reminds me of when Felix and I got the bus to the ballet school. We'd be on the bus, him by the window and me next to him, and we'd talk and point at things outside the window for the entire journey. One thing I never got tired of was chatting to Felix. A woman appears and she heads straight for the man and his son. They both look up, delighted to see her. She sits beside the man and kisses him on the cheek while ruffling the boy's hair. My heart aches for both Emily and Felix. I want to be with them. I want to find them. I want to tell them I love them. Wow – I've never had such a powerful urge before. They've always been a part of me. No matter how many women I have chatted up and kissed in bars Emily has always been on my mind. She's the only woman I want to spend the rest of my life waking up to and Felix is like the son I would have wanted.

St Pancras station is heaving. Lifting my eyes up to the departure screen I see that nearly all the departures are either cancelled or delayed due to the snow. I hope Emily and Felix are safe and well.

I need to find the Lost Property office and track down Jack's scarf. Judging by how busy this huge station is I think finding Jack's scarf is going to be like finding a needle in a haystack. When I get there, the woman on the information desk explains to me that I must fill in an online form about the lost item and it can take several days or even weeks for them to track the item down if it's been handed in. My heart sinks. There's no way I am going to get Jack's scarf back and the chances of it being handed in are slim.

Perhaps I could find the two public pianos and see if there's a yellow scarf tied to a seat nearby. I know they're located in the main arcade of shops as Emily and I once listened to one of the piano players back when we first started dating. We'd been to an event in London and somehow ended up in St Pancras. While she stood and listened to the man who played I remember taking the opportunity to watch her fiddle with her earring, twirl a strand of hair around her finger and gently sway to the music. I loved everything about her.

As I head for the arcade I am distracted by the sight of a man and a woman running across the station towards each other at speed, dodging queues of festive commuters staring gloomily up at the departure screens, runaway toddlers making a bid for freedom and navigating the busy station floor festooned with piles of orphaned luggage and sleeping travellers. Open-armed and goofy happy they launch themselves at each other. Their tearful reunion looks like something from one of those romantic films Emily used to make me watch.

How I wish Emily and Felix had been in Brighton this morning. What I do know is that my journey is no longer about simply handing over the locket. It's become much more than that. Emily and Felix are my family. I know that now. My days of partying and drinking as a single man are over. Somehow, I need to come up with a plan to get them back.

The first piano at one end of the arcade has no nearby seating. My heart sinks as I look around to see whether a yellow scarf has been kicked into a corner or is laid out somewhere prominent for its owner to find. As I turn away, I spot a familiar face at the piano. It's Michael from the train. He nods at me, and I find myself heading over to listen to him play. He's playing a beautiful and captivating version of Greensleeves. Everyone around him has stopped what they're doing and is standing listening to him. Once the song he's playing comes to an end he gestures for me to come closer. 'Rory? We saw you lying on the floor on the station. Are you alright?'

'I'm fine. A bit of concussion and some embarrassment for colliding with a ticket barrier.'

Michael grins. 'You looked like you were auditioning for a TV hospital drama.'

I point to the piano. 'Is this your celebration?

He nods and replaces his sheet of music. 'My sister died of Non-Hodgkin's Lymphoma the year after I'd met Alfie. She was a pianist too and played like a dream. It was Lilly, my sister, who taught me how to play. This is my way of celebrating her and keeping the memory of her alive. She was very special to me.'

I watch him prepare for the next song. Listening to him makes me think about how Lawrence and Vivi were very special to Emily and me. When I find Emily, I think I will suggest we do something to keep their memory alive.

I listen to his second song and look around for Alfie. With a wave to Michael I make my way across the arcade to the second public piano. As I get nearer and can hear the notes of the piano filling the air, I overhear snippets from a grandfather's conversation with his two little grandchildren. 'Magical things always happen at St Pancras, children.'

The only magic I need right now is to find Jack's scarf and meet Emily and Felix.

As I get closer, I can see a small group of shoppers stood around the piano. Alfie is playing, and is wearing a yellow scarf. No, that can't be Jack's scarf – can it?

Soon I am stood at the side of him. He looks up at me and smiles. Once he's finished his beautiful version of 'Amazing Grace', he turns to me. 'Hey, Rory, that's some head wound you got there. You okay, mate?'

'I'm fine. Some idiot pushed me and I got extra close to a station ticket barrier.'

Alfie smiles. 'That's a lovely bruised look for your Christmas photos.'

I nod and pat him on the shoulder. 'I've just seen Michael – is this your celebration too?'

He nods. 'My dad played the piano and when he died after I'd got married, I was broken. He loved Christmas and spent it sat at the family piano playing carols and festive songs.'

'So, you two come here every Christmas and play the pianos?'

Alfie nods. 'This is how Michael and I keep the link to our loved ones alive. It's important to do that when you lose someone. I do feel like he's with me and if he could speak, he would give me feedback on my crappy performance.' He laughs. 'Also, this station is magical. I hope you won't forget that, Rory.'

I stare at the yellow scarf wrapped around his neck. It's Jack's. 'Can I be rude and ask you where you got that scarf?'

He peers down and touches it. 'Found it tied to a seat.'

'That scarf – I know who it belongs to.'

'Who?'

'Jack, the missing kid, the one I helped on the train.'

Alfie's face lights up. 'Was that you who helped the little lad?'

'Yes, it has given me a new perspective. Look, can I have the scarf as I want to give it back to Jack and make him happy. His grandpa is dying and he's the one who bought him the scarf. I want to make someone happy this Christmas and the kid has been through a lot.'

Fiddling with it Alfie asks, 'Did you see your ex-girlfriend?'

I shake my head. 'She wasn't at home, but I have decided to try and win her back, no matter what it takes. Now, I need to make Jack happy again.'

He smiles at me and then removes the little scarf. 'Happy Christmas, Rory.'

CHAPTER 45

EMILY

*A*bove our heads the train announcer is apologising for the cancellation of another train due to the snow, which is flooding me with anxiety. We're not even at the right station. Felix wanted to go to St Pancras station one last time. I was too weary and upset about Rory to put up a fight.

If trains are being cancelled here due to the snow, they will be almost certainly cancelled for Brighton. My stomach starts feeling queasy again. Felix and I might be stuck in London for Christmas Eve. All the hotels – the ones we can afford, at least – will be booked up and we'll end up having to sleep on a bench in a station. What a mess!

There hasn't been a chance to watch the interview with Rory and his new girlfriend as Felix had to put the iPad away when the train got into Kings Cross. I don't want to watch it. Over the past twenty-four hours it feels like my broken heart has been stitched, unstitched, stitched again, and finally ripped apart by the interview clip. I don't think my heart's fabric can withstand any more damage.

Surrounding Felix, Baxter and I are groups of agitated Christmas travellers staring up at the departure screens with

LUCY MITCHELL

devastated expressions. The air is full of unhappy children crying, anxious conversations about whether the trains will be back in action later when the snow has been cleared, heated discussions with train personnel and mobile phones ringing out festive tunes which no one wants to listen to right now.

'Felix, we've seen enough now, come on, let's head for the underground.'

He casts me a look of desperation. 'Please can we stay here a bit longer?'

'Why?'

I watch him sit down on a plastic seat and place Baxter on the floor. 'Rory might be here.'

Sinking down into the seat beside him I blink away stinging tears. 'Rory's with his new girlfriend.'

Felix shakes his head and starts to rummage in his rucksack.

'Don't take the iPad out here, Felix.'

Felix ignores me and turns the iPad screen to face us. My heart sinks. Am I kidding myself by thinking Felix and I made progress with each other over the past twenty-four hours?

'I have to watch the interview,' he says, with that familiar look of determination on his face.

'Well,' I say, with a sigh, 'I don't want to watch it.'

Felix ignores me. I watch him take out his earphones, plug them in and press play on the video clip.

Taking hold of Baxter's lead, I turn in the other direction and wonder where Rory is now. My heart is aching for him and if it doesn't stop soon, I might have to go buy some painkillers. I think back to Felix mentioning Rory's brother, Lawrence. Why did I never get to meet him and was it Lawrence his mum was referring to in that postcard in his drawer? An uncomfortable feeling takes hold of me. If I recall she was talking about someone in the past tense as if they'd died. Felix also revealed Rory had been taking him to secret ballet lessons. I can see why Felix loves him so much. From the way Felix was talking about Rory, my ex-boyfriend had become a hero in his eyes. Rory had encouraged him to dance, and knowing this lights me up inside. Rory had been there for Felix when he needed him. Isn't that the sort of thing which makes a great parent? I don't think I knew Rory properly when we broke up six months ago.

Felix nudges me on the arm. 'SHE'S NOT HIS GIRLFRIEND,' he shouts. 'THEY ARE NOT TOGETHER.'

'What?' I gasp, flicking my eyes to the iPad screen and jolting with shock which in turn results in me accidentally letting go of Baxter's lead. Rory is *not* with the woman on the iPad screen. If I am honest, they're not giving up any romantic vibes as she's glaring up at him.

Felix yanks off his headphones. 'Rory kept telling the journalist he and the woman are not a couple, Emily.'

What the hell is going on? My heart has gone berserk inside my rib cage.

Felix points at the screen. 'Rory is a hero because he talked the missing boy into going home.'

'What?'

Nodding Felix beams at the screen. 'He looks like he's been in a fight. Rory is so cool.'

'A fight? Rory?'

I watch Felix lift his eyes for a second and flick them to the floor. Then he screeches so loud I am almost deafened. I follow his finger. Baxter is free of his lead and is racing off into a crowd of people. Shit!

'Stay here,' I bark at Felix, before letting out a blood-curdling scream and racing after tiny Baxter. Given the tin-can size of Baxter he is bound to get trodden on. 'BAXTER!'

If that little dog gets hurt, kidnapped, or flattened I will never forgive myself.

'BAXTER – where are you?' I wail.

'Emily?' A familiar voice behind me makes me jump. Turning on my heel I find myself staring up at Rory's summer blue eyes.

In his arms is a proud Baxter, who is sat on top of a bright yellow scarf.

'Rory?' I can't believe he's stood in front of me.

Without hesitation he pulls me into his arms and kisses the top of my head.

'Where have you been?' I say, with a sob as Baxter licks my face. 'We've been looking for you.'

He steps back with shock. 'What do you mean?'

'Felix and I went to Leeds to find you...'

Running his hand through his curly black hair he stares in amazement. 'Emily, I went to Brighton to find you and...'

We both stare at each other in shock.

'It's true, Emily,' he says. 'I had an accident at King's Cross last night, spent half the night in hospital, went to Brighton and had a brief cup of tea with Miss Hemingway after knocking on your door and getting no reply.'

My eyes notice the huge violet and green coloured bruise on the side of his head. He points to his injury. 'At King's Cross an excited traveller pushed me into a ticket barrier.'

'Ouch. Rory I can't believe what I am hearing. Felix and I travelled all that way to Leeds, and you were in Brighton the whole time. Did you come to Brighton to see me and Felix?'

I watch him place his free hand on my shoulder. 'Yes, I came to say I love you both... very much.'

As Rory's face goes blurry Felix comes hurtling towards us. 'RORY!'

Tears stream down my cheeks as I watch Rory lift Felix with one arm and hold Baxter in the other. 'Hello, Felix.'

We all walk towards the seats where Felix and I were sat. Rory hands a wriggling Baxter to Felix and kneels on the floor between us. He takes hold of my hand and Felix's. 'Listen, I love you both dearly and I want to be a part of your lives.'

Tears fill Felix's eyes, and he buries his head into Rory's shoulder. 'I love you, Rory,' he cries.

When Felix lifts his head Rory wipes away his tears and plants a delicate kiss on his forehead. 'I've missed you, buddy, and I love you too.'

Rory turns to me. 'I also love you, Emily. There was never anything between Anna and me. I want you to believe me.' He lowers his head and takes a deep breath. As he lifts his eyes to mine, I feel like I'm looking deep into his soul. 'Emily, ten years ago my little brother, Lawrence, died in a car accident. He was eighteen. I was in the passenger seat when he lost control of the car.' He stops and gently squeezes my hand. 'Lawrence was a great brother, and I was so messed up after losing him like that I stopped talking about him. I'm sorry I never told you about him.' I stroke his face as he takes another breath. 'Anna knew Lawrence from when he used to go to her mum's ballet school as a child.' Rory turns to Felix. 'Does Emily know about...' Felix nods. 'I told Emily everything last night.' Rory smiles and takes a deep breath. 'You remind me of Lawrence and going back to the ballet school brought back all my memories of Lawrence.' I watch Rory flick his eyes to the floor. 'When Anna joined my company, she told me she and Lawrence had been close at university. Best friends, in fact. I spent a lot of time with her because I wanted to hear about her memories of Lawrence.' His voice is thick with emotion. 'She made it feel like Lawrence was alive again.'

Felix throws his arm around Rory's neck and hugs him.

Rory stares at me. 'Last night I met up with Anna because I wanted to understand to why I had been such an idiot.'

'An idiot?'

He caresses the top of my hand with his thumb. 'I spent far too much time with Anna. I see that now. I can understand why you thought we should split up.' Pointing to the huge purple and green bruise on his forehead he says, 'I had an accident and ended up in hospital. Anyway, after that Anna and I went for a coffee. She told me she'd never been close to Lawrence.'

'What? I don't understand.'

Rory nods. 'It was all lies. There were no memories. She thought if she lied to me about her fictional friendship with Lawrence, I would fall in love with her.'

My mouth falls open in shock. 'She lied?'

'Lawrence and Anna were not best friends at university. It was all a trick. Emily, I want you to know that the night Vivi died I was with Anna.' He hangs his head. 'She wrongly assumed I wanted to be in a relationship with her and got upset when I told her I was in love with you. I should have been with you and Vivi. The guilt over that will stay with me for the rest of my life.'

I touch his face and can see the guilt written all over it. 'It's okay, Rory.'

He holds my gaze with his summer-blue eyes. 'I'm sorry for not telling you about Lawrence. It wasn't a great plan of mine.'

'Oh, Rory,' I say, my eyes filling with tears again.

He nods and reaches into the pocket of his shirt. 'I also came to give you this.'

CHAPTER 46

RORY

*E*mily's smile upon seeing the gold locket is unforgettable, and will now be etched onto my mind forever. Her honey-coloured eyes are shining as light glistens off the twirling locket, hung from my fingers. 'This is a belated birthday present from Vivi,' I whisper.

She casts me a puzzled look. 'Vivi?'

'Before Vivi died she asked me to buy you a birthday present. I knew you wanted this locket. So, she sent me the money and told me to buy it for you.' I stop and take a breath. 'This was the locket we always looked at in the jewellers in Brighton.'

'You remembered,' she says, softly.

'But your birthday was two days after she passed away.' I swallow back a wave of hot emotion.

Emily gasps. 'I told you I didn't want to celebrate my birthday.'

I hand it to her. 'Look inside.'

With shaking hands, she carefully opens the little locket and bursts into tears. I take her into my arms and rock back and forth. 'I hope you like what's inside. Your wonderful sister bought it for you and even though she left it blank I wanted you to remember her.'

For a few seconds she sits back and gazes at the locket. 'It's so beautiful.' Felix gasps when Emily shows him the photos inside. 'Mummy,' he whispers.

Emily is staring at me. 'You had these photos put in it?'

I nod. 'I knew how special Vivi was to you, Emily. Happy birthday.'

She cups my face with warm hands and peppers my cheeks with tiny kisses.

When she's composed herself, she sits up and gazes at Vivi's face inside the locket. 'My beautiful sister and your fabulous Mummy, Felix.'

He nods and rests his head against her shoulder.

It's time to put things right. I take both their hands again. 'Why don't we all make *this* work.'

'This?' Felix and Emily say in unison.

I shake their hands. 'This. Us. Our little family.'

Emily gasps and Felix flings himself at me.

'What, be a... family?' Emily croaks.

Nodding I take them both into my arms, plus a sleeping Baxter. 'Let's be a family. I love you both and I want us to be a family.'

'The best family.'

Emily leans in and we engage in a tender kiss. After, we go silent and gaze into each other's eyes. 'But you have your life in Leeds...'

'I'm not going back to Leeds, Emily and Felix. I'm not spending another day without you both *ever* again. It's time Tom and I parted ways. I'm on a different path now.'

Felix gestures for me to sit down next to Emily. Once seated he climbs onto my lap and squeezes himself between us. Baxter moves onto Emily's lap as she sits and strokes the locket.

'We met Tom,' announces Felix, making me stare at him with surprise. 'He showed us your kissing challenge.'

I can feel the blood drain away from my face. 'He told you about what?'

Emily touches my arm and raises the eyebrows. 'The *kissing* challenge – remember?'

'Ah, yes.' Oh, God – I am going kill Tom when I see him.

'He told us you kept calling girls Emily,' chuckles Felix, 'that's why you were not doing as good as him.'

Scratching my warm cheek, I curse myself for ever participating in Tom's challenge.

Emily squeezes my hand. 'It's all right, Tom told me the truth.'

'Did you kiss Beth?' Felix asks.

I can feel Emily's eyes on me. My cheeks now feel like they are being heated by a hundred tiny campfires. 'I did kiss Beth, but she left soon after.'

'Why?' Emily asks.

I turn to her. 'I couldn't stop thinking about you and Felix. At one point she shoved my favourite photo of you both in a drawer which made me angry.'

Emily smiles and I lean over for another kiss.

'Will you come home with us, Rory?' Felix is staring at me. His hazel eyes are wide and dancing with excitement.

'Yes, is that okay?'

I laugh and Emily gasps. 'The house is in chaos.'

'Why?'

She takes a deep breath. 'I started my online fashion company, and it has got out of hand.'

'What do you mean out of hand? I have been following you on Instagram and your stuff looks amazing.'

Felix taps me on the shoulder. 'It's everywhere. Dresses are everywhere. All over the house and I can't sit in the living room.'

Emily wipes her teary eyes. 'I was thinking about closing my business.'

The word 'no' flies out of my mouth. I know how much Emily loves dressmaking. She's dreamed about having her own business ever since I met her. It's also the link to Vivi, who had been a supporter of Emily's dressmaking and sewing skills since she was little. 'No, you are not doing that, Emily. Your dressmaking is your link to Vivi.'

'Yes,' she whispers. 'It is my link to Vivi.'

I kiss her hand. 'When I said we are going to make us work, I mean it. Look, I lost my job a few weeks ago in Leeds so there's no need for me to stay there. Plus a few of my old media contacts will still be around in Brighton and London. We can do this together.'

'What about Felix?'

I high five Felix. 'What about him? He's also part of our new team.'

Felix lets out a cheer.

'I don't care what the house looks like, Emily. What I care about is being with you, Felix and Baxter. We're a family now.' Her soft lips find mine and I know I have finally come home.

'I have not got any Christmas decorations, presents or anything,' says Emily, pulling away and running her hands through her hair.

Felix sits up and a huge smile spreads across his face. 'Having Rory back is the best Christmas present.'

I give them both a cuddle. 'This is what Christmas is about. Being together.'

Emily presses her forehead against mine. 'Do you really mean it about being a family?'

Nodding I press my lips against hers. 'I love you all. Always have. Always will. There's no one else like you, Emily. You are a rare edition.'

'Happy Christmas, Emily and Rory,' says Felix, jumping off my lap and onto the station floor. He picks up the yellow scarf which has fallen off with him. 'Is this your scarf, Rory?'

'No. Did you hear about the missing boy, Jack Gardener?'

Felix grins. 'Yes, we did, and Emily thought that woman you were with was your girlfriend.'

I let out a heavy sigh and curse that annoying journalist for the hundredth time. Both Emily and Felix are waiting for me to continue. 'Well, I was coming to London from Brighton this morning because Miss Hemingway gave me a fright. She thought it was Felix who was missing.'

'Oh no,' gasps Emily. 'We better call her and put her mind at ease. Rory – can I use your phone?'

I shake my head. 'No battery. Don't worry, we'll find a way to get her a message.'

Felix screws up his face and turns away. I ruffle his red hair. 'Apparently Felix told her he was planning to run away.'

'He did run away at this very station,' says Emily. 'Felix boarded a nonstop train to Leeds from King's Cross. That's how we ended up in Leeds.'

Felix turns back around. 'I wanted to find you, Rory.'

I stroke his cheek. 'Well, you should not have run off like that. You probably scared Emily witless.'

'He did,' adds Emily, rolling her eyes.

'Well, I raced back to London and on the train, I found the missing boy Jack. He'd run away because he was upset about his grandpa dying. His grandpa bought him this scarf which he lost when he ran away. I've now found it for him.'

Emily and Felix both glance at the scarf and back at me. Emily leans in for a cuddle and I kiss her forehead.

Before we both can say another word, Felix comes to stand in front of us and takes out his phone.

'Rory, Emily knows all about this. Ever since Mummy died, I have been recording videos on her old phone. I talk to her when I am feeling sad. When I was planning to run away from Emily at the station, I spoke to Mummy a lot.' He takes a breath. 'I know she's not coming back from heaven, but I hope God lets her see my videos.'

I reach out and give his shoulder a gentle rub. 'That's amazing, Felix. I'm sure your mum has been watching them.'

He smiles. 'Would you and Emily record a video with me?'

'For your mum – definitely.' I shift up and make a space between Emily and me. Felix comes to sit between us. He nestles in and fits perfectly. Holding out the phone he puts on the video camera, but he can't hold it far away enough to get us all in the picture. 'Shall I hold it?'

Grinning he hands me the phone and cuddles up to Emily.

'Ready, family,' I say, making Emily gasp and reach out to squeeze my hand.

'Hello, Mummy,' says Felix with the biggest smile I have ever seen on his little face. 'Look who we found at the station.' I wave into the camera which makes Emily giggle.

Felix continues. 'Mummy, I have the best news. We are going to be a family.'

We all press our heads together and cheer into the camera.

'These two are going to look after me,' says Felix, wiping a stray tear from his cheek.

I point the phone camera toward me. 'Vivi, I'm going to look after these two precious people for you and I am going to make them both very happy.'

Emily's sobs fill the air. Felix jumps out of his seat, allowing me to take Emily into my arms. Gently I push a strand of her hair to one side and plant a loving kiss on her forehead. She buries her head in my shoulder and I realise Felix is filming us. 'Mummy, look they are together again.' He points the camera on himself. 'I told you I had good ideas. Now for my secret.'

Emily lifts her head out of my neck and stares at Felix. I nudge her. She whispers, 'He wants to tell her about his love of ballet.'

He hands me the phone. 'Will you record this?'

Turning to Emily he says, 'Will you play my favourite music on the iPad. It's from Swan Lake.'

I press play and Felix launches into a dance. Holding Emily close to me I stroke her hair and watch Felix light up St Pancras station with his magical dancing. Behind him I can see the shocked faces of commuters watching in disbelief as Felix twirls, leaps, and soars through the air. Soon there is a crowd around Felix, and it feels like everyone has forgotten about the cancellations and is more interested in Felix's enchanting dance. Once he finishes and bows to his audience everyone cheers. Emily and I get up from the bench to give him a standing ovation and to my surprise all the people sat around us also stand and clap. With tears in our eyes, we go over and hug him tightly.

Upon returning to our seat Felix walks over to us holding out Vivi's phone. 'Mummy, that's my secret. I am going to become a ballet dancer. Rory never took me to football. He took me to ballet lessons. All those bangs and crashes I used to make in my bedroom were from my dance practice.'

I turn the phone to me. 'Vivi, I'm sorry I told you a few white lies about the football.'

Emily takes hold of the phone. 'Vivi, I am going to make sure this boy dances on a big stage. I am sure you are as proud of him as we are.'

I pull Felix into a hug. 'I'm so proud of you, buddy.'

After we have all said goodbye to Vivi and kissed the screen (including Baxter) Felix puts his phone away.

Felix sits on my lap and cuddles Baxter. I look at them all and it hits me. This is my home. With these three.

Emily lifts her mouth to mine and kisses me. 'Happy Christmas, Rory,' she whispers.

'Happy Christmas, my gorgeous girl.'

I hug Felix. 'Happy Christmas, Felix and Baxter.'

Felix beams at both of us. 'This is the best Christmas ever.'

CHAPTER 47

FELIX

Five months later

'Hi, Mum, it's me. I'm sorry I have not recorded anything for ages, I've been busy. Emily and Rory found me a new ballet class which is great. There are three other boys who go to it, and they want to be ballet dancers like me. I also have the BEST news. Rory asked Emily to marry him, and they want ME to dance at their wedding. My ballet teacher is going to help me with my routine. Uncle Bill is going to walk Emily up the aisle and Aunty Lizzie claims she's going to be the best bridesmaid in the world.

'Jade has joined our friendship group and we've been having lots of fun. We all think Sai wants her to be his girlfriend as he says he feels dizzy when he watches her play football. He also says Jade is making him want to do crazy things. The other day he asked me whether I would go with him on an adventure to see Jade play football in Blackpool. He wanted me to teach him how to run away from his mum at a train station. I told him that I am a good boy now and I talked to Emily and Rory when I got home. They were pleased about what I'd told Sai.

'Rory has put wooden flooring in my bedroom and Emily threw away the purple carpet which you loved. Sorry, Mummy.

'Emily and Rory have decided to travel to London this Christmas but this time we are going to stay at a hotel. We're going to visit St Pancras station. Rory says he wants us to do this every year and think of Vivi and Lawrence.

'I'll film again soon but don't worry if I don't. Rory and Emily keep me safe and happy. Bye, Mummy. I will love you forever.'

THE END

ACKNOWLEDGEMENTS

Dear Reader,

A BIG thank you for taking the time to read my book.

This story was written during a series of train journeys I took between Wales and Leeds following the death of my father. The characters and the journeys they take in the story gave me some respite from the pain of losing Dad. He was a huge supporter of my writing and I know he was smiling from heaven at the sight of me hammering out the words in a quiet train carriage, with a box of tissues to the right of me and a Twix chocolate bar to the left. Dad and I shared a love of books and he was always my wingman when we used to go into bookshops together. Like me, he always bought far too many books, and he also appreciated having a delicious coffee after a book purchase. Well, Dad, I wrote the book and it's been published. I will send you a book link so you can read it in heaven x

A huge thank you to Betsy Reavley, Shirley Khan, Abbie Rutherford and all the team at Bloodhound Books. You've been so supportive and the beautiful cover makes my heart sing every time I look at it.

To my fabulous husband, Huw, who has been amazing throughout my book writing career. You are also the person who came up with the title for this book. I know you say you don't like reading romance but I think one day I will catch you diving into an emotional romance – ha ha!

To Seren and Felicity – thank you for the emergency retail therapy sessions to Newport Retail Park during the editing stage of this book. You were right, I did need to have a break and get out of the house, however, I'm not sure buying you both make-up, hair products and clothes was part of my editing therapy!

To Mum and Vez, thanks for all the love, laughs and emojis on our family WhatsApp and in Majorca (Mum). Looking forward to seeing you in London for my fiftieth birthday celebrations and I can't wait to see you both carrying my bags of birthday book purchases – ha ha!

To Catherine and Sue, you are fabulous friends; you take no notice of me when I am moaning about my writing, you tell me to, 'get a grip' a lot on WhatsApp, you make me laugh a lot and you both have read and edited far too many of my romance stories over the years. Thank you x

To Jeff Mitchell, my favourite father-in-law. Thanks for all your support.

To Bettina Hunt, thank you for being a great writing friend and making me smile.

To Jodie Homer – thank you for reading the very first draft of this and encouraging me to carry on with it. Thanks for all your support and writing friendship.

To Lucy Keeling, thanks for being at the end of an Instagram message when revision got tough.

Thanks to Goku Uruthi for helping me with the characters of Felix and his friends.

To Candice Coates, my wonderful American writing friend. Thanks for making me giggle.

To Sandy Barker, thank you so much for your continuing support x

To Kiran Kataria, thank you for all your wisdom and support on this story during our time working together in 2022.

A NOTE FROM THE PUBLISHER

Thank you for reading this book. If you enjoyed it please do consider leaving a review on Amazon to help others find it too.

We hate typos. All of our books have been rigorously edited and proofread, but sometimes mistakes do slip through. If you have spotted a typo, please do let us know and we can get it amended within hours.

info@bloodhoundbooks.com

Printed in Great Britain
by Amazon

30052340R00169